LEAD ME
BACK

ALSO BY CD REISS

Hollywood Romance

Bombshell
Bodyguard
Only Ever You
Shuttergirl
Hardball

Dark Romance

His Dark Game
Edge of Darkness

The Drazen Family

Submission
Corruption
Broken Souls
Pretty Scars

LEAD ME BACK

CD REISS

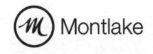
Montlake

Published by Montlake, Seattle

www.apub.com

Amazon, the Amazon logo, and Montlake are trademarks of Amazon.com, Inc., or its affiliates.

ISBN-13: 9781503905344

ISBN-10: 1503905349

Cover design by Hang Le

Printed in the United States of America

For anyone who can't see the light at the
end of the tunnel.

CHAPTER 1

KAYLA

"Are you sure you want a new number?"

The guy behind the counter looked away from his screen long enough to give me a weighty, dark-eyed stare. His sparse goatee sprang black coils, and his half smile clearly communicated that he understood things I didn't.

"Yes."

"There's no call forwarding. You'll have to tell all your friends and family you changed it. I'm just warning you, it can be a real pain in the ass."

What he called a pain in the ass, I called a relief. If I kept that number, I'd never ever be able to pick up an unknown contact and hear a friendly voice on the other side.

"I'll be living in 310. I'd like a 310 number, please."

Swiveling away from me, he speed-typed with two pointer fingers. My new, unboxed phone lay naked on the glass case in front of me, SIM card gutted, screen flashing greetings in a dozen languages as if it were casting a wide net into the world hoping for someone . . . anyone to claim it.

"I have a West LA with the last four digits of your old number: 8813." He shot me another serious glance. "Easier to remember."

"That sounds fine. Thank you."

He put the SIM card back in and did some more fancy finger work.

"Once I hit 'Enter,'" he said, his final tap hovering over the keyboard, "that's it. No going back."

I reached across the counter and hit the "Enter" key.

~

People talked about new beginnings as if you could start them with a single step anytime. Sure. Getting out of bed was a new beginning. Blinking hard once and deciding to do things differently could be a new beginning. But the big ones took effort. You had to wipe out old decisions and give up stale emotional investments. Stuff had to go. Physical objects. Furniture that wasn't worth moving across the country. A rent-controlled apartment on Second Avenue. A guy who was super nice but sucked the life out of you. The last drops of a career that had been drained.

Gone, gone, gone.

"Hello?"

"Talia," I said, leaning against the side of the white van with the blue stripe. "It's me."

"Kayla?"

My sister must have recognized my voice, but she was a confirmer.

"New number. You like it?"

"Where are you calling from?"

"Uh." I craned my neck, looking for a street sign. "Santa Monica and Western."

"You're across town."

"Is that far? You said Santa Monica."

"I meant the city, not the street. Head west on Santa Monica until you can smell the ocean and you need a sweater. Three blocks past Lincoln is Seventh. Can't miss it."

"Cool."

"I'll meet you after work. Six fifteen or so."

Just seven hours to kill. There was a Starbucks across the street. Nice to see some things were the same no matter where you were.

I'd been to Los Angeles once on business. I'd been too busy to leave the hotel for more than one dinner. Apparently, I was born in Beverly Hills, but that didn't count. The first four years of my life were a complete wash. My memories started in the far reaches of Queens with Talia and our heartbroken mother trying to look cheerful in our little house. Talia said a mask of happiness fused to Mom's face. My older sister was a cynic. She'd always wanted to move to Los Angeles. I'd told her she'd never fit in. Once Mom died, Talia had packed up as if she couldn't prove me wrong fast enough.

The billboard situation was insane. They were everywhere. They were the subway advertisements of Los Angeles. Dentists and personal injury lawyers, movies and TV shows, energy drinks and radio stations.

When I started the van, my phone rang again. Talia was the only one with my number, so I answered without looking.

"Justin?" An old woman's voice crackled on the other side.

"I think you have—"

"Who is this?"

"This is Kayla, but—"

"You must be the new girl. It's Louise. Justin's grandmother."

"No. I'm—"

"I didn't mean to forget you, but the old brain isn't working the way it used to. It's getting all full of little holes like that lacey swiss they have in Ralphs. Have you had it?"

"No. I—"

3

"Right. Well, you should try it. Benny—that's short for Benito—he used to melt it on sourdough with caramelized onions, and oh goodness was it delicious. Justin used to beg for it at lunchtime, but I could never get it quite right. If you want the way into his heart—"

In an effort to not be sick over the idea of a cheese and onion sandwich, I pulled out of the spot and almost smacked into a guy on a motorized scooter. Couldn't blame him for flipping me off.

"—melt lacey swiss on a nice sourdough from La Brea Bakery. My new boyfriend? Ned? I call him Ned the Bed because he's so good in it."

"Bed?"

She giggled. And I figured her for over seventy. The image of her shredding the sheets with Ned the Bed was distracting.

"Got a dick like a battering ram, and that's a fact."

I hit the brakes even though traffic was flowing. The car behind me jerked to a stop.

"Damn."

"That's what she said."

"I—" The sound of a police siren cut me off. It was immediately followed by a bullhorn.

"White van with New York plates. Pull over to the right."

"Okay, ma'am," I said as I put my blinker on. "I'm sorry, but you have the wrong number, and I have to go."

"Is this 310-555-8813?"

"Yes, but—"

"Tell Justin to bring a dozen red roses. For Ned's birthday, but leave the card blank."

"Where?" I said, talking to the cop in the car behind me as if he could hear me and find me a place to pull over that wasn't a red zone.

"The house! Oh, you're new. Right. I'll text you the address."

I wrangled my way to the right and parked at the only available space. A fire hydrant.

"Listen," I said, opening the window. "You seem really nice, but this isn't Justin's number."

But she'd hung up. The phone lit up with the default chime, and an address came through.

In the rearview, the cop got out of the car. The mirror showed only his waist, where he unclipped the strap on his holster.

"Okay." I tossed the phone onto the passenger seat just as the cop leaned into my window, one hand on his gun, the other on the driver's-side door. He had ebony skin and big brown eyes that were windows into a soul that had no patience for my nonsense.

"Hi, Officer."

"I see you have New York plates." He snapped a flashlight from his belt and used it to light the back of the van.

I was suddenly very conscious of the fact that he was looking at the artifacts of my life.

"I just got here. To Los Angeles."

"Do you know that in the state of California it's illegal to drive and use the phone without a hands-free device?"

"Um, no, but I'm not surprised?"

He snapped off the light and regarded me with a mix of suspicion and disdain.

"License, registration, and insurance, please."

~

All told, with fees and other junk, a $162 ticket was shut away in the glove compartment, and I didn't even have a job. I made my way west on Santa Monica. I was already halfway to my destination and had six hours to kill.

My phone rang again. I wasn't picking it up. No way. Not even at a red light. It could just go to the default voice mail, and I'd figure it out later.

It was probably the old lady with the boyfriend. Lacey Cheese Louise + Ned the Bed 4E.

If I didn't get the flowers, would she not have a present for him? Would he mind? Or would he shrug it off the way I'd shrugged it off when Zack forgot my birthday?

A little flower shop was just past the intersection, and there was a parking spot right in front.

What the hell? I had time, and making Justin's grandma happy would be a decent way to start a new life.

~

The van had gotten me over the Rocky Mountains with a steady, complaint-filled effort. Getting up the hill to Louise's house should have been a piece of cake. But the weight of my stuff had stressed the shocks and made the van ride so low the converter scraped against bumps. The engine knocked and rattled as if it had reached the tolerable limit of my ambitions.

When I got to a wrought iron gate, I had to put the emergency brake on so I could hold the roses upright with one hand and punch the code she'd left with the other.

Louise was fancy. She'd better shell out for the flowers.

The keypad beeped, and the gates churned open as if I were being admitted to Oz, closing behind me with a clang.

The hill got steeper from there. I passed three houses overlooking Los Angeles. Her address was at the end of the short drive. I parked next to a Bentley in front of her house and yanked the emergency brake.

"Everything all right back there?" I said to my stuff. None of it answered. The huge bolt of fabric I'd brought was pushed up against the back doors. "Good."

I got out with the flowers and rang the bell. I could hear it gong seven times, loud enough to wake the dead.

"One minute!" Her voice came from an upstairs window.

I waited. And waited. Paced a little. I could hear a pool filter and the whoosh of the freeway along with the birds and the rustling of the breeze. When the front door opened, I was by the side gate, admiring the sliver of a view I could see from there, imagining how amazing it must be from the back.

"Hello?" she said.

I rushed to the front. Louise was in her midsixties with spiky bright-pink hair, high-waisted stonewashed jeans, and white sneakers. Her horn-rimmed reading glasses hung from a rhinestone chain and rested against her dolman sleeve floral-print blouse.

"Hi," I said. "I don't know your grandson, but I didn't want you to not have a present for Ned."

"Oh!" She reached for them and gave the bouquet a requisite sniff. "They're perfect!"

"Thank you, I . . . uh . . ."

"Louise!" A man's voice came from inside the house. Young. Ned was the Bed for all the usual reasons, apparently.

"They were seventy-five dollars, so . . ."

"Justin!" Louise called into the house. "Your girl's here. Don't you pay her?" She turned back to me. "Come in, please." I stepped into a narrow alcove that went up two stories to a pyramid of skylights. A glittering chandelier hung in the center. The walls were decorated with generic gold-framed oil landscapes and still lifes of flowers. Louise put the vase on a table and regarded me as if I were a piece of art she was considering buying.

I'd just spent three hours in a van with crappy air-conditioning, driving in from a hotel outside Vegas, and hadn't been self-conscious until that moment.

"Look at you," she said. "Aren't you adorable?"

Either she was completely serious, or she was a great actor, because there was no sarcasm in her tone.

"Here's the receipt for the flowers," I said, taking the yellow slip of paper from my back pocket.

"Jus*tin*!" she yelled, emptying the bottom of her lungs.

"Take a fucking pill, Louise!"

Where I was from, you didn't talk to your grandmother like that. But where I was from, Grandma didn't tell strangers about Ned the Bed either.

"Those shoes!" she exclaimed, pointing to my wedges. "I had a pair like that in 1985. Shredded my pinkie toe like a Cuisinart, but that didn't stop me from dancing, I'll promise you that."

"They're really comfortable. But, anyway, I should get the money and get going."

As if she hadn't heard me, Louise picked up the flowers and made an immediate left, out of sight. I followed her into the kitchen, where she'd put the vase on the island's countertop and pulled the flowers out.

"My husband red-rosed me to death until our ninth anniversary. I got cut bloody." She laid them, dripping wet, across the marble, destroying the arrangement by checking each stem for safety. "He died young, but it wasn't me. Swear it. Though by that point there was no saving the thing. Did you know thirteen percent of wives cheat on their husbands? Can you guess how many husbands cheat?"

I unfolded the receipt and pushed it toward her, fearing my first day in Los Angeles was going to cost me more than $162 and a moving violation.

"I really need to settle this and get going."

"Twenty percent! I was in that seven . . ."

"Weeze"—a male voice came from behind me—"you gotta get that faucet fixed."

I spun around to look at him and, in the middle of his sentence, gasped so hard I sounded like a drowning victim.

Standing right there in bare feet, white tattoo-exposing tank, white basketball shorts with an orange stripe down the side, with his blond hair so precisely bed-headed it had to be on purpose, and a gold chain that was the icing on the cake of a look every fashion and celebrity magazine called "douchecore" was Justin Beckett.

From the band Sunset Boys. *That* Justin.

From the cover of *GQ*. Twice before age twenty-two.

I wasn't a fan or anything. I was a New York fashion designer—

Not anymore.

—and club scene onlooker—

Until the eyeballs turned on me.

I considered myself too much of an adult to listen to his music, but I wasn't *dead*. The Sunset Boys breakup that spring had drowned Twitter in sobs and DMZ in clicks. Justin Beckett, with his ghostly pale-blue eyes, had been the front man who'd thrown it all away for a crazy night at the Roosevelt Hotel. There had been a party at the pool. He'd beaten a bandmate bloody, gotten caught with another bandmate's wife and a bunch of drugs in a hotel bathroom. It was impossibly salacious. Like watching a car wreck where everyone was fine except the one guy who deserved to get hurt.

The clean-cut, silky-smooth boy in the band wasn't so silky smooth anymore. Maybe it was the rough night at the Roosevelt. Maybe it was just adulthood, but he'd transformed into a fully muscled, square-jawed man. His size and presence dazed me.

"Weeze," he said to his grandmother. "Who is this person?"

Louise gathered the smooth stems into a bouquet and put on her glasses.

"You're such a big deal you don't even know your own assistant?"

He shot his gaze to me.

"All right." He snapped his fingers and pointed to the door. "Get the hell out."

"Wait," I snapped. I didn't want to stay, but I wanted my money.

"I mean it. You got this far. Now get out."

"You don't have to be so rude," Louise said, inspecting a stem.

He grabbed my upper arm and pulled me out.

"Don't touch me!"

Ignoring me, he opened the door and pushed me outside, joining me in his bare feet and closing the door behind us.

"How did you find me?" he demanded, letting me go.

"I wasn't looking for you!"

"You one of the ones who parked on Laurel Crest?" He pointed to some street over thataway that I was supposed to know. "Because you're violating an order of protection."

"No! You stupid jackass!" With my finger pointed and an insult hurled in a decisively unfannish tone, his face softened for a moment. He had a tiny pimple on his forehead. It was so real, so human on a guy so handsome and undeniably magnetic, I almost lost my resolve and smiled.

But he was still the guy who'd gripped my arm so hard it hurt, and that guy could suck it.

"You're from what paper?" he asked.

"I just got a new phone, and your grandmother dialed the wrong number. She insisted it was you. And I was like, here's a nice lady who's not going to have a present for her boyfriend, so I went to get the flowers, which cost seventy-five dollars after I already got a hundred-and-sixty-two-dollar ticket for talking to her in the first place."

"I like your accent," he said. "New York?"

"Round it up to eighty." I held out my hand. "The receipt's on the kitchen counter."

"And I'm supposed to believe she just called you?"

"I told you. Wrong number."

"Louise can't see shit. She uses speed dial."

"You change your number recently?"

His mouth twisted, and he looked at me from shoes to hair. I wished I'd showered after the drive from Vegas. Zack never noticed when I was slobbing out, and for a moment I wanted that back.

"So, you're saying she called my old digits?" he asked.

"Maybe." I focused on that little pimple, but it was close to his eyes, which were a color no photo did justice.

"Prove it."

"Are you asking for my number?"

"Give me a break."

So snide. As if to say, "I only date models, and you're no model."

I put my hands on my hips. "It's eighty bucks to find out."

"Prove it first."

He had me. I needed the money more than he needed to know. And all he'd have to do after I drove away empty-handed was look at Louise's recents.

As I took my phone from my back pocket, his phone dinged with some kind of notification.

Any normal, courteous person would have finished our conversation and looked later, but Justin Beckett's reputation as an asshole was obviously earned. He looked at it, swiped, curled his mouth in thought, and typed something in.

Then he waited for a response with me standing right there.

Some humiliations weren't worth even seventy-five dollars, and this was one of them. I got back in my van and slapped the door closed. Justin didn't even seem to notice when I started the engine and backed down the street.

"Wait!" He ran toward me, bare feet on the pavement, phone to his ear, baggy poly shorts flowing.

"What?" I asked when he got to my open window.

He held his hand out to me. "Give me your phone."

"You're not serious."

"Give me your phone," he demanded in the silence between rings. "Please."

"Eighty dollars," I said.

"You're a raging bitch, but okay." He took out his wallet and pinched out a hundred-dollar bill as the phone rang a second time. "This is for the flowers." He missed my hand on purpose and dropped the cash in my lap. "And this," he said, dropping another hundred, "for the ticket. Here." He flicked a third at me. "Get Bluetooth speakers. Okay? Good. Now." He put his palm up. "Give me your phone."

Bought and paid for, I handed him the phone. He turned away to answer it so quickly he didn't see me giving him the finger.

No good deed goes unpunished, and getting flowers for Ned the Bed was no exception. Had I known the favor was for Justin Beckett, I would have gotten lunch instead of a dozen red roses. But there I was after seven days driving cross-country, parked in a private driveway I was going to have to back out of, waiting for some jerk to return my phone.

I folded the hundred-dollar bills and put them in my pocket. This was a bad start, but it was my start. The new number was just a symbolic gesture. No more calls from the temp agency with grinding jobs at fashion houses that dried up as soon as they realized who I was. No more cold looks or turned backs waiting in line at 38th Street Diner. No more Zack asking what laundry setting to use before proclaiming his undying love.

Just me and a portfolio of sketches and swatches. Dreams in a folder. I'd even created a label. KAYLA MONTGOMERY in white block letters woven into gray tape. From this day forward, I was a fully formed fashion designer and would accept no less.

I was feeling pretty good about that when Justin made his way back to the van with his signature slouch and a far-off look that made him seem almost human.

Almost.

Only a man that gorgeous could style his hair like a tardy middle schooler, dress like a dirtbag, and inspire women to scream for him.

He came to my door and handed me the phone.

Was the pimple gone? I couldn't find it.

"I need you to take messages," he said. "I'll call you to get them."

"Are you kidding?"

"How much do you want?" He was looking past me to the back of the van, probably to determine how hard up I was.

"To be your phone servant?"

"What do you have back there?"

He was going to try and charm me by showing an interest in my situation, and I was in no mood to feel better about doing him any favors.

"My life." I put the van in reverse. "It's my first day in LA. Thanks for the welcome."

"No, I mean that." He reached in the window to point at the rolls of denim wrapped together in plastic.

"It's four bolts of fabric. Step back before I take your arm off."

"That's nice selvedge."

"Wrong. It's fully saturated, red-cast, plant-based indigo from Japan. It's not nice selvedge. It's extraordinary selvedge."

"Who you delivering to?"

"It's mine."

That was all the answer he was getting. The person who had given it to me hadn't exactly owned it. I wasn't telling him how I'd had an hour to get it out of the office, so I'd had to hire a guy to move it because Zack was playing softball at the Anchor Banking Memorial Day picnic. God forbid he miss that.

I was halfway down the drive when Justin appeared in my rearview. I braked hard to avoid swiping him.

"What?"

He took two quick but not-quite-urgent steps to my window.

"I need you to answer calls."

"No." I let my foot off the brake.

"You need a job, right?"

I stopped.

"What makes you think that?"

"You had time to get flowers. You just moved here. You're begging for eighty bucks."

The fact that he was right didn't mitigate my anger, nor did his big icy eyes mitigate my humiliation.

"Bye."

When I moved, he moved with me. I couldn't go in reverse any faster without hitting something.

"You do fashion. Stylist or what? Never mind. It doesn't matter. Listen. Here's the deal. You work on costume for this thing I'm on. Union gig. Come on as an apprentice. Outta my pocket."

The gate must have been on a sensor, because it opened slowly behind me, and I had to stop to avoid crashing into it.

"Just . . ." He paused with his hands out, as if he wanted to hand me a bundle of explanations. The pimple was back, and redder than before. I hoped it found a mate and made pimple babies all over his face. "If that phone rings," he said, "you come get me on set or take a message."

The gate clattered when it was open all the way.

"Does anyone ever tell you no?"

His hypnotic smile chased away every thought in my head.

"Nah."

Even his honesty was so charming I almost agreed to his offer.

Almost.

"Well," I said and leaned over the doorframe to get a few inches closer to him, "I'm going to pop your cherry."

Before I could gauge his reaction, I twisted around to see where I was going, which had the advantage of moving my attention away from his smile. Harder than it looked, but doable.

Once I cleared the gates, I popped the van into drive and looked forward. He was on the other side, standing in the center of the driveway with his fist to his ear, pinkie and thumb extended in the international sign for "I'll call you."

I gave him the international sign for "go fuck yourself" and drove back down the hill.

CHAPTER 2

KAYLA

It was a long way down Santa Monica Boulevard, and the maps app kept trying to put me on the freeway, which was south forever and not the way Talia told me to go.

After seven days on the road, I was sick of highways anyway.

Once I was in the right neighborhood, I got something to eat at a fast-food chicken joint I'd seen twelve times on the way and went to the library.

A billboard with a pout-faced seventeen-year-old covering her bare chest with a handbag hovered over Santa Monica Boulevard. The designer was Josef Signorile, my last employer and a first-class scumbag. I sat with my back to the window to sketch from fashion magazines.

And of course there was a Justin Beckett spread in Italian *Vogue*.

When he looked out at me, he wasn't really looking at me, and no one saw me bend over the page as if inspecting every inch of him. His skin was clear, of course, and his tattoos rippled and curved over the muscles of the arm he had slung over Thomasina Wente's shoulders. They each had similar expressions of entitlement. Hers was shaded with vulnerability. His with disdain to any alpha who dared challenge him.

I was supposed to be looking at the clothes. Instead, I read the profile and tried to square it with the douchebag I'd just met.

FACTS:

Justin Beckett's parents were currently sailing around the world on a boat he bought them.

When "My Heart's Desire" went platinum, he bought his grandmother a house.

He's totally ready to up his game and win an Oscar.

He had to actually (gasp) audition for the role of Darcy in the new *Pride and Prejudice*. When the director, Gloria Wu, didn't ask for a callback, he begged.

"I, you know, I had to have Gene [Gene Testarossa, his agent at WDE] call her agent to make it happen. I really felt connected to this character. Everyone thinks he's some kind of creep, but he's not. He's a good guy. I said, let me play him frustrated with that this time."

"So, someone *has* told you no, you liar," I mumbled.

I moved on to his lovers, which he wouldn't discuss. Not that he needed to.

Though he won't talk about his relationships, Beckett has been photographed with model Rachel Stoker and—quite recently—the Sunset Boys' answer to Yoko Ono, Sienna Holden.

"When I'm in love, I'll let you know," he says. "I'll shout it from the rooftops. For now, I'm just having fun."

Beckett declined to discuss whether the affair with Heidi Collins, the wife of Sunset Boy Gordon Daws, was rooftop-worthy.

Climbing over women to crest the peak of Mount Adulthood. A real prince among men.

I was glad I'd refused his offer. I could make it a month on what I had in the bank. All I had to do was find a factory for the rolls of denim and I'd be halfway to my first small run.

Success or bust.

My phone buzzed in my pocket. I checked it. Blocked number.

I'd bet my bolt it was Justin.

"Denied," I said, hitting the red button.

It was almost six. I packed up and left just before the library closed.

∿

At six fourteen, I parked in the alley behind the CineSquare Theater, where Talia waited next to her BMW.

"Boogersnot!" She enveloped me in a full-body embrace before I was fully out of the van.

"Hi," I said into her shoulder. "It's so good to see you. Traffic here's no joke. And I got a ticket." I let her go, and she stepped away to look at me.

"In trouble with the law already?" She brushed her razor-sharp bangs, as if they were anything besides pin straight.

"Talking on the phone."

"Ouch." Her fingers rubbed together in the international sign for *big money*. "Spendy."

"Yeah. So." I cleared my throat and swept my hand over the length of the van as if I were working a car show. "Ta-da! My life."

Talia cupped her hands on the glass to cut the glare. "What do you have in here?"

"My stuff."

"What's the stuff in the plastic?"

"Four bolts of selvedge denim."

"Why?"

"To make samples."

"Okay." She nodded, arms crossed. She was a lawyer. Sensible. Hard-nosed. She never understood the "creative thing" her little sister "insisted on."

"I'm blocking the alley," I said. "I don't want another ticket today."

"Sure. Well. At least you won't have to pay rent for a while." She kneeled to the bottom of a solid black gate and, with a yank, pulled it up with a loud rattling noise. Behind it was a loading dock with two dumpsters, collapsing cardboard boxes, a row of silver soda canisters, and a car with a canvas tarp over it.

There was just enough room for the van.

"Get your life in here, my little booger."

~

The CineSquare Theater was wedged between a wig store and a café, limiting its size and, by extension, its scope. As movie theaters went, it had failed to evolve, just like the man who had owned it and lived in it until the end of his life. Our grandfather, who died and was buried before we even got a phone call from a lawyer.

The CineSquare was our inheritance. Not a cent of liquid cash had come our way when our last grandparent died, but my older sister and I were part owners of a movie theater that hadn't done a lick of business in a decade. The land it was on was worth millions, but it was hard to sell it when Grandpa wouldn't let it go unless the new owners signed off on keeping it a theater. No one would promise their future in service of another man's past.

So Talia and I got it in the will but weren't allowed to sell it. It was less an inheritance and more an encumbrance. But I could live in it, and that made it worthwhile.

"We'll get your stuff once I give you the lay of the land," Talia said as we walked past the empty concession stand. The carpet was decorated in blue and gold art deco loops.

"You thinking of reopening?" I asked.

"No parking," Talia said. "Not for love or money. Who goes to the movies and doesn't need to park the car?"

She backed into a red door marked EMPLOYEES ONLY, revealing a short hall with a janitor's bucket with a bone-dry mop inside it. At the other end was a long staircase.

"In New York you don't need to park the car."

"This ain't New York, booger." She looked back at me from above. "Drive or die. Grandpa had his apartment up top."

We hit a landing with a door marked PROJECTION ROOM, passed a floor with double doors marked STORAGE, and came to the topmost floor. My new home for the time being. The space our grandfather had lived in until the day he died.

"This is great," I said. "Like living in a Stephen King novel."

"And free. Kind of."

She opened the door before I could ask her what she meant.

"Wow," was all I had to say, so I said it again. "Wow."

Twenty-foot ceilings with huge skylights. Exposed brick walls. Open kitchen. Warehouse casement windows on both sides of the space. It was absolute heaven.

"Busted pipes," Talia said, closing the door behind me. "Cracked walls. Clogged gutters. Broken skylights. The leaks in the roof are so unsurprising they're almost a relief." She picked up a moldy carton.

"And more Grandpa stuff than I can fit in the dumpsters on any given week." She dropped the box in front of me. It looked like a dozen other containers were piled up against the walls. "If he hadn't been such an asshole, I'd lovingly go through every item."

I opened the flaps. Dust and grit slid off the cardboard.

"Has Dad been up here?"

"He wants nothing to do with any of it."

I took out an orange box with a white projector icon on the front.

"Reels?" I asked, opening the side. "*When Harry Met Sally*. Oh my Lord."

"Dad wants to see you. Dinner tonight, if you're free. And you are."

I hadn't seen my father in years. He and Mom broke up when I was four, and by "broke up" I mean Mom packed up one day and moved us out. She called him when she'd driven us far enough away that he couldn't follow. For years, she didn't say his name, answer questions, or tell us why she'd split like that. She just cried all the time.

When I was old enough to be angry, she dropped little hints about his contribution to her brokenness. I held on to a toxic resentment I couldn't shake. Talia called him after the accident, but I wasn't having it. Talking to him on the phone made me angry for no real reason, so I ghosted him like a coward.

"Sure. I can put off . . . I don't know . . . everything for half a day."

"Good." Talia went behind the kitchen bar and filled the teapot. "Do you think it'll be a problem to find a job?"

"Don't care. I'm not putting myself in that position. I'm going to look for a sample factory and start my own thing." I opened drawers and cabinets, taking inventory of the Corelle cups and plates. "God. So vintage."

"Do you need me to set you up as a corporation?"

"Good idea," I said, holding open two cabinet doors so I could stare at a collection of water glasses. "I wish we'd known Grandpa died. I would have gone to the funeral."

"He hated everything and everyone. He's probably haunting this building just to stay mad."

"I feel kind of bad, though. Living here without knowing him all that well."

"Don't." She stuck her nose in an old box of tea bags. "Dad and I tried talking to him when he was alive, and he wanted nothing to do with us. Does tea go bad?"

"I don't think so."

"Besides," she said, plucking out two. "He's screwing us from the grave. We can't sell this thing. You're sure you have enough to live on without working?"

"Yeah. A month maybe."

"And enough for utilities?"

"Yeah."

"And property tax?"

"Uh—"

"I told you about the property tax."

Had she?

She must have. She was thorough. Talia didn't miss stuff like that.

"How much is it?" I asked.

"I've been shelling out two thousand a month."

"Oh my God!" I'd lived in New York. I'd paid three grand a month for a loft bed over a doorway to my roommate's bedroom. We'd had six inches of counter space and two electric burners. But this wasn't Manhattan, and I wasn't prepared to lose what added up to two weeks of freedom.

"I can't anymore," she said. "I have things coming up."

"Things?"

She didn't elaborate. Talia was an entertainment lawyer, and her girlfriend, Soledad, was a public defender. I thought that made them half-rich.

"The repairs too." She pointed to the ceiling, where a brown stain grew around a crack in the plaster.

"I should have taken that job," I grumbled, still glad I hadn't.

"What job?"

"It's a long story."

"I'm not going anywhere."

My phone rang.

"I'll tell it if you give me some of the schnapps in the cabinet."

Sliding my phone from my pocket, I checked the screen, expecting a blocked number.

It wasn't blocked. Wasn't Louise. Wasn't Talia, because she was right in front of me, sniffing the schnapps to see if it had gone bad.

I picked it up, ready to tell someone they'd dialed the wrong number.

"Hello?"

"Hello," a woman said. "Is this Kayla Whitevan?"

Kayla Whitevan?

"No, I—" White van? "My first name is Kayla. Who's this?"

Talia gave me a quizzical look as she spiked my tea. I shrugged.

"Ah, my name is Francine Glick. I'm doing costume for a historical film in production now with Overland Studios. I got your number from Justin Beckett's agent. Gene Testarossa."

Wow. That guy really wouldn't take no for an answer.

"Motherfu—" I stopped myself. "Montgomery. My last name's Montgomery."

"You're a costume designer looking for work?"

I looked up at the stain in the ceiling. It was June. When did it rain in Los Angeles? Would we have to patch the entire roof? How much money could I count on Talia for when I was living in the apartment?

"It's complicated."

"I could use another truck girl. It's not that complicated a job."

Maybe not for her. I was the one who had to be Justin Beckett's secretary. That was complicated, but needed too much explanation.

"I'm a designer. I can make clothes, but I've never made a costume."

"Make clothes?" she asked, as if I'd surprised her. "You can do alterations?"

"Yes."

"Quickly?"

The more I agreed the deeper I got, and I didn't even know if I wanted this.

"I'm pretty fast if I don't have to finish every seam."

"This will save me so much time. Where have you worked before? Can you send a résumé?"

Could I . . . ? No, actually. I couldn't send a résumé. That was the point.

Hang up.

Hang up.

I can thank her and hang up.

Talia checked her phone. The glass was cracked. I knew she didn't have a ton of money, and here I was, showing up for the free rent and the fresh start.

"Excuse me?" Francine asked. "I didn't hear you."

"You don't need a résumé," I said. "Let me come in and show you."

"Tomorrow," she said with finality. "You come on set and show me."

CHAPTER 3

KAYLA

"She's here two hours, and she meets Justin Beckett," my father said after Talia and I told him the story over dinner. In his fifties, he was tanned and buff, handsome as a model with more sway than I remembered as a child.

"And got her a job," Talia said, cradling her latte. "To keep her close."

"Must be love." He waggled eyebrows that had been meticulously lightened to match his full head of blond hair. "Is he as hot in the real as he is in *GQ*?"

"I never felt so used in my life," I snarled.

"It's Hollywood." He waved his hand. "We're all valued for our usefulness. If you wanted a costuming job, I could have helped you."

He'd been in the finance department at Overland Studios for ten years, so maybe he wasn't overstating or showing off, but I didn't want to ask him for anything. Not yet.

"She would have had to call you," my sister grumbled.

"I don't want a costuming job. It's just what happened. And even if I get it, which I might not . . . it's only for a few weeks."

"After that, then. You call me."

"Dad. I don't like being used. I'm not going to turn around and use you."

"It's not using if we have a relationship. Which is all I ever wanted."

I stared at the sludge at the bottom of my cup.

"I know you're mad," he said. "But that was a long time ago."

"For you. You didn't see Mom cry all the time."

"Because she took you guys and left. What was I supposed to do? Chase a woman who couldn't stand the sight of me?"

"No." I pushed my cup away.

"Is that what you wanted? Me to chase you?"

I crossed my arms.

"Honestly?"

"Honestly."

"You're in trouble now," Talia said.

"Until I was a teenager . . . I wished you'd stayed married and just pretended you were straight. Then I met gay people and realized you'd be miserable. But I just wanted you to be as miserable as Mom was, because why should you be the happy one?"

"I wasn't happy."

"Well, that sucks for everyone."

"I was glad she took you away, to be honest. Your grandfather disowned me, and I was afraid he'd do the same to you guys. This way, he'd help your mother financially as long as I had no contact with you."

"What?"

"You look shocked." He swirled his coffee around his cup. "It's cute."

"Why didn't I know that?"

"Part of the deal. But, ding-dong, the homophobe is dead." He downed the last of his drink and clicked the cup into the saucer. "Meanwhile, I'm still here, and so are you."

The waiter brought the check. Dad snapped it away before Talia could get her fingers on it.

"So," he said as he got his card out. "We friends or are you going to drag around a set of Louis Vuitton luggage with my name on it the rest of your life?"

My anger at him was baggage at that point. I didn't need it. Mom had died six years ago. Grandpa was dead. Dad had done his best. But, for reasons I couldn't explain, I was attached to it.

"I'll drop the day bag."

"Good!" He handed the check to the waiter. "Unless you're partying with Justin's entourage next weekend, you come to my place."

~

Grandpa had no friends to want any of his stuff, and we were his only family. So his clothes were in the drawers and closets, and his sheets were on the bed. I changed them, but moving more to make room felt morbid. I left my clothes in the containers I'd brought from New York and kept my toiletries in the second bathroom, where his aftershave and soap didn't take up space.

Even with the bed facing the back alley, I'd underestimated how loud traffic could be. Fast cars whooshed by, or rumbled at the light, and the constant hum of the freeway kept me up.

Dad and Talia had told me I was supposed to call it *the* 405. And I was supposed to *hop on* it and complain about traffic with a sense of resignation. I had to listen to people when they gave me directions somewhere even though we all used an app.

She said I wasn't supposed to take public transit. "No one" took the bus. But we could barely budge the bolts of denim from the back of the van and onto the loading dock. They were thirty-two inches long, wrapped together in plastic, and heavier than they looked. In the dead of night, four guys had carried them across 39th Street to load into my newly purchased van. I hadn't asked myself how I was getting them out.

Talia and I were never going to be able to move it, and I wasn't risking someone stealing it. I planned my bus route without telling her.

Eventually, I fell asleep and woke in the morning during a dream where I opened my van to find Justin Beckett fondling my selvedge.

Even half-awake, I had to laugh.

~

The interior sets for Gloria Wu's *Pride and Prejudice* were in an Elysian Heights Victorian. By the time I arrived at seven a.m., the street had already been blocked off and was lined with trailers. People with headsets and clipboards ran back and forth, putting out fires I couldn't see.

I approached a long table with coffee and bagels, where a bearded white guy dressed neatly in a polo shirt and jeans was sniffing the contents of a carton of milk. He wasn't tall or short, dark or light, and had a pleasant, but ordinary, face.

"Hi," I said.

"Hey." He took his nose out of the spout. "Coffee's hot. Get it while it's fresh."

"Okay. Sure." I slipped a paper cup off the tower. "I'm looking for Francine Glick?"

"Costume lady?" He put his cup under the urn and poured.

"Yeah. It's my first day, so . . ."

"Welcome!" He snapped the lever up to cut off the flow. "I'm Eddie."

"I'm Kayla."

He handed me the coffee and took my empty cup.

"I left you some room for cream. Happy to fill it if you like."

"It's fine." I dressed my coffee. "So, where do you work? On set, I mean."

"I'm an actor." He smirked. "I'm playing George Wickham."

"Ah." He did look familiar. "Sorry."

"Don't be. It's the curse and blessing of being a character actor. I'm the face you've seen a million times but can't place." He held his hand out. "Edward Ainsley."

"Nice to meet you." I shook his hand, then turned my finger in a spiral to mirror what my mind did as it hunted through memory files. "Uh, you were the guy with the cane in—"

"*Dr. Jones.*"

"Right! And the cop in that movie? With the lighter fluid."

"You're two for two."

He didn't seem insulted or annoyed, so I decided not to feel bad.

"Wickham's a good part for a man of my limited talents," he said after a sip of coffee, and my face must have shown my surprise, because he laughed. "Don't look like that. I work a lot. A *lot.* That's more than most actors can say. So. I've never seen you. How long have you been in costume?"

"Sorry?" a woman in her twenties said from behind me. She wore a T-shirt dress under a beige cardigan, white sneakers, and pom-pom-heeled socks. When we turned to her, she looked as if she wanted to crawl under the table. "Hi. I, uh . . . I work in costume, and we're expecting someone new today so . . . you're maybe the new alterations person?"

"Kayla." I held my hand out.

"Evelyn." She shook. "I'm the truck girl."

"Um . . ."

"She racks and tags," Eddie said. "Can I pour you a cup, truck girl?"

"Sure," she replied with a nervous titter before turning back to me. "What have you worked on?"

"Nothing."

"Nothing?"

Of course that was impossible, so I backpedaled.

"No movies."

"TV?" Eddie said, handing Evelyn a paper cup.

"Thanks." Her eyelids fluttered behind her glasses.

"No TV. I'm just a fashion person and a decent tailor."

"Just a decent tailor," Eddie said. "Like being a decent engineer."

"Hardly."

"I bet you're great," Evelyn said. "Francine's super picky."

I cleared my throat and sipped my coffee. I needed to change the subject before they found out I didn't get the job through normal channels, whatever those were.

"Quite an accent you have," Eddie said before I could come up with a segue to anything else. "New York?"

"Yeah."

I had to think of something to ask before they asked why I came to LA, but luckily Evelyn got distracted by something behind me. I could feel the change in energy, as if the entire street were being pulled in one direction.

"Gang's all here," Eddie said. I followed his gaze to about half a dozen young men striding down the street like a pack of alpha wolves, and at the center was Justin Beckett. Same gold chain, with a new black tank top and knit pants baggy at the hips and tight at the ankles.

He scanned the street as if looking for something, and when he found me, he stopped.

Shit. Was he going to come toward me? I didn't want to start this job as an attention magnet.

He raised his fist to his face in the "call me" sign and I went completely rigid. I didn't want him to do that. No one would understand it, and things would get very weird, very quickly.

But when his hand got to his face, he spread his fingers and ran them through his hair, turning to shake hands with someone. Then, without another glance in my direction, he disappeared into a trailer.

I exhaled.

"Come on," Evelyn said, snapping me back to reality. "I'll show you over to costume."

~

There were two costume trailers. The one Evelyn took me to was air-conditioned, with a kitchenette, a space with a sewing machine, rolling racks, a desk, and a fitting room in the back. The other was apparently storage.

Evelyn picked up a clipboard and checked the costumes on the day's rack with a *squeak-click-squeak-click*, showing me how things were arranged and tagged as if I'd been hired already. Francine showed up a few minutes later and dropped her white floral Tory Burch bag on the desk.

"Francine," Evelyn said. "This is Kayla, the alterations person."

Evelyn continued checking with a *squeak-click-squeak-click*.

Francine held out a hand with rings on four fingers. I was immediately convinced she'd sprung from her mother's womb a fully formed professional with a profound vision. She had straight blonde hair to her waist that she kept sliding away from her shoulder with one finger and wore a leather blazer and bell-bottomed jeans that were totally out of style but worked on her so well I wanted to run out and buy a pair.

Squeak-click-squeak-click.

"Kayla Montgomery," she said with a hint of an accent I couldn't place. "I am Francine Glick. Nice to meet you."

"Hi." We shook. She was strong. "Thank you for trying me out."

"We don't say no to Justin Beckett."

The squeaking and clicking stopped. If I were prone to blushing I would have been deep crimson.

"So," I said. "I guess I have a fitting? Soon?"

Evelyn's hanger shuffle resumed.

"Yes," Francine answered, digging around her bag and coming up with a box of mints. "One for you?"

"Thanks." I hated mints, but on the off chance she was dropping me a hint, I took one. She offered Evelyn one.

"Nine thirty." She snapped the tin closed. "You'll show me how you fit on Justin."

Of course it had to be him.

CHAPTER 4

JUSTIN

The first time I auditioned for Darcy, I hadn't read the book, and I had zero intention of doing so. I was pissed about having to audition in the first place. My name should have generated an offer. I wasn't going to take three hours to read something written when guys wore ribbons and bows.

Then I didn't get the part, and as annoying as that was, it was fine. Gene had sent me out for Darcy as a warm-up before putting me in for what I really wanted—the Bruckheimer thing, *Speed Junkie*.

Meanwhile, Brad Sinclair's agent was getting him my part on *Speed Junkie*, and in four hours DMZ was throwing him a parade, and I was getting dragged all over the internet for losing a job in a period piece I didn't want. This was before the Roosevelt Hotel Incident even happened, which we are not talking about right now because it's irrelevant. The reason I didn't get Darcy the first time was because I phoned in the audition. Period.

So I read *Pride and Prejudice*. It wasn't bad. More girl-style than I like. But Darcy was my man. I felt him hard. My second audition was so on point they coulda just handed me my Oscar right there.

Sure. Sinclair got *Speed Junkie*, but I'd snapped victory from the jaws of defeat.

The champagne was barely flat before reality hit.

My old-timey British accent sucked. I had to get a voice coach. Gloria Wu was a drill sergeant with the rehearsals. Then the Roosevelt Hotel happened, and she loaded the contract with clauses that could get me fired. No drinking. No smoking. No bad press. Like I didn't quit Boy Scouts in third grade.

Gene said I had to take it, or I was going to have to forget movies altogether.

Some days, I wished I'd just taken him up on forgetting acting. They shot the outdoor scenes in Ireland, which was buggy as a jungle, and you couldn't get bottle service in the clubs. The costumes squeezed my balls, and girls had a weird-ass sense of humor that made me wonder if I was the butt of a joke or just dumb. The accent started creeping into my regular speech, so when I got home, I sounded like a tool. Louise liked it. Louise liked everything.

But I just kept doing my best. I was so good the entire shoot I thought I shoulda stayed in Boy Scouts. Everyone was high-fiving me as if I'd walked through a fire that had cooked off my bad reputation. I wrote a song about it, and another. Once I was done with this shoot, I was going to record a solo album that was going to do fine, and no one would come at me about the Roosevelt Hotel ever again.

The last two weeks were in a local location in Elysian Heights. Then Chad messaged on Insta . . . just "I'm going to call you. Pick up."

It was possible he didn't know I was on contract-clause probation. Also possible he didn't know he was the villain in my story.

That was what Gloria Wu said about Darcy. He was just living. He didn't know everyone thought he was some kind of rogue asshole. He also didn't have a team of people whose paycheck depended on what people thought.

I did.

Ken Braque wasn't only my public relations guy . . . he was everyone's PR guy, and he had the chateau in the south of France and the Bentley in his Malibu garage to prove it.

He also had my old phone, which was signed into all my accounts.

Ken didn't want to meet in a restaurant, because he didn't want to be seen. Hungry as a dog, I sat in his conference room, picking at the fruit tray while he sat across from me scrolling through my messages as if I was paying him to keep track of me. Which I was.

Every room in Ken's agency looked the same. Shiny wood. Chrome. Black office chairs. Windows from all the way here to all the way there. Not exactly cool or sharp, but expensive looking. Just like the man himself, who was some age between forty and fifty-nine, a height between five ten and six one, with a head of hair that wasn't graying but wasn't youthful.

"Chad messaged you on Instagram," he said, holding my phone so I could see what I knew was there.

"So?"

"How?"

"What do you mean how? The paper airplane in the corner."

"Your messages are locked to the public."

"I forgot to unapprove him." I snapped the phone away and navigated to settings, where I had a list of the very few accounts allowed to send me a message. Would have been hard to miss Chad, considering I'd cut off everyone else, but maybe it was a little bit on purpose. Chad was the only one of us who'd disappeared after that night, and the one who'd never contact me unless it was life or death.

"Did he call?" Ken asked.

"How should I know?" I put the phone down and picked a piece of toothpick-speared pineapple off the tray. "He doesn't have my new number."

I popped the fruit in my mouth and flicked the toothpick on a napkin, trying to look casual. I half reclined in the chair with my ankle over the opposite knee.

"Your limitations are for your benefit," Ken said.

"Are we doing the thing where you lecture me?"

"We're doing the thing you retained me for."

"Keeping me clean." My foot rocked at the speed of my annoyance.

"Keeping you from falling into the abyss of irrelevance. If you were a different kind of musician or you had a different look." He flicked his hand toward me, up and down to indicate the look he was talking about. "If you'd started your career after adolescence, we could sell you as the dangerous kind and lead into a redemption narrative in your fifties. You don't have that luxury. No one has ever successfully rebranded out of childhood stardom. Sorry, kid."

"Cool. I'm out." I uncrossed my legs, but Ken didn't move.

"You start shooting again tomorrow?"

"Yeah."

"Has Gene gotten you anything else?"

"He wants the edit to go out first."

"Good. Let's review."

I pushed into the back of the chair and turned it so he was to my side. Even then, seeing him in my peripheral vision was like a buzz saw an inch from my balls. I pressed my fingertips against one temple to block him.

"No contact with anyone involved in the incident. This includes, but is not limited to . . . Gordon Daws. Heidi Collins-Daws. Chad Westwick. Shane Huang."

That list of names hurt every time.

"I know."

"When you're out, you will either drink zero alcohol or use a driver. Zero drugs, period. Carter Kincaid will be your bodyguard. He reports to me. Keep your middle finger in your pocket and pretend you like everyone you speak to. And we need to add a rule about women."

"I haven't gotten laid in months."

"In Cork? Red hair?"

"They're all redheads."

"This one cost you a few grand in shut-the-fuck-up money. She had video of you in a pub getting handsy with two of her friends."

"That was one night in like . . . May." It was the only night I let loose in Ireland, paying to keep the bar open. And yeah, there were three girls, and we all had a good time. "Did she say it wasn't consensual? Because it was."

"No one's saying that, but if the video had gone viral before we got to it, we'd be putting out a fire. This is the point, Justin. Never forget this is about directing people's attention away from your conduct and toward your work."

"Dude, this is too far. I can't date?"

"I never said that."

"You said there had to be a rule about women."

"I did. Here's the rule. If you like someone, they come through me."

"Nah." I spun my body and the chair in his direction and leaned across the table. "That's a full nope."

"You're vulnerable, and you're not in a position to trust your own judgment. The studio has stuck with you on this film, but all it's going to take is one unscrupulous woman with a Twitter account and a lawyer and like this . . ." He snapped his fingers. "Your brand is shot, and Slashdot Records cuts your marketing budget. You make music no one hears about. Justin Beckett becomes someone people google when they're wondering if any of the Sunset Boys made another album. DMZ will make money talking about every stupid thing you do for the rest of your life, but as an artist, you're finished."

"You're exaggerating."

"It'll cost you your career to find out."

I stood up and held my hand out like I wanted to shake on it.

"I'll think about it."

Ken took my hand, smiling because he knew I didn't have a choice.

~

I figured Kayla, Hot Girl With Selvedge, would fold as soon as I had Francine Glick call. No one resisted Francine. She did the heavy lifting of making me feel like a man while wearing froufrou shit all over. She told me the more powerful the dude, the finer the lace. She was so convincing about the badassery of grosgrain ribbon that I had it put on my hoodies. If she could convince me of that, getting a jobless, broke-ass designer on set would be a piece of cake.

And I was right.

Monday. I was walking onto the location with Bern (my manager), Victor (my PA), Carter (my bodyguard), and Humby (my stylist) when I saw her talking to Eddie Ainsley by craft services.

She was as hot as I remembered. Curly black hair. Brown eyes. Full lips that had a little hole in the center when they were closed. I gave her the "call me" sign, then flipped it into a head scratch when her eyes went wide with "don't do that."

I could take a hint.

~

"You have a fitting for scene 21 at nine thirty." Victor sat on the bench across the table, tapping the eraser side of his pencil against his clipboard and puckering his lips, meaning he was deep in thought.

"Noted," Humby said in a thick British accent as he stood in the corner, flipping through a magazine.

"Meet with Gloria at eleven thirty on set to prep for scene 19, which is shooting at eleven forty-five. When are you supposed to eat lunch?"

Leaning to look out the tinted window, I saw Kayla walk away from Eddie and into the costume trailer with the truck girl. I checked my watch. My fitting wasn't for another hour.

"Not acceptable," Bern said as he leaned into the fridge. "She knows better than to call Justin's scenes between twelve and one."

"You had the schedule last night," Victor bit back. "This should be fixed already."

Bern came out with his breakfast Tab and popped the cap. "I was busy."

"So was I," Victor said. "Doing my job."

"Your job's ordering lunch."

"Nobu," I said more than asked, trying not to look like I was staring at the costume trailer.

"Of course," Victor said. "Your grandmother called. She said she was surprised. Thought you fired me and hired a girl with curly hair?"

"Oh snap," Bern said.

"No." I waved it away. "She's got a bunch of numbers for me on speed dial. It's a long story that ends with oncoming dementia. Whatever she wants, just say yes."

"She wanted to thank me for the roses."

"What did you say?"

"I said, 'What roses?' and she said, 'The ones that got me laid.'"

Bern laughed while I watched the costume trailer for a girl who wasn't coming out for a while.

"I have a fitting."

"Right." Humby snapped the magazine closed. "Early bird and all that."

"I'm good," I said to him. "Hang here."

"What?"

"It's just a button," I lied. "Go check on the shirts with the lace, would you? I want one for the thing on Saturday."

I left before he could ask what thing. Carter fell in behind me without a word.

Just about the only time I could walk around on the street was when it was closed off for a video and now a movie shoot. Even then, it wasn't like I was just walking along the street. People had questions, script revisions, and gossip. It was like trying to get across the quad in high school after our first album went platinum. It took forever to go a hundred feet, but I acted rushed and eventually got up to the costume door.

Kayla was on a ladder, holding a Victorian undergarment that looked like a bedsheet. The phone made a rectangle bump in her pocket, and I had to admit she was even cuter when she wasn't growling at me.

The truck girl stood beside the ladder, checking her clipboard.

"Not my size," I said, sitting in Francine's chair, eye level with Kayla's cowboy boots.

"Not everything's about you," she replied, flipping the tag on the hanger.

"Justin," the truck girl said with a glance at her watch. "You're early."

"Came to see how Kayla was doing. So. How you doing?"

Kayla got down from the ladder carefully. Making me wait. Still cute, but still growling in a way.

I put my feet on the desk, because I was feeling chill, even if she wasn't.

"I'm fine." She kicked the steamer on with the toe of her boot.

"Truck girl," I said to the chick with the clipboard. "Can you grab me a doughnut or something?"

"Her name's Evelyn." Kayla hung the garment on a hook above the steamer.

"It's fine," Evelyn said, pushing her black glasses up her nose. "Doughnuts from the cast table?"

"Yeah."

She left. It was just me and Hot Phone Girl.

"No 'thank you' for getting you a job?" I said. "Cool. Cool. You do you."

"I will."

"Any calls?"

"No." The steamer gurgled as she ran it under the skirt.

"You sure?"

She put her phone on the desk. "There. Code's 2019."

I took the phone and opened it. Scrolled through the messages and notifications. Nothing. I flipped it back onto the desk blotter.

"It's absolutely amazing to me that you just felt entitled to go through my phone like that."

"You gave me the code."

"So?"

"Isn't that what you wanted me to do?"

Not answering, she ran the steamer handle under the garment with an intensity that had nothing to do with me. I was sitting right there, but I wasn't even in the room as far as she was concerned. Or so I thought.

"What are you looking at?" she said.

"Why are you so pissed off at me?"

"For one? You manipulated the situation to get me here, and you won't tell me why."

"Why do you care?"

"Because you just scrolled through what could have been really personal stuff."

All I'd seen were a few *yeses* and *thanks* and a yellow emoji.

"There was nothing."

"That's not the point." The water in the steamer was doing its thing. Steaming. And so was she. I'd just tried to reassure her it was cool, and she was mad. What did she want out of me, already?

41

"What's the point then?"

"The first point is, don't look in my stuff. The second is . . . What if I pick up and I don't know what to say? And am I supposed to just wait until you ask me who called? I mean, what is this? You're controlling a piece of my life, and for all I know you're using this number to sell drugs or . . . I don't know. Fuck your best friend's wife."

My reputation preceded me. Denying everything wasn't even on the table, but letting her think the worst wasn't either.

"Hold up." I took my feet off the desk. "I am not that guy."

"Sure you're not."

I'd walked through fire, and all she could see was the stupid headlines about the Roosevelt Hotel. What happened to the benefit of the doubt?

"A'ight," I said. "Here's the deal. You get a call from Vegas, don't answer it. Just come get me. Anywhere on set. You find me." I plucked a pen from a mug full of them and wrote my number on a sticky note. "If we're not on set, you call this." I stuck the note on her phone and slid it toward her. "Guard that with your life."

She looked down at it. Then at me, as if she knew what my personal number was worth.

"Take my phone," she said, turning back to the steamer. "I'll use my old one and get another number."

Did that work?

No, that wasn't gonna work. Ken could find out I had two phones. I needed a buffer.

"What do you want?" I asked. "Money?"

"Not from you."

"I can tag you on my Insta."

She scoffed. "Why?"

"Maybe you got a SoundCloud or something. I tag you, you get followers."

"No thanks."

"What, then? What's a guy gotta do?"

42

She hung up the steamer rod and leaned over the desk as if she were the boss and I was in some kind of trouble. Which was a no. She wasn't the boss of me. I leaned back and put my feet up. She could sniff my soles or back the fuck up.

But no. She looked me right in the eye.

"I have a pretty good ear for bullshit," she said. "But I don't need it for this. You want me to pick up calls to your old number, and I want to know why."

"That's it?"

"That's it."

"I tell you and you'll just do it?"

"You'll owe me, but I'll do it."

"What'll I owe you?"

"To be determined."

I shrugged. I could live with a TBD. Wasn't much she could ask for that I couldn't deliver. And if it was a bad ask, I could just say no.

But blowing my wad wasn't going to work either.

"I stuck my foot in it. Got put on blast. You read about it. The Roosevelt Hotel. My band broke up. The record company threw a hissy fit and invoked this thing in my contract. I had to cut myself off from certain people and get counseling."

"That was in your *contract*?" Her expression settled somewhere between a sneer and genuine curiosity. "Who you can be friends with?"

Anyone who couldn't be accused of "exerting negative influence," but I was in no mood to define Chad by the accusations against him.

"Yeah. You handing out free legal advice?"

"No." She took her knuckles off the desk and crossed her arms over her chest. "And these people? The ones you cut off? They have your old number?"

"Yeah."

God, the way she looked down at me as if she was trying to see inside my head. She was so damn hot. Not my type. Too tough. But more of a challenge than any millionaire model on my old (or new) phone's contact list.

"Look," I said. "It's an old friend. It's not my dealer or anything like that. And . . . you know I thought it wouldn't be a big deal. But I'm not the guy who just cuts people off. Doesn't feel right."

"You're asking me to help you breach your contract."

Roadblock. I wasn't asking for a service, I was asking her to stick her neck out. But being right didn't make her *right*. What was going to happen to her if she was found out? What did she have to lose? She wasn't going to get sued. I mean, mostly maybe. And it wasn't like she needed a working relationship with my record company.

I was about to point this out when the door at the end of the trailer opened and Francine came in with a coffee cup.

"Hey, Frannie," I said.

"Get your feet off my desk, Justin."

I got up and gave her a hug.

"You're early for your fitting," she said, getting into her chair.

"Yeah, I was bored."

"Welcome to Hollywood." She turned to Kayla, whose arms had dropped to her sides. "You can go now? Yes?"

"Yes."

"We don't recut," she said to Kayla. "We work with what we have, and we're not fancy about it."

"No problem."

"Good. Get JB21. Mr. Darcy's lost a little weight since we made the trousers." With a flick of her wrist, she ended the questioning.

Kayla nodded and casually picked up her phone, shooting me a glance before she put it in her back pocket.

CHAPTER 5

KAYLA

I was a sucker for people who love their friends. I didn't make friends easily, and I lost them like earring pairs. Carelessly, while I wasn't looking. I guess that was one of the reasons it was so easy to leave New York.

Brenda was the only one I really cared about. We'd met at Parsons School of Design, and eighteen months after graduation we were working at Josef Signorile together.

I hadn't seen her in a long time, but I'd never forget her. In first-year draping class, she'd brought her own dress form. We all had to work on size-eight forms, but she wasn't having it. She'd hauled in her own size fourteen and dared the instructor to tell her otherwise . . . which he did. He brought it right to the dean and she fought tooth and nail to work on large sizes, which didn't make her any fans in the class.

They didn't want to think about big women. Wanted to pretend they didn't exist. I'll admit to being uncomfortable with anyone doing their own thing while the rest of us followed the rules and were all graded on the same size model. But she grew on me. She was tough. She knew what she wanted to get out of that class, and by hook or by crook, she was getting it.

I started to admire her, and by the end of the semester, she'd sold me on the million ways large-size people were erased, and that draping class was number one. She deserved a better grade, because she could do magic with a square of muslin and the right size form.

New York could suck a bag of dicks, but Brenda? I missed the way she could set me straight, and I was sure she would have given me an earful about being Justin Beckett's personal message taker.

I flipped a hanger tag. JB21 was the actor's initials and the scene number. I found the pants where Evelyn said they'd be and brought them into the fitting room for my test.

The fitting room.

Where the trouble back home had started.

I slid the stuffed blue tomato with pins sticking out of it onto my wrist and laced a tape measure around my neck.

This was my job, not just today, but for my life. What had happened would never happen again.

The fitting room at the end of the trailer was shielded from prying eyes by covered windows and a locked door. Two mirrors were set at a right angle in one corner.

Francine sat in a little folding chair by a table with her legs crossed. I could see Justin's bare feet under the changing room curtain. They say famous people put their pant legs on one at a time. Not Justin. He sat on a chair and shoved them both through.

"Do we measure them first?" I asked.

"We go fast," she said. "We're not making hundreds of these. Alter for fit and for the camera."

I pushed the hanger past the curtain, and when he took it, his hand brushed mine for a second. A totally unnecessary touch that sent a wave of shudders through me.

"Okay," I said, pulling my arm back as if I'd been caught in the middle of a sexual fantasy.

"The machine's in the rack room. You can use it?"

"Yes. No problem."

Justin came out of the changing room in nothing but trousers, as if he wasn't somehow bending light toward him looking like Michelangelo's *David*. The definition of his body was exactly that sharp. Marble carved to the shape of every muscle and vein and painted with tattoos on his right shoulder and arm, with a relaxed posture of defiant arrogance.

It was my job to look at him, but I turned away for my own sanity. I had to get it together. He was still an ass, and his looks made it that much more likely he was always going to be an ass.

He got on the platform in front of the mirrors. There was work to do. He was just a form, and his waistband was sagging where his lower back curved.

"Okay," I said more to myself than anyone else. "This is easy."

"Good," Francine said, picking up her vibrating phone.

I could feel the heat of his body and the weight of his eyes on me in the mirror. His back bowed above the swell of his ass, with a soft, sueded matte I had to make an effort not to touch.

I pinched the back of the waist. "Is this comfortable?" I asked.

"Yeah." He watched me kneeling behind him. I pinned the back rise carefully from the bottom.

"I have to go on set," Francine said, standing. "Kayla, do the alteration. Finished by ten fifteen. If I'm not back in time to see it on him, take a picture."

"Okay."

Before I could ask another question, she was gone, and I was alone with Justin's stare and the magnetic pull of his shape.

"This is a lot," I said, pinching out the waist.

"I stopped partying." He crossed his arms to get them out of the way.

"After the Roosevelt Hotel thing?"

"Yeah." I adjusted the excess from the rise below, feeling the firmness of his butt under my fingers. My face went hot, and I hid behind him so he couldn't see me in the mirrors. "But it changed my life."

"Was it hard?"

"Of course it was hard."

I stopped at the last bit of fabric. While I loved a good double entendre as much as the next girl, I was already too close to nervous giggling. Or maybe he was still on the subject, and I was being silly.

Looking around him, I checked his expression in the mirror.

Smirking. Was he trying to make me uncomfortable?

Fine. Two could play at this.

"I bet it's quite hard." I pinched the last tiny bit of excess. "Every time you look at yourself in the mirror."

My fingertips, informed by the delight of my eyes and the need to experience the smooth perfection of his skin, thought they could get away with something inconceivable. Before I could override the decision, they brushed the indent of his lower back.

He jumped with a quick laugh, spinning to face me.

"I'm sorry!" I cried, confused by the laughing and the sharp twist away.

He's ticklish.

"Are we done?" he asked.

"We're done."

"Good."

He stormed into the dressing room and shut the curtain.

I didn't care if he liked me as a person, but I didn't want him to think less of me as a professional. And yet I could still feel the softness on my skin. Part of me—the nonsense animal part—wanted to see just how ticklish he was.

"I've never done that before," I called. "Really. I'm so sorry."

"Forget it." He kicked the trousers under the curtain. "It's not that big a deal. Just make sure my pants don't fall down when I'm in scene, okay?"

I picked up the costume.

"Okay." I hated being wrong, especially in opposition to someone I thought so little of.

My phone rang, and Justin snapped the curtain open, fully dressed. I took it out of my pocket and looked at the screen.

Unknown number from Las Vegas.

I handed it to him, and he answered as if it were his phone.

"Hey," he said. When he heard the voice on the other side, he shooed me away as if I were a child, and I hated him all over again.

I left to make the adjustments on the dinky machine we had in the trailer. I could hear his voice on the other side of the wall. The words were too muffled, but the tone was sober. He wasn't making dinner plans or trash-talking. He was serious.

The alteration didn't look great, but I kept the mess to the back, where his jacket would cover it. It took seven minutes, but when I went to the changing room to have him try the pants on, he was gone.

Thank God. Now I could work.

~

The assistant director, a woman named Renee with a constantly attached headset, came to bring me on set for a quick steam on a petticoat, then Francine needed a slip stitch to keep a lapel down so the light didn't shine on it. I managed to gobble down lunch before I was sent to makeup so I could remove a foundation stain from Eddie's shirt.

"How's your first day?" he asked, chin pointing up so I could rub his collar with a bar of soap. People were constantly in and out of makeup for adjustments. The chatter was constant except when a scene was shooting upstairs. Then it was quiet as a church.

"Eventful."

"Never a dull moment," Hector, the makeup guy, said as he screwed a cap on a pot of blue. "Not when you're living the dream."

"Is that what this is?" I said, trying to do the impossible without a bleach stick.

"If your dream is watching the Beckster lose his shit," Eddie grumbled under his breath.

"What happened?" I asked, wondering if it was the phone call.

Eddie just shook his head as if he'd said too much. Hector cleared his throat as if changing the subject.

"One minute!" Renee called to the far corners of the house.

"Good enough." I stepped back. "I hope."

"It's fine," Hector said. "We're not selling it at Nordstrom. We're selling it to America."

Eddie took off to get to set. I sighed and folded the packaging over the soap.

"You haven't been doing this long." Hector arranged his table. He was in his late thirties and already bald and jowly, as if he were born old enough to know when someone was new.

"First day."

"Let me give you a hair and makeup tip. If you want to keep working, your job is to listen and let it go. Don't ask questions if the answers might be of value to someone."

"Okay. I'll take it under advisement."

"Kayla?" a handsome guy in a suit asked. I recognized him as one of the men who had come on set with Justin.

"Yeah?"

"I'm Carter, Justin's security."

"Hi."

"He asked me to get this to you."

He handed me my phone and was gone before I could thank him. Hector looked at the phone with a raised eyebrow. I expected him to ask about it, but he was a man who took his own advice.

"We're going out Friday," he said as an actress plopped herself in his chair. "Makeup. A few of the girls in hair. You should come."

"Sure."

He'd already turned his attention to the actress. I headed for the costume trailer and opened my phone. I had a text from Justin.

—*Thank you*—
—*And yeah. It was hard.*—

CHAPTER 6

JUSTIN

There were four of us. Me, Chad, Shane the Pain, and Gordon.

Echo Park was our kingdom, and the Beckett house on Valentine Street was the castle.

I had an Xbox, a PlayStation, and a fraternal twin brother, Justice, who wound up on a minor league team in Florida. Mom and Dad let us run all over the neighborhood from the time we were in kindergarten at the Montessori school around the corner. Justice and I were wild animals. Gone all day and home for dinner covered in dirt and scrapes. Chad, Gordon, and Shane started coming over around third grade, right about when Dad made us take piano and play a team sport—because balance was a thing with him. We could climb fences all over Echo Park as long as we did those two things.

Justice begged me to join the Wilshire Warriors with him, but those baseball uniforms with the stirrups in the pants were humiliating. After one season, I couldn't do it anymore. So Mom talked Dad into letting me take guitar instead.

My father making a compromise meant I had to prove he'd made the right choice. So I practiced like a madman, and I got over the hump of learning how to read music and play my instruments before I realized it was hard.

He owned a restaurant in Silver Lake, so he was out at the markets at the crack of dawn, home between lunch and the first seating, then working all night. So he was *around* but only sometimes. If the guys were over after school, when I was supposed to be practicing, they had to wait on the porch until four o'clock while Justice was at baseball practice with Mom.

That one day, in the spring of seventh grade, I could see them through the big front windows, killing fifteen minutes. They laughed about a thing I wasn't included in, and I snapped.

I turned my keyboard amp up and let her rip. I played the stupid Beatles song I was learning. "The Long and Winding Road." And my friends stood on the other side of the window and sang it with me. We'd never sung together before. That wasn't a thing. But we landed on some kind of harmony, maybe because the keyboard wasn't so loud on the other side, and the guys could hear each other.

Dad came up the steps, holding a paper bag with baguettes sticking out of the top. I stopped playing because even though I wasn't officially breaking the rules, I wasn't obeying the spirit of the thing either. The guys were facing me, so they didn't see him and went on another verse until I stopped and pointed behind them.

In unison, Gordon, Chad, and Shane stepped away from the glass and greeted my father. Gordon called him Mr. Beckett, which he hated. Chad and Shane waved and said, "Hey."

Dad flicked his wrist at our front door. I read his lips saying, "Get inside." He could get a pit bull to back up and roll over, so my friends obeyed. Dad followed them in without a word and brought his baguettes to the kitchen.

"What now?" Gordon asked, throwing himself on the couch.

"If he calls my mom . . ." Chad finished the thought with a quick shake of his head.

Shane sat at the piano and played a cadence pattern. He took piano, but his parents weren't militaristic about it.

"Just chill," I said. From the kitchen, I heard the bag land on the counter. "He won't call."

He wouldn't rat on them for distracting me or tell their parents to keep them away before four. Raising kids took a village. He'd rag them out himself, which would suck.

Dad came into the living room and crossed his arms.

"I'm sorry—" I started to explain but shut my trap with a hard look from him.

"You three," he said. Chad chewed a nail. Shane stopped playing. Gordon straightened up ever so slightly. "You taking music at school?"

"Nah," Gordon said. "Got cut last year."

"Of course," Dad said. "So where have you sung before? Together?"

We looked at each other. Had we sung before? What kind of question was that? Was it good or bad? Why was my father such a dick?

"Thought so," Dad said, checking his watch. "All of you go home. I'm calling your parents."

Wide-eyed, they shuffled out, and I was left alone with my father, whom I'd never really hated until that moment.

"I'll clean the toilet," I said, turning off the keyboard amp.

He let me go do the adult thing even though I wasn't in trouble.

~

Hot Phone Girl left the fitting room, and I answered the call.

"Chad?" I said, pacing across the tiny room.

"Yeah. It's me." Trucks rumbled in the background. Wherever he was, it was windy.

"Where are you?"

"A pay phone. Dude. I'm fucked. So fucked."

"You're not fucked. You just have to get out of Nevada."

"And go where? Dude. This is federal, okay? I brought my stash over state lines."

I pressed my forehead on the mirror as if I were trying to double my brain. It didn't work. I wasn't any smarter, but my head was cooler.

"You need to come back."

"Why?" He wasn't asking, really. He was accusing. This was going to get weird if I didn't give him a good reason to come home.

"Because everyone who gives a shit about you is here." I snapped a little too much, but the revisions I had to memorize were on the floor, and convincing Chad to come back to LA could take an hour.

He didn't answer right away—as if he was trying to decide between believing me or the voices in his head.

"You all want to put me away," he said, siding with the voices. "You think that's giving a shit. But you don't know what it's like. You don't know what they do to me. They're trying to steal our songs. Right out of my head. Before I even write them."

"No, dude. That's impossible."

"They did it already! Why don't you listen?"

"Chad. Just come home and we can talk about it."

"I have it under control."

"Are you taking your meds or nah?"

"They make me stupid."

Chad was a bright guy, which was the problem. If I focused on the meds the doctor was giving him instead of his self-medication, he'd bolt.

The sewing machine on the other side of the wall started pounding. That would be Kayla doing the alterations. I didn't want her or anyone to hear me, so I left the trailer, talking low so my voice would get lost in the chaos of the closed-off street.

"We can write new songs," I said. "Better ones."

"You got a solo deal."

"I had to take it. But if you came back, we can work together. I promise."

"That's why you want me to come home."

"It is. Dude. Listen."

"No. You listen. I'm not safe there. Not around you or anyone. I know you. You're just a vacuum sucking my energy out of me. You want me dull and stupid so you can tell me what to do. And I called to tell you . . ." He drifted off.

"What?" I stood in the middle of the street with my head bowed. Carter's feet were in my vision and not much else. "Tell me what?"

"I know why you did what you did."

"What did I do?"

"You think you covered for me. But I know it was all so you could break us up and go solo. That was your plan from the beginning. We all know it."

The sound of the trucks and the wind cut off. I'd lost him. Again.

CHAPTER 7

KAYLA

Francine gave me the job. My first week on set went okay. I did another fitting on Justin where I managed to keep my fingers off him. He texted every day to ask if I'd gotten a call from Vegas. Late Friday, the texts started the way they usually did.

—Anything?—

—Nothing—

—K thx—

I pocketed the phone and took in Caroline Bingley's stays, like a corset but more comfortable.

"You coming out tonight?" Evelyn asked as she tagged a hanger. She was wearing baggy jeans from the nineties and a blue T-shirt with rectangle-cut sleeves.

"Sure. Who's going?"

"Hector and Jenny from makeup. Susan, maybe? Hector says he can get us into NV."

"What about Eddie?" I asked. The tension between them had been thick enough to touch.

She pushed her glasses up and kept her eyes on her work. She'd denied anything was going on with her and the actor, but refused to talk about it further.

"Maybe," she muttered, snapping hangers on the rack. "The big shots hang in the VIP room anyway, so whatever."

"He doesn't seem like a big shot," I said.

"Yeah, well. That all just depends on who you're seen with."

I had a hundred questions about who Eddie was seen with that she may have answered, but my phone buzzed again.

Justin.

—If you get a call this weekend you'll let me know?—

—Yes—

—Thanks—

—You hitting NV with the BTL?—

"What's BTL?" I asked Evelyn.

"Below the line. You. Me. The grips. Camera. Movie grunts, basically. Why?"

"Nothing. Just heard it around."

I tapped out a quick answer to Justin.

—Yes—

—Maybe I'll see you there—

~

Friday night, I was making a quick dinner in what I still considered Grandpa's kitchen. Behind the things he used most was a level of filth

I couldn't leave alone. He had a garlic press he must have thrown back in the drawer without cleaning sometime in 2005. I was getting the impression he'd had a mental decline none of us had known about, and it made me sad for him.

The phone rang as I cleaned the grime off a coffee mug. I held the phone in my palm, recognizing the caller as someone I'd gotten a new number to avoid.

But he was irresistible, and that was always the problem.

"Hello," I said.

"Kayla baby," Zack answered. His voice, so smooth and melodic, used to lull me into a sense of well-being.

Now it was just annoying.

"Hi."

"You changed your number."

"Yeah, I was going to call you, but it's been busy."

Lying was easier if I focused on the truth. It had been busy, and I was going to call him eventually.

"That's all right. Talia gave it to me."

Talia obviously found him irresistible as well. I hadn't explicitly told her not to give him my contact information, so I couldn't blame her.

"I'm just checking in on you," he said. "How's LA?"

"Fine. The weather's everything they say."

"I miss you."

Sure. Now he missed me. The guy who'd spent three years treating me like a piece of furniture suddenly missed me. Some days, I'd wished he'd just cheat on me so I'd know why I was an afterthought.

"Yeah," I said, putting the last mug on the rack. "So, how's Buster?"

"He misses you, too, don't you, boy? He's wagging his tail."

"He must want a treat." Zack's Chihuahua liked me well enough, and maybe he missed jumping on my lap for a stroke or eating my shoes, but I wasn't giving his owner the satisfaction of admitting it.

"I think he does." I heard him pop the box open. "So, Friday night and you're home."

Did I want to tell him I just hadn't gone out yet? I didn't owe him an explanation, and I didn't want to deal with twenty passive-aggressive questions.

"So are you."

"It's midnight here. I just got back. Laura and Jeremy say hi."

"Hi."

My phone rattled in my hand. Another call. I looked at the screen, and sure enough it was from Nevada. Not Las Vegas. Just Nevada.

"I have to go," I said.

"Yeah. Hey. You know Laura said Sartorial X Jeans is looking for someone."

"And?"

"You should call her about it."

"Did she tell you to ask me?"

"I'm just putting it out there."

The phone vibrated again.

"Why?"

"You could come home."

Pure Zack. It had taken years for me to realize he didn't hear a word I said. He just batted those thick black lashes over his sapphire-blue eyes, and I mistook that for attention. Even when I left New York and was crystal clear that meant I was leaving him, too, he didn't hear me.

"I have to go."

"I'll text you Laura's number."

I switched lines without responding, but I'd missed the Nevada call. I'd promised Justin I'd let him know if something came in. So I did.

As soon as he picked up, a blast of loud music and voices hit my ear.

"Did you get a call?" he shouted.

"Yes, but I didn't answer." I was shouting as if I were the one in a nightclub.

"You coming to NV later?"

"Yes!"

"Come around the back entrance. I'll put you on the list."

"But—"

He hung up.

~

Hector, Evelyn, and half a dozen people I recognized from set were almost in front of the shorter line at the club. I hopped out of the cab and rushed to them, passing a line that went around the corner.

"How are you running in those shoes!" Evelyn exclaimed. My neon-yellow Vivienne Westwood shoes had a front platform as high as a textbook and a thick heel in back.

"They're really comfortable," I lied. The bouncer sent the group in front of us to the line on the other side of the door.

"Not good," Hector muttered.

"What's not good?" I asked.

"They're picky tonight." He glanced at Evelyn's shirt, and I understood the problem right away. Her hair was falling out of her ponytail, and she was wearing a brightly printed cowboy blouse over the same jeans she'd worn to work.

"How many in your party?" a redheaded whip of a guy in a white satin shirt asked.

"Nine," Hector said.

The redhead looked us over.

"We'll take eight." He pointed to Evelyn. "You can wait on that line."

We looked at each other. Evelyn looked like she wanted to die. This posed a conundrum for everyone. I'd seen it before. Some things were the same no matter which coast you were on. We'd all wait in the long line to support Evelyn, and at three a.m. we'd go to a twenty-four-hour diner and complain about stupid bouncers and hot clubs. It wasn't fair, but nothing really was.

"I'm tired anyway," Evelyn said. "I'll just—"

"Seven," I said, then turned to Hector. "I got it. Go on."

"We'll all go," he objected.

I pulled Evelyn back.

"We're good. See you later."

"But—" Evelyn started.

"Come on," I interrupted, looping my arm in hers and pulling her down the block. "Trust me."

"Where are we going?"

A guy with a camera blew past us and whipped around a corner, behind the building.

"Follow him."

We walked fast to catch up. Another guy with a camera and bag came from the other direction and turned the same corner.

"Are you sure you're okay in those shoes?"

"I'm fine."

We turned into the back alley and walked toward a pack of paparazzi behind a velvet rope, in the middle of a right-of-way between the building and the parking lot. They shouted questions at Brad Sinclair, the actor, who was getting out of a matte-black Ferrari. He waved, flipped them the bird, and was escorted through the back door.

I was the only one wearing black except the woman in a tuxedo and a wire over her ear.

"We don't belong here," Evelyn said.

"Yes, we do."

"If they didn't let me in the front, they won't let me in the back." She stopped. "Kayla, just quit it, okay."

"Why?"

"It's not going to work."

"Trust me."

"No. You don't know what it's like to be humiliated in front of everyone."

"I do. Evelyn, I swear I do and—"

"When did it ever happen to you?" She crossed her arms, demanding I tell her things I hadn't told anyone on this side of the country.

"In New York."

"You were picked out of a group as the only one not cool enough to get into a club?"

"No. It was worse. No one would even wait on line with me."

"Why?"

"Miss," the woman in the tuxedo said. "Line's out front."

"I'm on the list." I kept my chin up as if I was sure I belonged there. "Kayla Montgomery."

Tuxedo checked her clipboard, flipping pages back and forth. A bearded paparazzo jostled me, trying to get a better spot.

"Whose list is it?" Tuxedo asked.

"Justin Beckett. And I have a plus-one."

She flipped three pages back. The bearded guy leaned away, and when I looked at him, I caught him eyeballing me as if memorizing my face.

"Problem?" I said. I stopped myself from telling him to take a picture because it lasted longer. He just nodded as if he didn't have a single problem I wasn't the solution to. Great. Now I was associated with Justin Beckett.

"There's no plus-one," Tuxedo said.

I took out my phone. "I'll call Justin and have him add one."

I hoped the threat would be enough to get her to let us in, but apparently not.

"Oh my God." Evelyn hid her face in her hands as I hit the green dot on my phone.

"Yo," Justin said. "You here?"

"I need a plus-one."

"One sec."

He hung up, and we waited as Tuxedo went about the business of letting someone else in.

"What is happening?" Evelyn whispered with urgency.

"We're going to have a good time," I said. "We just have to wait a minute."

"What if they let me in?" she said. "They're going to realize it was a mistake and kick me out, and it'll be worse."

"They won't because it's not."

Tuxedo opened the rope for us. When we were through, she closed it behind us, and the paparazzi took a few shots as if we were stars.

"Left hand, please."

We held out our wrists, and she wrapped a hot-pink wristband around mine, then Evelyn's.

"VIP room's up the stairs." She opened the door. "No pictures or video."

"Thanks." We went into the carpeted vestibule. The walls vibrated in a rhythm that seemed both far away and readily available. The door into the club and the stairway to the left were manned with bouncers. Right in front of me, as if they were even human, Brad Sinclair was chatting it up with Michael Greyson and a few others I didn't recognize.

Maintaining the seen-it-all attitude was going to be hard. Once, while interning at Jeremy St. James, I'd done a fitting for Gwen March's Emmy gown. I'd been competent and undaunted by her fame, yet I'd beamed with pride when she won. Her hem was straight because of me. I was background, but I'd touched something seen by millions.

Being in that lobby was the exact opposite experience. With nothing to do—no pins or tape measure and nothing to express my competence—I was background, and somehow ineffectual and awed.

Evelyn had frozen in place—that was something I could manage.

"Hey, so what's that history you were doing?"

She snapped out of it.

"History?"

"Yeah. Tell me about your master's."

"I was studying the intersection of fashion and technology. Like why cotton is so cheap and how you have to analyze changes in supply chain so . . . oh my God, they're coming this way."

Michael and Brad were making their way to the stairs, and I snapped out of it. We had someplace to go. I turned to the VIP entrance, and the bouncer opened the rope to let us through.

"Nice shoes," Brad Sinclair said from behind me.

"They clash with the wristband." I ended the quip by nearly tripping on my long, drapey pants. I grabbed Evelyn so I wouldn't tumble.

Brad chuckled at either my joke or the near pratfall.

"You all right?" he asked.

"Yeah. I'm fine."

This is what you get for wearing long pants in July.

Head down, I opened the heavy curtain at the top of the stairs.

Though dark and well designed with dark woods and ambient light, tables and chairs were still fashioned for mere mortals.

"This is so cool," Evelyn whispered.

"Yeah."

"Eddie's here."

I followed her gaze to Eddie, who was standing at the bar with Thomasina Wente, the runway model. He was three inches shorter than her, but looking up while he spoke didn't seem to bother him.

"Go say hello. I have to find Justin."

"No way!" She clutched my arm.

I was about to ask why but would only hear the obvious. She had a thing for him but didn't want to battle a German fashion model. Completely reasonable.

"We should go downstairs," she said. "Everyone's there."

"Later. I'm going to get a drink."

As we headed in that direction, Eddie turned and saw us. He was in a loose white shirt and tight tapestry vest. Evelyn clutched harder, even when he waved us over.

Thomasina Wente said something I couldn't hear, and by the time we got to the bar, she'd moved on to something else.

"Kayla," he said with a nod before moving to my companion. "Evelyn."

He looked at her as if she were the only woman in the world.

"Hi," she said.

"Can I get you guys something?"

Justin wasn't visible right away, but I saw Carter standing against the wall with his hands in front of him. Then I caught sight of one of Justin's entourage walking away from the bar with a drink in each hand and followed him to a bank of couches in the corner.

"I'll have a beer," Evelyn said.

From the back couch where Justin held court, he saw me. For a split second, I didn't recognize him. Not by name. Not by reputation. Just a man whose presence radiated outward.

"Anything for you?" Eddie asked from a million miles away.

Justin Beckett, in a weird moment, wasn't the fallen boy-band superstar or the entitled asshole who peeled three hundreds off the stack and dropped them in my lap to buy my secretarial services. He was immortal and he called.

"I'm good," I said, walking toward him.

"Hey," Evelyn said. "Where are you going?"

"Just over there."

Eddie leaned over the bar in a deep drink-related discussion. I took the opportunity to give Evelyn the thumbs-up before the crowd parted so I could see Justin fully. His sweatpants hung low on his waist, and his gold chain flashed. The overcompensation of his outfit shut down my trance like a TV on static. Shoulders slouched, fingering an empty glass, he was unbearably human and startlingly beautiful, with a sore melancholy that was the core of every sad song ever written.

He was the kind of guy I could really fall for, which meant he was garbage.

"Kaylacakes," he cried with his hand out, fingers curling back and forth in a hand-it-over gesture. The silly nickname broke the spell, erasing his approachable magnificence and turning it into the irritating injustice of genetic accidents. That was his talent. Being whatever you wanted to see in a man.

With two hands, he shoved the woman sitting next to him and patted the empty space she left behind as if I were a puppy dog.

I hated doing what I was told, so I sat on the table in the center of the U of couches and unlocked my phone.

"You look nice," he said a little too appreciatively, flicking a fold in my pants. "All dressed up in black like a real New Yorker."

"Here's the call," I said, opening my recent calls before handing the phone over. He looked at the number and the ones around it. His seductive appreciation of my outfit was gone. "You really should just take the phone. This is silly."

"Who were you on the phone with when it came in?"

"None of your business."

He leveled his gaze at me, and I met it without flinching. Both our jaws were set, but I was right, and when he looked down, it must have been because he realized he didn't have a leg to stand on.

"Hold on," he said, swiping to text messages. He replied to the call I'd missed with a text. "We got this. We got it."

—Hey. Where u?—

"*We* don't have anything, Justin. I didn't sign up to be your secret receptionist or for twenty questions about who I'm talking to when a call comes in. I'm just trying to live and have a life, and you think you can take over. It's not enough that I got dressed up to come halfway across town because I basically did your grandmother a favor. You act like I owe you something."

He nodded, sucking his left cheek between his teeth.

"Let me get you a drink." He looked over my shoulder. "Vic, get her a . . ." He turned back to me. "What do you drink?"

"I don't want you to buy me a drink."

He put his elbows on his knees and leaned into me. I still expected him to smell like Axe body spray, but he smelled like the ocean. "You're gonna make me surprise you?"

"Nothing about you is surprising."

He smirked, glanced at the phone to find no reply, and turned back up to me.

"You're so tough. So, I'm guessing scotch or straight rye. Something that makes you want to punch kittens. Maybe on the rocks since it's July." His tongue flicked to lick his lower lip. "But you're here. Dressed in black all up and down with big yellow shoes. Still talking to me when you despise me and every word out of my mouth. Like you want to be sweet but it's so damn hard."

"We're back to hard?"

I tried to hook him away from an intimate come-on that was uncomfortably real and into something manageably shallow.

He didn't take the bait, leaving me with the possibility that he was as attracted to me as I was to him. I suddenly felt like a balloon inflated to the point of breaking.

"Old fashioned," he said.

"What's that supposed to mean?"

"It means I have a guess." He looked over my shoulder. "Get her the Star Slider. Another club soda for me."

"I don't have to drink it."

"You should try it. It's sticky and unsatisfying. Sour at the back." He gave half a shrug. "Like my apology."

"What apology?"

"The one I owe you for being a dick."

That was it. No actual apology followed. He just waited for me to accept something he never offered. Maybe that was as good as it got with him. Too bad it wasn't good enough.

"Pay up," I said with extra pop on my *p*.

He nodded, sucked his cheek in some more, looked away, stalling like an old car.

"I'm—" He stopped as my phone lit the bottom of his face, vibrating in his hand. When we looked down at it, the tops of our heads touched.

—On the 15. Driving. Text later—

"Yes!" he cried. "Hell, yes!"

He grabbed my face and went to kiss me, but we both turned just enough to land his lips on my cheek.

"Yes!" he said again with a smile that could sell magazines off the rack faster than they could be stocked. "Thank you! Thank. You. Kay. La!"

Laughing with happiness bordering on delirium, he hugged me so tight that his gold rope chain pressed into my chin. His joy was so contagious I put my arms around his waist and my palms on the curve of his lower back, swaying with him as I surrendered to his moment.

My eyes were open, and over his shoulder I could see Evelyn and Eddie laughing. She seemed relaxed and chatty until she saw Justin hugging me and she put her hand over her mouth.

This looked weird. Everyone was going to think we were together. Kayla the Nobody and Justin Beckett—who was either loved or reviled by anyone with an internet connection.

Not the way I wanted to start fresh.

When I released him, he unwrapped himself. I thought it was over. We could just sit, and he could tell me what he was so happy about.

But he wasn't done. He bent over and scooped me up, one arm under my knees and the other holding up my torso. I sucked in a breath, and he spun me around like a cyclone, whipping my head to the right, then the left when he changed direction.

"Hold up!" I shouted as he was about to change direction again.

He stopped. Smiling at me in a way that wasn't rehearsed or manipulative. My arms were around his neck for leverage, but damn if it wouldn't look like affection.

"You," was all he said. "You did it!"

"What did I do?" I asked, letting my curiosity get the better of my desire to be put down.

Instead of answering, he looked around at his friends, as if realizing they were there for the first time. A sea of faces stared back at us with wide eyes. A bubble of humiliation welled up from my chest, as if I'd left the house without pants and didn't notice until I was between stops on the subway.

He put me down, and I assumed he felt the same shame at his naked emotion.

I was wrong.

"Problem?" he asked the strangers circling us with his palms out at his sides, looking at each of them in turn with a challenge.

Shamelessness and entitlement had its advantages.

"What just happened?" I demanded.

"Come on." He took my arm and tried to pull me away.

"Where are we going?" I leaned in the opposite direction. He took the hint and let my elbow go. I was afraid he was going to pick me up again, but he just smiled and spoke softly in my ear.

"The Emerald Room." He nodded as if I was supposed to know what he was talking about, and I shook my head to let him know that not only had I never heard of the Emerald Room, I wasn't going anywhere without a full description of his expectations.

"It's fine," he said.

"I'm not going into some strange color-coded room alone with you."

He held his hands up, laughing.

"It's not that. We can talk." He tilted his head to the crowd that was breaking up but standing close to see if he lost his mind again.

"Don't pick me up anymore."

"Okay. Sorry."

"And no touching."

"No touching. Really. You can trust me."

He went around the table and looked back at me to see if I was following. My clunky yellow shoes were rooted in place, and everyone was pretending to pay attention to something else.

I picked up my bag and walked beside him to yet another roped-off door.

~

The Emerald Room was pretty cool. Smaller than the VIP room, with soft lounge music and curved tufted booths tented with deep-green velvet curtains, it was quieter and less crowded. Some of the curtains had been drawn over the couches to hide the occupants. A slim white woman with penciled-on eyebrows led us to an empty booth.

"Can I get you something to drink?" she asked as we slid in.

"Club soda for me. She'll have—"

"Same."

Eyebrows started to draw the curtain.

"No," I said.

"Leave it open," Justin added, taking my signal. The woman nodded and left us sitting on opposite sides of the circle, my phone glass-up between us. Justin leaned forward without his usual slouch. He bounced his knee fast enough to make the heavy tabletop vibrate.

"So," I said. "That was embarrassing."

"Really?"

"You're that unaware?"

He shrugged, glancing at the door.

"Sorry," he said. Whatever elation his text had brought on had drained out of him.

"You're forgiven."

"What do I owe you? For everything you've done for me."

"An explanation."

He fiddled with the phone, spinning it on the tabletop before stopping it with a flat hand.

"I can't." He pushed it toward me.

"Look, it's obvious what's going on." I left the phone there. "I just want you to say it."

"Oh, really?" He looked more alarmed than curious.

"Sure. You're half–bad boy, half-heartthrob. If America knew you were gay—"

"What?"

"Chad's your lover. Right?"

He laughed and leaned back.

"It's okay," I said quickly. "It's not like I care. And I know how people are. Your secret's—"

"Hold on there."

"—safe with me."

"I'm not gay, and if I was . . ." He leaned forward again and folded his hands on the table. "I wouldn't be banging Chad."

It was my turn to fiddle with the phone, turning it glass-side-down and mirroring his knotted fingers.

Our drinks came. He sipped his. I put mine to the side.

"You going to drink it?"

"I hate club soda."

"You're a weird girl, you know that?"

"Yeah."

"Okay." He rubbed his thighs. "You want me to tell you everything? That what's on your mind?"

"Yup. From the beginning."

He looked around the room.

"I shouldn't trust you."

"You already did. Might as well finish the job."

He chuckled, rubbing his palms together.

"Arright. Yeah." He cleared his throat, and I let him stall. "I guess I owe you that." His leg shook again. "From the beginning."

He was really going to tell me. The enormous responsibility of my demand was dwarfed only by my desire to carry it.

"From the beginning."

He shifted closer to me on the perimeter of the circle so he could talk at normal volume.

"Stop me if you know any of this."

"I know nothing."

He nodded once and began.

"I grew up in Echo Park. My parents were pretty strict about me and my brother doing sports or music and nothing else. I couldn't hang with my buddies until I finished practice. So. One day . . ."

~

Justin Beckett was a good storyteller. He talked about his life without the thousand-watt charm or douchey dismissiveness. He wasn't doing an interview for promotional sound bites or laying himself bare for the sake of fan sympathy.

"My dad has this sense of what's gonna fly and what's a waste of time," he said, ring tapping his near-empty glass. "Like, no one, and I mean no one, thought Silver Lake needed a French restaurant. But they were wrong, and he was right. So when he heard us all sing together, he knew it was something. He'd spent years boozing up the right guys in the restaurant. Just in case. We were his just in case, I guess. He got in a coach. Hired a songwriter. Got releases from the guys' parents." He flipped his hand to indicate all the intermediate steps that weren't interesting to him. "We went into Slashdot Records polished like Louise's silver. I mean, we glowed in the dark."

"I bet."

"And I'll say it again. These guys . . . you have brothers or sisters?"

"One sister."

"So you know what I'm talking about when I say these dudes were my brothers."

"Yeah. Sure."

Technically, I did know what it was like to have a sister, but I had the feeling Talia would never be to me what Justin's three bandmates were to him.

"But. Okay, that was all background. This is the thing. It happened really fast." He stopped himself and twisted his mouth as if blocking more words.

"Everything I say after this . . ." He pushed his index finger against the table. "It goes in a locked box."

"My locked box?"

"My box to yours. It's secret. You got it? You tell nobody. Not even your diary." He held up his pinkie. "Swear."

I hooked my pinkie in his, and he curled it around so tight it felt like a permanent chain.

"I swear," I said. "Locked box."

He pulled back, drawing me closer before letting go.

"All right," he said. "Good."

"Good."

I had a secret with Justin Beckett. Almost as surreal as having his phone number.

"We were sixteen," he said. "And after *Boys on Valentine* we were playing stadiums. It scrambles your head if you're an adult. But we were kids. And Chad . . ." For the first time since he began, Justin faltered. ". . . he couldn't deal. He kept disappearing. He always made shows and sessions, but, if we weren't working, he was completely fucking off. A week would go by, then one of us would get a call from a police station in fucking Hemet or like . . . once he called me at four in the morning from a broom closet in Dodger Stadium. He was locked in and pissing in the . . . you know the yellow bucket with the mops that attach? And he was gonna wait until the janitors showed, but he had to take a shit, so . . ."

"What was he doing in there?"

He lifted his glass to his mouth and tipped it until a piece of ice dropped in. He crunched it against his back teeth like a walnut.

"He grew up in this building up in Elysian. Big yard they grow vegetables in. Apartments pretty nice. Kind of a commune. All hippies and conspiracy theorists. They don't bother anyone, but it's not like they're bothered either. They just do what they want. Like smoke so much pot you get high sniffing the couch cushions."

He let another ice cube drop past his lips and slapped the glass down.

"Did you know?"

He scoffed. "Sure. And it was fun until it wasn't."

"And his parents did nothing?"

"They gave him vitamin C." He slapped his hand on the table and looked away. "They loved the hell out of him, and I'm not here judging . . . Club soda's trash. I need a goddamn drink."

He craned his neck around and waved at Eyebrows. Our server arrived with a smile, but telling the story had turned Justin's joyful mood into surly agitation.

"Get her a—"

"Coke," I said, too thirsty to waste a club soda and too intent on keeping my wits about me.

"Same but put Jack in mine."

"One coke, one Jack and coke." Eyebrows turned on her heel and left.

"So," he said once she was gone. "Connect the dots."

"Chad disappeared, and you were happy he agreed to come back."

"Yup." Elbows on the table, he rubbed his hands together. "You glad I dumped that on you?"

"Kind of."

He had to look over his shoulder to see me. He regarded my face as if a two-word answer had illuminated me for the first time.

"What's that mean?"

"You hated every minute of it."

He pushed his body away from the table and twisted himself on the couch to face me, draping his arm over the back.

"Tell me how else I feel then," he said.

"That's cheating."

"I'm a lot of things, but a cheater ain't one."

"You sure are a lot of things."

"Such as?"

"A narcissistic egomaniac."

"Ouch."

"Enough about me." I imitated his voice. "Tell me what you think of me."

The drinks arrived. He took a quick sip from his and put it down, turning his full attention back to me, starting at my forehead, drifting down to my lips before meeting my eyes.

"Well?" he said expectantly.

"You want me to tell you about you?"

"Everyone does it. It's a national pastime."

I took a moment to sip my drink. It was cold and fizzy, and I was glad it wasn't spiked with Jack Daniel's.

"When my sister moved out here . . . I'm not saying it was this way for you with Chad, but it felt personal. Like I was dumped. I literally grieved. Then I got mad because our father left. Kind of. And she was leaving me too. Anyway. What I'm trying to say is I'd hate to go through it over and over. Not knowing if he's coming back this time. So, I think you're worried, for sure. But I also think you're angry because he keeps leaving you. Which . . . you can't be angry because it's not his fault, and he needs you. So you pretend you're not angry, which . . . you know . . . doesn't help."

"That's not what I expected you to say."

"Do I want to know what you expected?"

"I thought you were going to tell me to get over it."

"What?" I laughed. "Why?"

"The tough-girl thing."

"That's what you need to get over."

"Yeah, you're almost kind of nice."

"Me? Kind of nice?"

"Yeah, you. The mean one with the . . ." He pointed to my face as if looking for the right word. "Those eyes."

"These eyes?"

"With the lashes that make you seem all girly and soft until you open your mouth to bite my balls off."

"You're the asshole who—"

"I know, I know. I'm the asshole who." I thought he was reaching for his drink, but he picked up my phone and handed it to me. "Unlock it."

"Why?"

"To show you something."

"You know the code."

"I want you to do it."

I'd fallen into the trap of offering consent by curiosity.

"I should bite your balls off."

"You'll break your teeth. Come on. Open it."

I pressed my thumb to the home button, and he turned the screen to his face. It lit up his cheeks, casting his skin in blue and his honey-colored late-night beard in black.

"What are you doing?" I slid into him to see him open text messages, and without either of us thinking, I was enfolded in his free arm with my shoulder against his chest.

"Putting my ass on the line," he said. "They have audit access to my cellular."

"Who's they?"

—Dude. New number. 310-555-7161
Don't call the other one.—

"Bunch of lawyers and guys in suits. They find out Chad's calling my new digits and I picked up they're going to break my ass."

We watched, but no dots appeared to confirm Chad was answering. Justin lifted the arm that was flung over the back of the booth and put his thumb on my bare shoulder, drawing a quivering line down my arm. When I turned to look at him, he was an inch away, already facing me.

"Maybe he's still driving," I said.

"Probably." His breath was still cool from the ice.

"You're firing me."

"Pack your things and get out." His lips were just about to touch mine when my phone buzzed in his hand. We looked down.

THIS NUMBER HAS BLOCKED YOU

"Wow," I said.

Moment broken, Justin took his arm from around me. I suddenly felt foolish for nearly kissing him and disappointed that we hadn't really kissed.

"There you go." He handed me my phone. "He's probably going to call me in a few minutes."

"That's fine. I should check on Evelyn."

"I'll walk you out."

"No, no, it's fine."

"Carter can bring you." He snapped his fingers, and like a shadow the handsome bodyguard appeared.

"Mr. Beckett?"

"Make sure she meets up with her friend, would you?"

Two feet tall and half-invisible, even in yellow platforms, I stood up. Having been encircled in his attention, moments before, I now felt shut out. This guy was giving me emotional whiplash, and I hated that I'd given him that power over me.

Carter nodded and motioned for me to go first.

"Kayla," Justin called.

"What?" I snapped. He had no right to make me feel like this with his douchecore getup and stupid tattoos, and I had no business letting him do it. I was too good for his trash ego and his irritating entitlements.

"Thank you for everything."

"No problem."

"You're amazing."

"I know."

"See you on set."

The bar wasn't as lively as when I'd gone into the Emerald Room, but Eddie was still there, alone. I thanked Carter and sat next to him.

"Where'd she go?" I asked.

"She just took off. Middle of her sentence."

"What were you talking about?"

I sounded suspicious, because I was. Women didn't just take off in the middle of a sentence without a reason.

"Something we had in common," he said. "Is it me? Do I come off wrong?"

"Were you coming off or coming on?"

He held his hands up.

"There was no touching, I swear. We were talking about costumes." He stopped himself and shook his head. "Putting them on." Again, he second-guessed his words. "Separately." His shoulders slumped as if he was giving up.

"Okay, okay. Stop." I rescued him. "I get it."

"Can you just make sure she's okay?"

"Yes," I said. "First thing. I'll take care of it."

"Thank you."

He seemed genuinely relieved, but I wouldn't give him any credit for being a decent man until I heard from Evelyn. I'd been fooled before.

CHAPTER 8

JUSTIN

The morning after Kayla met me at NV, I had a late call, so I slept in. Everyone thought I was some kind of man of leisure, but I didn't get to stay in bed much. Getting up early to work my ass off wasn't the brand. No one wanted to hear about that. They wanted their songs and their redemption story, not fourteen hours in the studio or the days in a room memorizing lines.

So, at six, when I usually woke up, I rolled over, figuring I'd skip my workout and sleep an extra four hours.

But nah.

My brain stayed in this in-between place where I couldn't move my body to get up and do something, but couldn't fall asleep either. There were dreams that weren't really dreams because I was watching them like an awake person and saying, "Yeah, that Kayla's pretty all right," because it was her face that was looking at me. Not saying anything. In the dream I couldn't move. Like she'd given me a drug that paralyzed me or something. I didn't want to move, either, because if I did, she'd go away, and my dream-self was like, no way. You stay here and look at this girl. Don't do anything to make her split. Not a word out of your mouth.

When she rapped her knuckles on the table, I didn't even look. She was trying to distract me. Get me to make her leave.

Rap-rap-rap.

Nope. Nope. Nope.

"Jesus Christ," Ken said from somewhere.

Kayla's face got drowned in light. I hadn't moved or done anything, but I knew she was leaving. It was like someone had rolled a yellow screen between us.

"Who wears their shoes to bed?"

That was Gene. Kayla blinked out, and I got 40 percent more awake.

"How did you get in here?" I asked, eyes still closed.

"The cook let us in," Ken said. The mattress tilted and my cheeks stung.

"Stop it." I pushed away the hand slapping my face. I opened my eyes. Ken was sitting on the edge of the bed.

"What time is it?"

"Time to get up," Gene said from behind me. I heard the band of his watch clink, but he still didn't tell me the damn time. I pushed myself up. I had my own damn clock, and it was eight in the morning. Ken got off the bed and straightened his jacket.

"We'll be on the patio."

~

Chad hadn't called. Probably crashed as soon as he got into town.

I looked out the window onto the pool and guesthouse. My agent and my PR guy were at a table by the pool letting Charlotte, my kitchen lady, serve them her mint lemonade. No one was paid enough to wait on two suits who strolled into my house uninvited.

Brushed teeth and showered bodies were for people who called before they showed up. I just put on a robe and sunglasses to go downstairs. Charlotte was in the kitchen unpacking groceries.

"Mr. Beckett," she said, nervously. "I recognized them, so I thought it would be okay."

"It's cool," I said. "Thanks for getting them something, but if you're busy, you don't have to."

"I'm not busy."

The grocery bags told another story, but what was I supposed to do? Call her a liar because she was being taken for granted?

By the time I got to the table, I was surly as a wet cat. I sat down, stretching my legs and letting my butt slide to the end of the seat so I could lean my head back.

"What?" I said. More a demand than a question.

"You went out last night?" Ken asked.

"Yeah."

"You have a good time?"

"Yeah. Thanks for asking."

"Dude," Gene said. "You want to sit up and take this seriously?"

"Take what seriously? There's no rule against me leaving the house. Which reminds me . . ." I picked my head up, as if waking. "You can call me, and I can come over there. I don't need a nurse in a Hugo Boss suit barging in to bust my balls. And leave Charlotte alone. If you're thirsty, look in the fridge."

"We wanted—" Ken started, but screw him.

I sat straight, took the glasses off, and tossed them on the table.

"You can call my office right now and ask for a meeting. I'll try and squeeze you in next week."

There was no way I was going to be able to crawl back into bed and pick up Kayla-face where I'd left off, but damn if I wasn't going to try. I'd just stood and gotten my back turned when Ken established why he was the most expensive handler in LA.

"You were in the Emerald Room with a girl," he said.

My morning was screwed, but I wasn't giving him the satisfaction of sitting back down or even turning around just yet.

"No rules against girls, dude." He couldn't see my face, but in the pause that followed, I couldn't see them, either, which put me off my game.

"Can you sit, please?" Gene broke first. No surprise there. So I sat, because a guy's gotta take the little wins to avoid the big losses.

"Get on with it," I said. "I have shit to do."

"The costume girl," Ken said.

"Yeah?"

"She seems nice."

"I'll tell her you said so."

"What's going on with her?"

"She's nice. I like nice people."

Funny thing was, *nice* wasn't a word I would have ever used for Kayla. Strong. Mouthy. Ambitious. Decent enough to bring Grandma Louise flowers. But nice? Not so much.

"Since when?" Ken asked. He had a way of seeming relaxed and intense at the same time, as if he were a dispassionate surgeon and his attention was the scalpel. I was the patient, and he was trying to cut information out of me. The question was, Did he know what he was looking for?

"What are you asking me?" If he knew about Chad, he was going to have to say it and then just accept my lie.

"She's a regular girl, right? Safe. Not a model or an actress. Not another princess."

"You're boring me, Ken."

"We think . . . ," Gene interrupted, then swallowed the rest of the sentence under Ken's glare and picked up his glass of lemonade.

"We think you have the right instinct," Ken said once Gene's mouth was occupied with drinking instead of talking. "We've been too focused on avoidance. Improving your brand with what you're not doing is going to keep you working this year. But it's not building anything.

You're being proactive, and that's what's going to build your career for the next twenty years."

"I know you're bullshitting me," I said. "But what I can't figure out is exactly what you think you're bullshitting me about."

He smiled and leaned into the conversation as if I'd opened some door he'd thought was locked.

"Your brand . . . your new brand is 'Justin from the neighborhood,' right? From bad boy to boy from the old neighborhood. Not a goody-two-shoes boy next door, but the guy you know who made mistakes, then grew up. The guy from high school who was trouble; then you see him at the ten-year reunion, and he's reformed and rich as hell."

"I'm twenty-five."

"You're already rich. You have three years to reform." He moved his glass three inches, as if his big payoff needed more table space. "Reforming isn't just about the past. It's about the future. And nothing says future boy next door like a relatable girl next door on his arm."

I laughed. I didn't want to, but I couldn't help it. Maybe it was nerves or maybe my PR guy was just plain funny.

"Have you met her?"

"No, but—"

"She curses like a fucking sailor, wears crazy-ass shoes. If you owe her money? Forget it. She will park on your lawn until you pay up. You sit her down and tell her what you just told me, and she'll tell you exactly how far to pack that shit up your ass."

This was supposed to scare him, but he was nodding and smiling as if this was what he wanted to hear, word for word.

"So you want what?" I asked. "You want me to date her?"

"You like her, right?"

"She's pretty hot," Gene said.

They wanted me to go out with Kayla to prove I was a better man. That the Roosevelt Hotel was behind me, and I was a sound brand investment for the studios and a safe role model for the kids of former fangirls.

The idea had its appeal. When I gave Chad my number, I'd pretty much let Kayla go. I hadn't thought about it like that in the moment, but in retrospect I should have known I wanted to see her again and made a plan. Asked her out or something. Not just cut her loose like that.

"Is she in on this or nah?"

"What do you want?" Ken asked as if it mattered.

"I have to tell her, man. It's not right." I put my sunglasses on and leaned back into the sun. "And I'm pretty sure that if I don't tell her and she finds out? She'll cut my balls off."

Ken rapped the tabletop and stood.

"It's decided, then."

"Good. Now get out."

"One thing, though?" Ken blocked the sun, and I couldn't see his face in the shadows. "Before you mention it to her?"

"What?"

"I'm judging her based on her job. Let my team do a little research first. Make sure she is who we think she is. Better we know now than DMZ finds out later."

"What kind of research?"

"You know." He shrugged as if I did.

"Google?"

"Yeah." He passed, stopping to pat my shoulder. "Google."

～

Gotta say, I was a little too pumped to try and go back to that dream.

In acting, they tell you that when you're feeling something in real life, you should take that feeling and catalog it so you can use it in a scene. In the shower, I remembered to do that.

A little surprised at myself for not realizing I wanted her sooner.

A little relief because I made it in time.

Some hope, a future-looking feeling like excitement but lower in the chest.

Final label: *Reverse Disappointment.*

I shut the water and checked my phone before I even toweled off. Still no Chad.

Okay. Whatever. I wasn't letting that ruin the reverse of disappointment. He'd ping when he pinged, which would hopefully be after I called Kayla and she agreed to go out with me. I hadn't been excited about seeing any particular girl in a long time, so though I was dried off when I navigated to her number, I wasn't waiting until I was dressed.

She was on set already, so she might not pick up.

My thumb stopped before hitting her number.

If she didn't pick up, I'd see her at work, where I'd have to look her in the eyes while I didn't tell her Ken was googling her. Or that anyone with a brain cell would know he was doing more than a Google search. Or that the wheels were in motion, and even if I told him to hold up, he'd do what he wanted anyway?

And was I supposed to call her and not tell her I just got the rubber stamp on seeing her? That she'd gone from convenient phone-answerer to potential brand management tool?

She was never, ever going to forgive me, and I didn't blame her.

I felt used every day, but I'd consented to at least 30 percent of it. Springing it on her later wasn't cool. Wasn't right. Annoying that I couldn't do what I wanted, but this was like my dad always said—pay your debt to practice now so you have music in the bank for later.

Mom had a saying too. Patience is a virtue. For a guy who wasn't interested in virtue, that didn't mean anything, but for this guy, naked in the bathroom putting his phone away before dialing? It meant a lot.

I'd wait for Ken, then tell her everything.

~

Ken and Gene had been out of my house five minutes when Grandma texted.

—I don't know where to put this piece—

A picture of her hand with a silver bolt in the center followed.

—Where'd it come from?—

—I'm fixing the upstairs sink—

"You mean you're breaking it," I muttered.

—I'll be right there—

I didn't know much about fixing a sink. I could probably change a tire, but I never had to. I believed in calling the right person for the right job, but ever since Grandpa died, Louise made me swear I couldn't fix whatever it was before she'd let me call anyone who knew what they were doing.

And I couldn't pretend to look at the shocks on her car or the dead burner on her stove. She could tell if I was phoning it in. So I had to get all the way under the sink, unscrew things, and declare the problem officially below my pay grade.

"It's still leaking," she said from her seat on the toilet. I was on the floor with my head under the sink and my legs sticking out of the vanity cabinet.

"Yeah," I said, loosening something that had a name a plumber knew, but I sure didn't. "How about now?"

"It's worse."

"Well, that's all I got." I crawled out of the cabinet. "Can I call a guy?"

"I'll have Ned look at it."

Ned was one of those old guys who saw something broken, rolled his sleeves up, and made for damn sure it was broken for good.

"Yeah. No." I stood, holding my greasy hands up like a surgeon. Couldn't use the sink. Couldn't wipe black gunk all over the towels. "Give Ned a break. I'll take care of it."

I went down to the kitchen and turned the water on with my elbow. The counters were a mess of unopened mail, coupons, and magazines. The flowers Kayla had gotten for Ned's birthday were dried out, still in a vase, sad as a kid who couldn't go out to play.

"Weeze!" I shouted, soaping my hands.

"I'm right here."

"Can I get someone in here to help you clean up?" I tried to sound casual as I rinsed and shook the water off.

"No. What kind of grown woman can't clean up her own mess?"

"You. All right?" I snapped a towel off the ring. That wasn't clean either. "Look, not for nothing, you're busy, and look at this kitchen."

"I don't need servants." Flustered, she made a stack out of a handful of mail.

"I'm not complaining, and I'm not criticizing."

"Could have fooled me." She took a yellow slip out of the pile and slapped it to my chest. "That's for your accountant, Mr. Hire-A-Guy."

When she moved her hand, the paper dropped and I caught it. Kayla's receipt for the roses. Not strictly a business expense.

"Louise, come on. I just want you to have it easy for a change. What's the point of having all this money if I can't give some to you?"

She smiled up at me and patted my cheek.

"Such a nice kid."

"Stop."

CD Reiss

Telling her to stop only encouraged her. She squeezed my face, and for a woman in her sixties, she had the grip of a man half her age.

"You're good to me."

"Mmpf."

"But save your money for your wife and children." She took her hand away. "Okay?"

"You win. This time." I kissed her on the cheek. "I gotta roll."

"Have a good day."

"I'll send a plumber," I said from the doorway.

"All right."

"Don't unscrew anything else."

"Go, already!"

I got in the car with the yellow slip of paper still crumpled in my hand and tossed it on the passenger seat, when I noticed it was the florist receipt. I couldn't shake that girl. It was as if she was sitting next to me, reminding me that I could call her anytime.

Chad didn't call all day. Didn't text. Nothing. Zip. He'd supposedly been on the 15 from Vegas, but by the end of the day I wondered if he'd just been messing with me.

I didn't want to bug Kayla.

I mean, no. I wanted to bug Kayla, but I didn't. I gave Chad my number so she wouldn't have to deal with my problems, and I told Ken I'd chill while he made sure she wasn't going to be trouble.

The whole thing would be easier if I could stop thinking about her. I'd said she was kind of nice, but she was more than that. She was quick on the draw. She surprised me. She was an open book in another language. Touching her was like touching a girl for the first time.

She wasn't going to be trouble. Anyone could see that. But in the time it took Ken to do whatever he was going to do, she could decide I was the one who was trouble and walk.

That wasn't going to work for me.

CHAPTER 9

KAYLA

I was in the trailer all day Monday tagging costumes and fitting stays for background players. Net positive on that front, because I didn't want to deal with Justin or my inappropriate feelings for him. Sure, maybe he wasn't half the jerk I thought he was. Maybe he actually had surprisingly deep wells of compassion and loyalty, but the fact was that guys like him didn't want girls like me. Maybe for a kiss in a private club. Maybe a distracting week of twisted sheets and neighborhood-waking late-night screams.

Stop.

Thinking about him naked wasn't helping, but I couldn't help it. That half kiss had awakened a buzz in my belly I couldn't get rid of. He made me feel like the only woman in the world. Like he understood me. Saw me. I had to remind myself that was what he did for a living. His gift was making every fan in the room sure that he was talking just to them, and I wasn't going to be fooled by it.

The upside of my run to Club NV was that Chad now had Justin's real number. My stint as a fake assistant was over, and I'd gotten a job out of it. Another week and this would be done. I could dedicate myself to the reason I'd left New York in the first place. At eight p.m.,

I was sweeping up the trailer and listing everything I had to do to make those dreams a reality. They were bigger than a costume trailer and bigger than Justin Beckett, if only I could stop thinking about him for one minute.

—Nothing?—

Justin texted as if I wouldn't tell him if I got a call or message from Chad. As if his story hadn't moved me to change my entire opinion about him.

—Sorry. I'm still blocked—

Then . . . nothing. I didn't know if he'd lost interest or was being a professional, but by Wednesday I was starting to feel as though his touch in the Emerald Room had been a momentary lapse on his part. I stared at the screen for a full five minutes, waiting like a smitten teenager instead of a grown woman who had stuff to do, then put it away.

He'd moved on. Fine.

"Is everything okay?" I asked Evelyn at the craft services table on Thursday morning. She was eyeing Eddie as he left his trailer. Again. "You split on Friday."

"I was tired." She stirred her coffee—her scarf wrapped around her neck in a florid, perfect bow.

"I just want to make sure. Eddie didn't do or say something to upset you?"

"No." She shook her head sharply, brows furrowed. "Not at all. He's really nice, actually."

I believed her, but I was also sure I wasn't asking the right question.

"Um, you've been running away from him at a full sprint."

"No, I haven't." She looked down, as if she couldn't face me when she lied. "Not a full sprint, anyway."

"Well, no one said you had to like him."

"I do!" she protested. "It's just that we were talking about something, and I started getting all melty, and I was sure he could see it."

I was about to encourage her, but the intercom at her belt squawked to life.

"Darcy's fussing with his jacket," Francine said through the static.

"I have it," Evelyn replied.

"Send Kayla," Francine said. "Sleeve cap's pulling."

The radio beeped out.

"Can't have that," I said, gulping coffee before I went into the house.

~

The crew bustled around, fixing lights that were bright enough for a parking lot. Justin stood on a piece of blue tape stuck to the Persian carpet, jerking his shoulder.

"Costume's here," the assistant director recited when I came in.

"About time," Justin said.

"How did you stand waiting ten seconds?" I stood in front of him and inspected the fit of his coat, adjusting the lapels forward to shift the shoulders, trying to keep my mind on the costume instead of the way he looked at me.

"It was like an hour," he said.

"Where does it hurt?" I ran my fingers along his shoulder seams and down the armholes, looking for excess in the cap. And yes, feeling the hard muscles underneath.

"When I do this." He shifted his right arm forward as if he were about to embrace me, with the blast of light melting his ice-blue eyes.

A woman put a beige device up against his cheek and pressed a button.

"So don't do that." I pushed his arm down and waited for the woman with the light meter to move. When she checked his left cheek, I moved to his right side and put his arm back up so I could see the problem with the sleeve cap, running my hand along the inseam.

"It's going to be hard to seduce Miss Bennet with my arm down."

The light meter woman moved away.

"You can do with one arm what most men can't do with their whole body."

"They can hear you."

"Who?"

"The mics are on." He smirked at me. "They pick up everything."

I looked behind me, and a bearded guy with a boom tapped his headphones and smiled.

"Well then," I said, blushing. "Take the jacket off so I can feel stupid and busy at the same time."

Justin unbuttoned it, and I slid it off him, letting the offending sleeve go inside out. He looked over my shoulder as I snipped open the fill inside the cap.

"What are you doing?" he asked. I could feel the deliberateness of his breath on my neck, and I leaned into its minty warmth.

"There's too much fill, and it's sewn too tight." I looked up at him. "It's fine if you're standing there, but if you want to seduce a woman like her you need to be open."

"Open to what?"

"To her saying yes."

"How's it coming, Kayla?" Francine asked, appearing suddenly.

"Done." I held the coat up. Justin turned his back to me, and I slid it over his shoulders.

"Better," he said, shifting his arm and facing me.

"Let me know how it goes with Miss Bennet." I buttoned the jacket. The assistant director called the scene, and camera and sound announced their readiness.

"I will."

~

After a few days of quick conversations, smiles, and stolen glances—but no more major on-set alterations—he called while I was in the grocery store.

"Hey, Kaylacakes." Crickets in the background. The hum of a pool filter.

"How did Darcy do today?"

"He was about to get some, but it's a PG movie, so he has blue balls now."

I laughed, checking a dozen eggs for cracks.

"Where are you?" he asked.

"Trader Joe's. Where are you?"

"Chilling by my pool."

"Sounds nice."

"I have to get into the studio soon."

"Okay."

"Do I get to see you or nah?"

"See me? I guess I'll be on set."

"Not like that. Not with people eyeballing us. Just me and you hanging out."

"Like a date?"

There was a pause from the other side. I was pushing the cart, but I'd passed the peanut butter two aisles ago, as if I couldn't choose a condiment and hold down my end of the conversation at the same time.

"Justin?"

"Yeah," he said as if woken up. "Let's take a drive or something. I can pick you up tonight."

"It's almost nine o'clock."

"You gonna turn into a pumpkin?"

"I'm a morning person."

"Call is late."

"I'm free Saturday. Take it or leave it."

"You're fucking with me, right? You're doing that thing where you put the guy off."

"Do I seem like a game player to you?"

"No. No, you don't."

"Saturday, then."

"All right. But it's gonna be hard to wait."

"I find it hard to believe you have nothing to do until then."

"Maybe I really want to see you," he said with an audible shrug that stopped my cart-pacing. "I like you, so I want to hang out. It caught me by surprise, but it's got me like . . . fine. Whatever. I'm going with it. I like you."

"That makes me happy."

"Why?"

"Against my better judgment, I like you too."

"Cool. I'll see you Saturday."

We said our goodbyes. I hung up and went back for the peanut butter with a smile on my face.

~

On Friday, Talia's Audi waited a block away from the set. I got into the back seat and closed the door.

"Hey, Soley." I leaned over the seat and kissed my sister's girlfriend, Soledad, on the cheek. "How's it hanging?"

"Low and heavy." She had long, dark curls pinned against the back of her neck and cheekbones for days. "You have your bathing suit?"

"Yup. Ready to laze by the pool like a champ. Hey . . . ," I said, noticing a sparkle on Soledad's finger. "What's that?"

"What's what?" Soledad replied. I reached forward and grabbed her hand so I could confirm the sparkle was a diamond solitaire.

"Holy crap! You guys are engaged?"

"You didn't tell her?" Soledad pushed Talia's shoulder.

"She's at work all the time now."

Soledad rolled her eyes and held her hand to the back of the car so I could admire the ring. It sparkled even in the low light of the streetlamps.

"It's gorgeous."

"She picked it," Soledad said.

"Congratulations. Does Dad know?"

"No," Talia said, then corrected quickly. "Yes. About the engagement. Yes."

"What doesn't he know about?"

"Nothing. Sorry. Stop asking questions when I'm driving."

Talia looked at me through the rearview, and I stuck my tongue out at her.

~

Dad lived in a three-bedroom house made of concrete and heavy sliding doors up in the Hollywood Hills. His friends Adam and Darren were over. They were in their thirties, married, in love. Adam was in real estate finance, and Darren was a drummer. They discussed how much salt went on the rim of a margarita glass, and I wondered if Dad would feel like a fifth wheel if I wasn't there.

Dad got on the edge of the diving board. I sat in the separated hot tub with Soledad—my half-finished margarita on the ledge and my toes touching the far wall—thinking about that drink, and my father, and how we'd missed the stage where he told me not to drink, then got mad when I did, and eventually accepted it as part of my adulthood. We'd skipped an important part of the process, as if we were jeans that had skipped a trip to the washhouse. We were well cut and sewn, but without the wash we were stiff, uncomfortable, working too hard to fit.

"Did you get the fabric out of the van?" Talia splashed me out of my reverie, reaching her arm over the barrier that separated the hot tub from the rest of the pool.

"Not yet. It's freaking heavy."

"If you need guys to help, I got guys," Dad said from the diving board on the deep end, then leaped in, swimming underwater until he got to our side.

"Who needs guys?" Darren asked.

"No one," Adam chimed in. "Call a mover, Raymond."

"Not a big deal," I said when Dad popped up. "I was thinking of just unrolling a few yards to make samples. But I have to find a small-run factory first, and before that I need cash, so . . ." I sipped my margarita. "Not an emergency."

"We should hook her up with Steve," Darren said, handing Dad a margarita. "His company invests in hot young talent."

"Stop." I kicked water at him. "I'm not hot."

"Of course you are," Adam said, stretching out in the sun. "You look like your father."

Dad was hot, apparently. I guessed he was, in a fiftyish guy sort of way.

"Steve's the CFO of Butter Birds," Darren said, sitting in a dry patch. "Your friend Justin Beckett probably wears them."

"He's not my friend, and duh." Everyone knew Butter Birds. Their jeans ran seven hundred a pop and were the hottest thing around, mostly because they kept production runs so small they were priced for scarcity. Even celebrities had to buy on the secondary market, where they were even more expensive.

"What's going on with him?" Talia asked.

"Nothing."

"I can make a call . . . ," Dad started.

"Talia told me you and Justin are like this." Soledad twisted two fingers together.

"We're not." I hadn't even told her or Talia about Club NV or the kiss that wasn't. And until he showed up on time, bathed and dressed for our date, I wasn't mentioning that either.

"I was talking, hello?" My father snapped his fingers in my direction. Did normal parents do this? Or was it me? Was it because he actually hadn't parented me that I could ignore him so easily?

"Sorry. Yes, Dad?"

"I know the CFO, if you want a meeting."

"Really?"

"Unless you want to tap your friend Justin."

"Yes, I do want a meeting, and he's not my friend."

"Okay, enough." Adam held his hands up as if he were stopping traffic. "The lady doth protest too fucking much."

"No—"

"Yes," three of them chimed in together.

"If he was an asshole to you," Dad said, "we can call DMZ and end him."

"You're so cute when you're protective," Adam said.

"He wasn't an asshole to me. At least, after the first time he was. Then he was nice."

My father's eyes narrowed.

"This is fascinating." Adam had gotten to a sitting position on the edge of the chair. "Look at him."

"He's really pissed," Darren added. "The vein in his temple's pulsing."

"Kayla," my father said.

"Dad."

"I will end him."

"Can you imagine if you had kids?" Adam was now crouching behind Darren. "With that woman you dated when you were delusional? Monica? Oh, your face would get like that."

"Dad," I said. "There's no ending anyone. He's very nice to me, and overall he seems like a decent person."

"Are you sure?"

"Of course not. But as of this moment, I believe he's all right."

"A lawyer's answer," Soledad said.

"Quit it." I put my arms behind me on the ledge and pulled myself out. "I'm not some delicate flower. I'm serious, Dad. Thank you. But until I come through the door crying, just assume I'm fine."

"Fine."

"Fine," Talia added. "Let's pick another celebrity for her to date."

"Mija," Soledad cooed, splashing water on her. Her fiancée kicked an arc back. A water fight ensued, and I slipped away from further questions.

~

After dinner, Talia drove me back to the theater. It was late, which meant that, even in July, it was chilly.

A Tesla was parked in the alley, blocking the loading bay door under the words No Parking.

"The rich can't read," Soledad grumbled.

"I'm too tired to call a tow on them," I said.

"That's what they're betting on," Talia said, pulling up nose to nose with the Tesla.

I kissed her and Soledad on the cheek.

"Later, sisters."

As soon as I got out, the Tesla door opened like a seagull wing. Justin fit in the driver's seat like a custom-made component.

"Hey, Kaylacakes."

"What are you doing here?" I looked into the glare of my sister's headlights and waved.

"I was in the neighborhood."

The Audi pulled up next to us, and Talia rolled down her window. She looked at Justin suspiciously, then at me.

"You all right?"

"Yeah, this is—"

"I know who he is."

Justin got out of his car and extended his hand to my sister.

"Hey, you must be Talia." They shook. "I'm Justin, and I know this looks weird."

"It does."

"I'm just saying hi. We . . . Kayla and I . . . we're friends, so."

"So you just parked here and waited like a stalker?"

"Two minutes. Just now, I was texting her to see if she's around, and here she is."

"I'm fine," I said. "Seriously, he's harmless."

Talia had plenty to say between "two minutes" and "harmless" but kept her lips sealed.

"Bye, guys," I said, waving my fingers. Soledad waved back, significantly less bothered than my sister.

"Be good," Talia said before she rolled up the window and pulled away.

"Harmless?" Justin said when the taillights disappeared.

"If you were evil, you'd be a better liar."

"I'm an excellent liar."

"You've been here two minutes?"

"How long do you think I can stay still before someone recognizes me?"

"So you show up a day early, unannounced—"

"Is it not Saturday? Damn. My bad."

"—wait 'two minutes,' then start texting me to see if I'm around?"

"This is an abandoned theater. I was trying to figure out if a person could even live here."

"How did you even know where I live? I was going to text you in the morning. Saturday morning."

"You wrote your address on Ned's flower receipt." He shrugged as if to beg the question of what a guy like him was supposed to do with information like that.

"Maybe you are evil."

"So . . ." He let the rest of the sentence dangle, as if I should know how it ended.

He pointed upward without looking, and I followed. The second-story lights of the building across the way were out, but the stripes of the blinds were bent as if someone was holding them open.

"So," I said. "There's that."

"Wanna go for a drive?"

~

The Tesla was more like a hovercraft than a car. The leather seat felt as if it were built for me, and the ride was so smooth it didn't feel as if there were a road under us. The screen in the center dash mapped our location, and a husky female voice came from every corner of the car in surround sound.

In three hundred feet, turn right.

He obeyed with dangerous enthusiasm. Somehow, I wasn't thrown against him. I stayed straight in my seat as if Elon Musk had suspended the law of inertia.

"You all right?" Justin asked after a shockingly hard left through a yellow light.

"Is there an emergency you need to get to?"

It didn't feel like we were going fifty on a side street, but numbers don't lie.

"This thing stops on a dime." He swiped the screen at a stop sign. "You like music?"

"No. I'm an animal."

He put on EDM that thumped and bumped.

"Where are we going?" I shouted.

"What?"

"Where . . ." I turned the music down. "Where are we going?"

"I wanna show you something cool." He turned the volume up. "The drop here is murder. Check this out."

The tempo rose, and the tension built up; then, as he moved his hand like a conductor at a rave, it dropped, and he spread his fingers like an explosion. I laughed. He was obnoxious but kind of funny. Not that he deserved big points for that. It was easy to be charmed by a man caught in the act of loving something.

In three hundred feet, turn left.

"She sounds like Catherine Keener," I said in the split second between the direction and the music coming back up.

"It is. Good ear," he said as he whipped the left with one hand on the bottom of the steering wheel.

With one turn, we'd moved from wide commercial boulevard to a darker, narrower street that went up into a hilly residential neighborhood. I turned the music down.

"Did you just say that your GPS is in Catherine Keener's voice?"

"Yeah, I like it."

"She sat in a studio and recorded lefts and rights for you?"

At the fork, stay to the right.

"Nah. You say a few specific things, and it does it."

The streets got twisty and so narrow there was only room for one car. On the right, houses rose above. On the left, the city looked blue under the orange sunset.

"So she said a few things?"

"I did hers. She did mine. It was fun."

Stay to the right, then turn right.

"That's uncanny," I said.

"Yeah. It's cool. This is my favorite kind of voice. Tons of undertone. You got the same thing when you talk."

"Thank you."

"But not when you're calling me an asshole. Then you go flat."

"And fuck you."

He laughed, then stopped the car at a crossroads so he could tap the screen.

"Check it out." A waveform opened up. "Just say what's on the screen up here."

"Are you serious?"

"When I tap this button, you start."

He tapped and started driving again. I was curious and flattered enough to play along.

ANACONDA

"Anaconda." The waveform rose and fell as I spoke.

HIGHLIGHTS

"Highlights."

BROOMSTICK

"Broomstick."

I said *symphony, egregious, vase, tomato,* and *shouldn't* before a progress bar came on the screen and a smoother, more default voice asked us to wait.

"Are we going all the way up?" I asked. The houses up the hill had thinned, and smog covered the city below.

"Almost."

He turned right without being told and stopped at a black metal gate. He put a code into a keypad to open it and drove through.

The lot was scrubby and pitted with a T-shaped hole in the middle. Rebar lined the edges of the pit like scaffolding on a building.

"Home sweet home, baby." Justin parked the car and got out before I could ask who it was home for. He came around to open the door for me, but I beat him to it.

"Let me show you the view."

I followed him to a narrow outcropping that overlooked the city. The sky was striped with colors, and a last crescent of sun hung at the ocean horizon. Lights flickered in the squares between the warps and wefts of brake lights on the streets.

"Wow. This is a view."

"Best in the city." His skin glowed in the sunset, and his eyes were darker and deeper in the warm light. He'd always have whatever he wanted. Even in solitude, he'd have the best of everything.

"Of course it is." Just below us, in the brush, something rustled. "What's that?"

"Just coyotes."

"*Just* coyotes?" I stepped away. "Aren't they dangerous?"

I was wearing a bikini top, flip-flops, cutoff jeans, and a T-shirt. There was nothing between me and the sharp teeth of a feral animal.

"Only if you're a little yippy dog."

"Ugh."

"There'll be coyote fencing all around." He waved outward, indicating the massive perimeter of the space, then to a corner of the little overlook. "I'm putting rows of benches right here and a . . . like a planter over here, but low so you can sit on it. And when they pour the concrete, I'm putting a fireplace over here so it lines up with the Santa Monica Mountains." He karate chopped the horizon.

I looked back at the property. The rebar was oxidized, and the porta potties had a layer of dirt on the roofs and in the crevices. There were no yellow digging trucks or new boot prints.

"Why'd you stop building?" I asked.

"You know." He ran his fingers through his hair, dipping his head to do it as if he didn't want his arm to go all the way up. "Dumb stuff. Band broke up. Everyone hates me. I don't know if what I got is what I got or if more's coming. I might not work after this."

I didn't mean for a short laugh to come out. He hadn't said anything wrong or funny, but my filter went down with the sun.

"What's funny?"

"I'm sorry," I said. "That was just a reaction to something else. Nothing to do with you."

"Okay? So? You're not gonna tell me? I mean, I'm showing you my house. I don't just bring people up here."

His hair flicked in the breeze, lifting away from his face in all its dissatisfaction.

"It's just . . ." I exhaled. "The idea you'll never work again because people know you and they know what you did."

"They think they know."

"I worked for Josef Signorile."

"Were you there when some girl me-tooed him up the ass?"

"My point was . . ." I cut him off. "He survived it when someone accused him. Business is better than ever."

"I don't like that preppy shit anyway."

I managed not to laugh out loud but had to scoff.

"I'm trying to tell you you'll come out on top. I know your pain is real to you. But when you said you don't know if you're going to work again, I want you to just know that you're going to be fine. People like you don't face consequences the way the rest of us do."

The last of the day had moved west, leaving a chill in the air. In the final gasp of orange light, I could plainly see the hurt in his face.

"I'm not saying you're a bad person," I said. "But you have a charmed life. All you have to do is understand that and make sure that what you do doesn't create consequences for other people." I crossed my arms and rubbed my biceps to warm me against the sudden cold I wasn't dressed for.

"Sorry," I said. "You didn't bring me up here for a lecture."

He took his jacket off, leaving him in a T-shirt that six months before would have been four inches too long and a size and a half too tight. He put it around my shoulders and tenderly smoothed the collar down. I was turned away, watching the horizon.

"You came out here because of Signorile," he said, fingers drifting from the collar to my bare neck.

"I couldn't take it anymore. The whole scene. Sure, his wife came out with an alibi, and he got off, but he stopped hiring women because we were too much trouble, and everyone said they didn't blame him. It was so toxic."

"So you came to Los Angeles, and you met me."

"You were such an ass."

When I turned to face him, he put his hands on each side of my jaw, as if cradling a bowl.

"I am an ass," he said. "But I think you like me."

"Sometimes you're not repulsive."

"Am I repulsive right now?" He spoke so softly he had to lean forward.

"No." An inch of tingling air separated our lips.

"I want to kiss you."

"Permission granted."

He didn't dive right in. I did. He pulled back a little, brushing the length of his lips along mine, taking it slow, touching my cheeks as a boundary for his mouth. My brain shut everything down except processing the way he felt, waiting for the flick of his tongue against mine. He calibrated the slow build of desire with impeccable precision.

We're going to do it in the Tesla.

Yes. I put my hands on his hard chest, accepting that if we could manage to have sex in the car, there was going to be sex in the car. Like teenagers with nowhere else to be alone, we'd wrestle on the leather seats and regret it later.

A crunch and a breath that wasn't Justin's or mine made me leap a few feet, gulping air.

Two coyotes were standing between us and the car, eyes glowing, low growls coming between sharp rows of teeth. I clutched Justin's arm, testing the hardness of the muscle by digging in my fingers.

"Hey!" he barked at the top of his lungs. "Out! Out! Out!"

They backed up. Justin stomped and shouted. "Get the fuck outta here!"

They ran into the darkness.

"You all right?" he asked.

"Yeah," I squeaked.

"Can you . . . uh . . ." He tipped his chin to his arm.

"Oh. Sorry." I let him go. "That was . . . Is that all you have to do? Yell at them?"

"Works once or twice before they wise up."

"Oh."

"You're shaking."

"I'm fine."

"Come on." He put his hand on my lower back. "I know what's going to chill you out."

He led me to the car. The doors opened like wings, and the lights flicked on. When I started for the passenger side, he stopped me.

"You have a license?" he asked.

"A driver's license?"

"I hear you don't bother with them in New York."

"In Queens you do."

"Good. You can drive."

"Really?" I sounded like a kid finding out she was going to Disneyland. I was surprised at my own delight. Fancy cars weren't my jam. I didn't fantasize about anything besides getting where I was going.

But I'd never ridden in a Tesla before, and I never thought I'd drive one.

"Go on," he said in the white flood of the headlights. "Get in."

If it was a hovercraft from the passenger side, it was a spaceship from the driver's. Justin leaned over me to show me the obvious turn signals and the less obvious button to make the seat fit my body. It shifted around me silently, tucking me in a cushion of ergonomic comfort.

"The gate opens automatically," he said, tapping the screen. "Go up here, and you can pull a U-turn—"

I popped the gears into reverse, slung my arm over the back of the seat, and twisted around to see behind me.

"There's a back camera," he said.

"I gotta see with my eyes."

The gate opened. Halfway into the dark street, a husky voice I recognized despite the fact that it wasn't famous came from the speakers.

Exit and turn left.

"Whoa!" I cried at the sound of my own voice.

Justin cracked up and clapped his hands twice.

"You should see your face. Gold. Twenty-four-karat gold."

"That's creepy." I sat straight and went to change it, but he slapped my hand away.

"Nuh-uh. It's perfect."

"I can't listen to me bossing me."

"You know the way back?"

"No."

"Come on. You backed out, so left is that way." He pointed down the hill. "Why are you looking at me like that?"

I put the car in drive and went up the hill.

Recalculating route.

In four hundred feet, turn left.

"See, you know your way around like a native."

"Really?" I turned right onto a curved, overgrown street.

"Whoa whoa . . ."

I snickered.

Recalculating route.

In one thousand feet, turn left.

"If you don't know right from left, you can follow the map." He tapped the screen with a knuckle.

I turned right.

"What's the fun in that?"

Recalculating route.

In three hundred feet, turn left, then make an immediate left.

I turned right.

"Where are you going?"

Recalculating route.

Go straight for one-quarter mile.

"Left." I turned left into absolutely nowhere. It was my turn to laugh hysterically as I cut a hairpin turn and slowed for a coyote crossing the dark road. I was as lost as I'd ever been and joyfully pushing deeper and deeper into the glorious unknown, where I could be anyone I wanted, and anything could happen.

Stay to the right onto Canyon Drive.

"You won't even listen to yourself," Justin said.

"Because I have no clue where I'm going, and I know it."

"We're going to end up at a . . . ah. See?" A reflective yellow triangle hovered with a black END in the center floated over a smaller red diamond. "Like I said."

"I may not know where I'm going . . ." I slapped the car into park. "But I wound up exactly where I wanted."

He regarded me as if for the first time, with a lopsided smile on those sensitive, careful, precise lips.

"All things considered," he said, "*you're* pretty evil."

"I'd like permission to kiss you again," I said with a shrug.

Bending forward, close enough to see the late-day growth on his cheeks in the reflection of the headlights, he put his hand on my left thigh.

"Permission granted."

This kiss wasn't slow and steady. We crashed like waves on the shore, groping and grasping, exploring and tasting, until he slipped his hand under my left knee and yanked upward, pulling me onto his lap with a leg on each side of him. I dug my hands under his sleeves to feel the smooth hardness of his arms. He slid down and jerked up his hips until I felt his erection between my legs. I groaned into his mouth. He reached under my shirt and probed under my bikini top.

So we were back to doing it in the Tesla, because I was an out-of-control wildfire, 100 percent contained.

Then. Naturally. My phone rang.

We ignored it, grinding our hips together.

Ring number two. He pulled the string holding my bikini top together. When he found my hard nipple, I buckled under the hot crack of pleasure.

"I want you," he said, using his free hand to push my lower back down hard against him. "I want you so bad. But don't be pissed."

He slid my phone out of the compartment between the front seats.

"Jesus." I leaned my forehead on his shoulder while he looked at my screen over my shoulder. "It's not Chad."

"Kayla." He shrugged me off as the phone rang again. "Open it. It's Louise."

With a sigh, I put my thumb on the home button, and he swiped to answer.

"Hey. Weeze. Whaddup?" He looked out the side window as he listened. "Did you call an ambulance?"

CD Reiss

I leaned back to give him room. Justin had great instincts. I would have let it ring.

"I'll be right there," he said, then hung up.

"Is she all right?" I asked, taking the phone back.

"She's fine." He slid from under me and got into the driver's seat. "She gave Ned a heart attack."

"Oh my God."

"He's not dead." Hand on the gearshift, he gave me one last appreciative look. "Buckle in, baby. I'm driving now."

112

CHAPTER 10

JUSTIN

Everything was under control before I even pulled off the 405. My handler was taking care of the hospital. They'd have Louise in a private waiting room and me in a parking spot near the executive elevator by the time I arrived.

Kayla heard the entire thing over the Bluetooth. I didn't think it was that big a deal, but she made a shaky jazz hands motion and said, "Whoa, watch out. We got a big shot here."

"What?"

"That was super uncomfortable."

"You want me to walk in the front door? I wouldn't get past the lobby."

"I know. Never mind." She tapped the center screen for music. "Oh, you have good stuff."

"Duh," I said. "You can pull up my Instagram on that. Make me follow you."

"Why?"

"So I can keep track of you? I don't know. Why do you follow your friends?"

"I don't have Insta." She put on Mazzy Star and sat back.

"Twitter?"

"Nope."

"You do Myspace or something?"

"What's Myspace?"

"You have no social media?"

"I used to, but now I don't. I'm much happier. And besides, if you want to know what I'm doing, you can call me and ask."

I pulled into the alley behind the theater and stopped under the painted No PARKING sign.

"Thanks for showing me your foundation," she said. "I'd kiss you, but I don't want to keep you."

Up ahead, two guys turned into the alley. Kayla reached for the door handle. My hand shot out and grabbed her forearm like it had a mind of its own.

"Keep me," I said, pulling her close.

"One minute," she said, putting her finger to my lips. "Louise needs you."

"Sure."

As I kissed her, I peeked at the guys coming down the alley. I didn't stop until they'd passed.

"You on set Monday?" I asked. "Late call for night scenes, I think."

"Yes."

"You taking the bus?"

She bounced out, slipping her keys out of her bag.

My favorite kind of girl knew what she wanted and didn't play games about it. That was already 100 percent Kayla, but what made her even better was the complete lack of starstruck desperation. She'd avoid me, go about her day, and take the bus home to Creeper Alley.

Once she got the door unlocked, I pulled up and rolled down the window.

"Kayla," I called.

"You better get going."

"I'm driving you home from set next time."

She put her knuckles on top of the door and leaned down.

"I stay after you prima donnas are all gone."

"This alley's shady. And you gotta walk under the 405 from the bus. I don't like it."

"I'm fine."

She went in for a short peck on the lips. I grabbed her by the back of the neck and gave her more than she asked for, but not more than she was willing to give.

"You better go," she said. "Say 'hi' to Louise for me."

"Done." I turned on my GPS, and her voice came on.

Enter destination.

"Hi, Louise," I said.

Hi, Louise.

Kayla laughed. I pulled her in and kissed her one more time.

"Go," I said.

Destination unavailable.

After a final wave, she closed the door. When the upstairs apartment lights went on, I split.

~

I found the waiting room near the top floor, behind a closed wooden door they'd given me a code to open. My grandmother's feet were propped up on a sage couch with clean lines and spotless cushions. Behind it, windows looked out onto Olympic, and in front a mahogany coffee table was dressed in flowers and fruit trays.

She was more broken up than I thought she'd be. Eyes puffy. Hands wringing a damp tissue. Foot bouncing so hard her slipper was nearly off.

"We weren't doing anything, really." She kneaded her tissue. "We were just—"

"Don't tell me what he does." I dropped onto the sofa and kicked my feet up onto the table. "I'm good."

"I wasn't going to, smart-mouth. And get your feet off the table. Your father raised you like a wild animal."

She never said stuff like that. She wasn't strict about manners, and she didn't get on my case. I knew she dug Ned, but he was going to be fine. He'd be his usual self in no time, doing all the things I didn't want to know about.

"It's all right," I said. "He's gonna be fine."

She shot me a death look. I took my feet off the table.

"I know that." She honked into her tissue. I slid down in my seat and tried to rest while keeping my feet off the furniture.

"Your grandfather died of a heart attack," she said. "After dragging us all over the world, he up and has a coronary right back home on Tremaine. Your father was in seventh grade and behind in math, again, of course, because we'd just spent two months in Cambodia on a garbage hunt. So he was with a tutor, not home to help move that stupid, stupid chest."

"I thought he had a heart attack reading the paper?"

"He was forty-five. Did you know that? Stupid thing wasn't that heavy either. It had a carved top with these birds that had stones for eyes. Camphor lined with brass fittings. He had a dozen of them in the store, but this one? Had to move it into the house with no one to help, because it was 'too good to sell.' We had a house full of crap that was too good to make money on."

I moved to her side, grabbing her a tissue as I sat.

"I wanted to stay home. Let him hire a buyer to run all over. But no. It was him, him, him. And I went along with it until it killed him. He died the next day . . . yes, smart-mouth, reading the paper . . . with that damn chest under the window. But it was the life before that did it. The life I allowed. Well, I'm not allowing it again. We're taking it easy from now on. Ned and I are going vanilla." She dabbed her nose.

I rubbed my eyes as if that could erase the visuals. On one hand, I wanted her to live forever. On the other, if she and Ned were swinging from the chandeliers on a regular basis, she'd probably outlive me. The words *Stay kinky, Grandma* were absolutely, positively not coming out of my mouth.

"Frankly," she said, considering her balled-up tissue, "you might want to give your dick a vacation too."

"I'll give you a million dollars to stop talking like this."

"You can shove your money. I was talking about your life. You're here. You're there. Up. Down. Have you thought . . . maybe . . . that this problem with your career is a gift you should accept?"

"No."

A knock at the door preceded a woman in a white coat poking her head in.

"Louise Beckett?"

We stood.

"Yes," she said.

"I'm Dr. Jackson," she said. "If you want to see him, you can."

Louise straightened herself, sniffed one last time, and followed the doctor. Left alone with the fruit trays and the view of Olympic, I sat on the couch and propped my feet on the table to text Kayla.

—*You up?*—

—*No*—

—*Just letting you know Ned's fine. Louise is too. TMI but fine*—

—*Thank you*—
—*Hey. You've inspired me to take the van to work.*—

***The alley's fine but it's all night shoots this week
and the buses don't run late—***

Honestly, I'd wanted to drive her, because I wanted to see her, but whatever. I wasn't going to push it. She wanted to go herself. As long as she was safe about it and I'd see her again, I had no objections. I didn't think for a minute she wouldn't want to see me again. That kind of thing just didn't happen.

—They say I'm pretty inspiring—

***—You're five-eighths less dirtbaggy than
I thought you were—***

*—You're half the nasty bitch I thought you
were. But that's my favorite half—*

—Good night, dirtbag—

—Have nasty dreams—

The green dot by her name went gray as she signed off. No long goodbyes for this one. No social media, and she didn't turn texting into an endurance sport. She was going to take some getting used to.

Bored, I stretched out on the couch and flipped on the TV. If I'd been home, I wouldn't have seen it. I avoided the entertainment celebrity-news bottom-feeders because I didn't need the aggravation. Ken had people to watch TV for me. But in the waiting room, the channel was preset, and I was knocked on the side of the head by three things at the same time.

One, Gordon coming out of St. John's Cathedral in a tux and an actual haircut next to his bride, Heidi. He looked really happy, and that was what stopped me, because I hadn't seen him with a smile in too long. I was behind them in my DITA sunglasses, doing the best man thing while cameras flashed like the worst lightning storm on record.

Two, the chyron said SUNSET BOY GORDON DAWS FILES FOR DIVORCE.

Three, the damn words the host used made me want to hurl the couch at the TV. *Infidelity. Justin Beckett. "Soul Mated" was written for Heidi Collins. Assault. The Roosevelt Hotel. Drugs.*

I hunted for the remote's channel button as the news lady went on and on about how the band had broken up because of my "bad boy behavior," which—to me—boiled down to an indictment of my complete disregard for anyone else's feelings.

Of everything, that was what really put my balls in a vise.

Gordon was hurting. He had to be. He loved that girl like he'd never loved another thing in his life.

Finding the button, I looked up to change it to something more palatable, like a slaughterhouse exposé or the Dodgers going oh for four. Before I could, the video had changed to me on the Grammy red carpet, pre–Roosevelt Hotel. Sunglasses. Backward cap. Cigarette behind my ear even though I didn't smoke. I'd left the bow tie undone and pushed the tux jacket sleeves up my arms as if I didn't give a shit, but getting that to look right had taken forty-five minutes.

Then, with a professionally developed grin, I turned to the bank of cameras and flipped them the bird.

I clicked off the TV and tossed the remote on the table. It skidded off the polished wood and landed on the other side.

Chad had disappeared into the desert of the 15 freeway and fallen off the earth. Shane was just back from knocking around Scandinavia with a bunch of metalheads. Gordon was probably at the bottom of a bottle of tequila. I wasn't supposed to talk to any of them. Shane had an order of protection. Even if I could find Chad, he was off-limits. Gordon hated me. They were all trouble. I had a career to start over. Things to do. I wasn't getting caught up in this garbage again.

I called Gordon anyway. He wouldn't know my new number, so he didn't pick up. His VM was a slow walk of who I'd reached and what I had to do.

What I had to do was hang up before the . . .

BEEP

"Hey, Gord. Ah, fuck. Dude. I'm . . ."

Not sorry.

Not "I feel bad."

". . . I'm bummed for you."

Even that was probably too easily twisted. It was time for me to shut up.

I cut the connection and stretched out to wait for my grandmother.

CHAPTER 11

KAYLA

Clearly, Justin wanted all the same things I did. I wanted him to drive me home in his spaceship every night. I wanted to make out in the front seat and invite him upstairs.

What I didn't want was all the other stuff that went with the rides. I didn't want to be associated with his reputation. I didn't want his entourage or "Beckettes" around, looking at me. I'd already endured being well-known for the wrong things, and the thought of doing it again made my chest constrict.

Outside the Justin-specific reasons for my anxiety, I didn't want to depend on a savior for what I should be able to do for myself. So the morning after he dropped me off to meet Louise, I went down to the loading bay and opened my van.

The back was empty except for an empty water bottle in the corner and four bolts of Japanese selvedge denim that had been wrapped in plastic in the Josef Signorile sample room. The bundle was deceptively heavy. I knew that from getting it in the van in the first place, which didn't keep me from trying anyway. I rolled it, angled it, and tried to ease it out the back without letting it drop on the dirty ground, where I'd have to roll it out of the way. The only way to do it was to lower it onto the dolly I placed against the back edge of the van. I should have unwrapped it so I could do the four bolts individually, but then they wouldn't stack, and I was an idiot.

"Okay, big guy." I grabbed each side and spread my legs on either side of the dolly. "One. Two . . ."

On three, I pulled. My right hand slipped off and flew away, hitting the edge of a detached part of the back door.

"Ow!"

Worse than "ow," I was bleeding from a gash on the side of my hand right below the pinkie.

Maybe Signorile had cursed the fabric when he'd found out it was gone. Or when his wife told him she'd released it to me out of guilt. Maybe the fabric wasn't cursed, and it was just me.

By the time I got to the apartment my forearm was covered in blood. I washed it off and found some gauze and tape from the 1970s in Grandpa's stuff. The tape wasn't sticky anymore, but I had some masking tape in my things.

I was about to go back down to attack the bolts again when my phone rang.

Dad. I picked it up.

"Hey," he said. "How's it going?"

"Fine. I just lost a quart of blood."

"What?"

"Joking. It's nothing. What's up?"

"So," he said, as if—less like a father and more like a best gay friend—he was ready to spill a cup of juicy gossip. "I ran into Steve from Butter Birds last night. The guy I was telling you about."

"By ran into him, do you mean you called him?"

No denials were forthcoming.

"I told him all about you. He wants you to come in and talk to their creative director."

"Really?"

"Would I lie?"

"Okay, but do you know for what? Informational meeting? Job opening?"

I said the last word in pieces, as if overstepping the possible.

"Just go."

My portfolio was six months old. I had no samples. No current sketches.

"Your personality speaks for itself," he said with all the confidence of a father.

"Dad, come on."

"I'm not wrong. I know we practically just met, but you're special, and that's the truth. Get yourself out there. Let everyone see it."

He was right on that point. Whether I was special or generic, I still had to leave the house. And there was no reason I couldn't schedule the meeting in enough time to whip up some ideas.

"Okay. It's not Vasto or anything, right?"

"What's that?"

Vasto was an Italian investment firm known for picking design winners, providing financing, mentoring them, picking them up, and kissing their boo-boos when they slipped.

"Dream investor, but inaccessible," I said. "Doesn't matter. Butter Birds does the same thing, and so thank you."

"Listen, Kayla . . ." He paused as if he had to take a breath before finishing.

"Yeah, Dad?"

"I don't . . ." He laughed at himself, as if remembering something. "I have this friend, Ari. I hope you meet him sometime."

"What kind of friend?" I said with a touch of gossip in my voice.

"Friend-style, friend. But he always says you can convince yourself there's a relationship that isn't there, but you can't convince the other person. Because I can get a little . . . let's call it *enthusiastic*. And right now, I'm enthusiastic about you, and, really, we don't know each other."

It was surprisingly painful to hear that particular truth.

"That's my fault. I didn't—"

"No, no. That's not why I started saying uncomfortable things. What I'm saying is . . . I'm going to do you favors because I can't help myself. But I don't want you to feel obligated to accept or . . . you don't have to fill some role in my life. I mean I want you to, but it'll be what it's going to be, and you can't . . . I don't want you to feel pressured."

He always seemed so at ease, it never occurred to me what this meant for him. He'd lost us, and though Talia was found, I'd been a love he'd never recover.

Then I was back.

If that happened to me, I'd be enthusiastic too.

"I'm glad you're in my corner," I said. "Enthusiastically in my corner."

"And that's where I'm staying."

"Good."

"Go get 'em, tiger."

He was giving me exactly what I needed, but I hadn't given him what he needed. I'd never wanted to fill that gap for him. Maybe that was a relationship, or the beginnings of one.

"Dad?" I said before he'd have the chance to hang up.

"Yes?"

"I missed you sometimes. Not 'having a dad' so much as I missed . . . I don't know. You smelled nice and you danced with me at Aunt Judy's wedding. Remember that?"

"I do. And you cried when I put you down to dance with Talia."

I didn't remember him ever putting me down.

"Just wanted to tell you . . . I didn't forget."

"If you don't hang up right now, I'm going to cry."

I laughed, because he needed that too.

We hung up after a few goodbyes.

I started sketching right away. I had two more days of shooting, then set breakdowns. I didn't have time to get the denim out of my van. I'd have to get a cab home.

~

The costume trailer was half-unloaded into the truck that would haul everything back to a warehouse. We were getting ahead of the last day of shooting by getting rid of what we didn't need anymore in the cracks of time we had available.

Francine was going through the night's rack when I came back from the set, where I'd tightened the stitching on a button.

"Kayla," she said, punctuating my name with the click of hangers. "Good. I wanted to talk to you."

"Okay."

"What are your plans after we're done here?" She flipped a tag, checking to make sure it was correct, and went to the next one.

Ambition was nothing to be ashamed of, but my plans seemed so tenuous and overreaching I felt silly.

"I'm setting up some meetings," I said. "With backers. For my own line. So, making samples and stuff."

And stuff. People like Francine never said "and stuff" to describe their job.

"Interesting." She checked the last tag and, finding it acceptable, let it drop with a nod. "You don't need a job, then?"

That was a complex question, because I needed money, but accepting a job in costume meant less time to pursue what I came to Los Angeles for in the first place.

In the pause I took to find my answer, she continued.

"I still don't have a fitting person for *Treasure Hunt*. Not one I trust. You're calm under pressure. You work fast, and the players look good."

"Thank you."

CD Reiss

"Fittings only. I can get someone else to manage tags and racks. You take it and a forty percent increase."

Working with the garments was always a good thing, and the money would be decent, but I'd been caught in this trap before. Taking the job now meant indefinitely delaying what I really wanted, because a related job would come after. And another. Then I'd be fifty with a 401(k) and nothing I wanted out of my life.

"I don't know," I said.

"You think about it." She slung her bag over her shoulder. "This is a huge opportunity. Huge. You'll learn a lot and meet people."

"Thank you. I appreciate it."

"Good." She nodded. "I'll be in the studio. Check on Evelyn, would you? She gets lost in the truck sometimes."

"Will do."

The truck was actually a shipping container that would be hitched to a tractor once it was loaded. The door was ajar.

"Evelyn?" I said as I came in. The racks were packed tight, and the lights were on.

"Here," she said from the back.

"Just checking—" I stopped short when I saw her. Her hair was down, and she was wearing Regency underwear—a plain white shift and petticoat. What made me stop was her change in demeanor. Her head was high, her shoulders were back, and her glasses didn't slip down her nose. She looked sexy as hell when she was clothed in confidence.

"Francine gives us first shot at buying costumes she's passing to resellers."

"Buy that," I said. "Buy it right now."

"You like it?"

"It's you. I mean *you* to the bazillionth degree." I inspected the fit as she spun for me. "How did you get the stay on?"

"I have ways."

126

"You've done this before?"

"Oh my God, yes. I do cosplay events. Meetups. Reenactments."
She flicked through a rack. "There's a Regency ball at the Roosevelt
Hotel in a couple of weeks."

Even the way she pushed the hangers around was more assured, as
if she'd know what she was looking for when she saw it.

"You know what I loved?" I slipped behind that rack to the one
behind it. "Susan had a summer dress with tiny stripes."

"I loved that one, but she's a size six."

"Here it is." I pulled the dress out and pushed it to her over the
rack. "Look, I can take some out of the skirt and add panels to the
sideseam. Boom. It's a ten. Just like you."

"You think?" She ran her hand over the fabric.

"Totally. And dropping an armhole on a sleeveless is nothing."

"I can pay you. How much do you want?"

"I just want to see you in it."

"You should get one and come! My friend had a last-minute job she
has to go to, so we have an extra ticket!"

Taken aback by the invitation, I shook my head.

"I'm not a big cosplay person."

"So?"

"I don't know the dances."

"No one cares. Come on. I can pay you with a ticket. It's so much
fun, and if you hate it, I won't be mad if you leave."

"Maybe?"

"You have to."

Her desperation seemed disproportionate to the problem, and I
must have had suspicion all over my face, because she started explaining
without being asked.

"That night?" she said. "At NV? I told Eddie I liked his waistcoat,
and I went on and on about the accuracy of the detailing, then asked

him if his shirt under it unbuttoned all the way down. Like, that just flew out of my mouth, and it was like he could see me imagining him with his shirt off.

"He said, 'Is it not supposed to?'" she continued. "And I said, 'No, but it's fine. If you come to the Regency ball with me on the twenty-eighth, no one will even say anything.' Which was basically like asking him out."

"What did he say?"

She laid her forehead against a rack bar, as if the answer was too much to bear.

"He said he was already going."

"That's great!"

She picked her head up. "It was as good as a no. So I ran out. I couldn't take it."

"I don't think it was a no."

"It wasn't a yes. And I was so embarrassed. I'm still kind of mortified. I can't go alone. I'll do your hair. There's a twist style that's perfect for curls."

My phone buzzed.

"Okay," I said, checking to find a number I didn't recognize. "I'm in."

"Yay!"

I stepped away to answer the call.

"Hello?"

I could hear breathing on the other side, and the background chatter of a restaurant or coffee shop, but no response.

"Hello?" I said again. I was about to hang up when a woman's voice came through.

"Who is this?" a woman asked.

This crap was on a long list of pet peeves.

"You called me," I protested.

"And who are you?"

"Who did you call?"

"I don't owe you—"

I hung up. If someone just couldn't say, "Sorry, wrong number," they weren't worth my time.

The phone buzzed again. Same number. Christmas on a cracker. I picked it up.

"You have the wrong nu—"

"Where is he?"

"Who?"

I knew who she was talking about, but I didn't owe her rude ass a damn thing.

"You tell him Heidi says thanks for the divorce. I hope he's happy he and his big dick ruined everything."

And bang, like that, she hung up.

Heidi had to be Gordon's wife—whose infidelity with Justin Beckett was one of the half dozen things that caused the breakup of Sunset Boys.

The same guy who worried over his lost friend to the point of distraction was the same one who'd had an affair with another friend's wife.

That was inconsistent, but plausible.

I'd have to tell him about the call.

I'd have to walk out of the costume trailer with a thousand tasks on my list, take time out of what I was hired for so I could help Justin Beckett manage his drama.

I'd moved to Los Angeles to make my life simpler and somehow gotten roped into someone else's complexities. It was hard enough to live my own life, now I had to live his?

The only judgment I should be making was whether I wanted to get romantically involved with a man who sucked the life out of me. And the answer was a flat no.

I had work to do, and taking Justin's messages wasn't in my job description anymore, so I got to him when it was convenient for me, which was after everything but the last shooting night's racks was loaded.

Carter was standing in front of the fancy trailer, stoic as ever.

"Is Justin in there?" I asked.

"He's eating," he said, not moving an inch.

"I have to talk to him."

"I'll let him know."

His loss. My desire for his body was being steadily eclipsed by my need to protect myself from him.

"Fine," I said. I got two steps before hearing a *rap-rap* from the trailer. Justin had seen me and was at the window, trying to get my attention. Carter opened the door for me.

Justin was in street clothes and full scene makeup, sitting at a table before a confetti-colored sushi spread. One of his entourage, a guy with a goatee and prematurely receding hairline, sat across, eating salmon nigiri with a fork and watching a YouTube video on his phone. Justin kicked him under the table.

"Let her sit."

He got up and slid onto a couch with his plate and his video, barely looking at me.

"Sushi?" Justin said, using his chopsticks to push a plate toward me. "They always make too much."

"I ate."

He popped a roll in his mouth and chewed, fixing his gaze on me. The makeup that made him beautiful on camera covered what made him beautiful in person. He seemed less intense, less present. Definitely less intimidating.

"How's Louise?" I asked.

"Good." He pointed his chopsticks at the bandage on my hand. "What happened there?"

"Flesh wound."

"I should see the other guy, right?" he said, shoving a piece of sushi in a puddle of soy sauce.

"I was trying to move something heavy out of my van."

"Did you drive it in?" He popped the sushi in his mouth and chewed.

"No."

"Then you're mine tonight."

How anyone could say that so casually, without even looking up, was a mystery I couldn't solve. As was why my insides got warm with anticipation.

"I got a call," I said, and before I was even done, his hand shot up to stop me from saying another word. He turned to goatee guy.

"Bern, can you get out for a minute?"

Attention on the screen, Bern walked out, leaving his half-eaten lunch behind.

"It wasn't Chad," I said before he could ask. "It was Heidi."

His chopsticks clattered when he dropped them. "Fuck."

"She says thanks to your 'big dick' for the divorce."

"No." He jabbed his finger at me. "No, no, no. She doesn't get to do that."

"Isn't she Gordon's wife?" I hadn't walked into the trailer intending to litigate his past or make accusations, but I decided that was foolish. I needed to know who I was getting involved with. "She's the one you—"

"I did not. Okay? I didn't. And here we go with the whole 'Justin's a douchebag so we just assume he does everything douchebags do,' right?"

"I didn't say anything like that."

"But I can see it in your head. You think I'm a garbage human who sleeps with his friend's wife."

"I didn't say I thought that either."

Having put me on the defensive, he slid down in the seat, stretching his legs to my side.

"So you believe me?"

His focus on what I believed or didn't was a non sequitur. I wasn't his doormat or an enemy combatant. I was a woman with a life that he either fit into or didn't, and if we didn't fit, my opinion of his excuses was irrelevant.

I wove my fingers together on the table, leaning forward in the opposite posture.

"It doesn't matter if I believe you."

"It kinda does."

"Not to me. Not at all. Because I'm not going to sit here for another minute listening to the life and times of Justin Beckett. You're a drain on me, and we're not even dating. I'm not going to expend any more energy figuring out if you are who you think you are or helping you solve your problems. I have my own problems. My future's up in the air, and the next, like . . . three choices I make are going to affect that future. I have a property tax bill coming, and unlike you, when I say I don't know if I'm going to be working, that means I don't know if I can pay it. And also unlike you, the property I'm going to owe the taxes on is the only place I have to live." I laid my palms flat. "I need to live the one life I have." Pushing against my hands, I stood up. "I can't let you take over. I won't."

"So what does that even mean?" he asked.

"It means thank you, but I'll take a cab home."

I got to the door, but just as I was about to push the lever down, he was in front of me.

"I don't get what your problem is," he said.

My fists curled into hard balls. If he touched me anywhere I didn't want him to, I'd punch him where it hurt.

"The problem is you're blocking the door."

"So last night? It was nothing for you?"

"We've both made out with people before."

"Wait a second," he said. "This isn't about me being some kind of scumbag?"

"No, Justin. But if you don't get out of my way, it's going to be."

He backed off, as if making the biggest concession of his life.

I stormed out.

I'd won the battle.

CHAPTER 12

JUSTIN

This girl.

Kayla ripped the rug out so hard my shoes came off.

I'd dated a princess—an actual princess—for seven months. Princess Ingrid of Denmark. She didn't give an inch, and from jump I knew the game she was playing. So I played it, too, because you can't win if you don't play. In the end, I said "nah" and Ingrid said "meh." We came to a draw, more or less, which was the best a guy can do when he's up against a girl who was born and raised for the game.

But Kayla was either more masterful than Princess Ingrid, or she was being honest. And here was the thing. Besides surprise and irritation, I had feelings. Real feelings. The kind that made me want to be near her, sure. But also the kind that made me want to be the opposite of what made her walk out the trailer door in the first place.

My feelings didn't lie, so she had to be honest. No woman played me like that.

All I had to do was show her that I wasn't going to take her life over.

Hard to do without being right in her face.

First thing, make sure she didn't get any more of my calls. They'd bring her to my trailer door, but she needed to come to me because she wanted to, not because she felt obligated.

Heidi wouldn't pick up an unknown number, so I had Victor make the call and set up a meeting. He got back to me without asking a single question he shouldn't have. Bonus points for being the best assistant in town.

Heidi and I hit dinner in the back patio of Pietro's the next day. It was blocked from the valet by hedges, and I got there first, so there wasn't much chance we'd wind up on the internet together.

Heidi had been the director of a swank private elementary school. She and Gordon had met at a fundraiser he got dragged to with his sister, and he'd pursued her even after her ex tried to sabotage them. We hadn't hit it big yet. Not that big. We'd all thought she grounded him. Maybe she did, but maybe not enough.

She strode in with such purpose her dark hair flew away from her face with each step. She sat across from me in black bug-eye sunglasses and put her bag down as if I'd told her not to. Then she set her mouth in a mean little red line and said nothing. That must be the look she gave parents of misbehaving students. I had my back on a planter and my arm on the table, facing sideways so I didn't have to deal with her full on.

"You're welcome," I said when I got bored. She didn't reply. "You called to thank me and my big dick. You're welcome."

"When we got married, I told Gordon that if we ever broke up, it would be because of you."

That was bullshit. I never even looked at her sideways, and she knew it.

"Hold on there, sister."

"It was always *Justin*. All their lives revolved around you. Like you were a deity they had to follow into parties and back out. It was your needs. Your habits. Your pathetic need for validation. So, yes. I was right. If we went wrong, it would be you."

"And what did he say?"

"He said you were misunderstood."

The waiter came and dumped a fully scripted list of specials on us. I ordered a burger. Heidi ordered the steamed asparagus as an entrée.

"This is months old already," I said when the waiter left. "I did what I could. I don't know why you're busting my ass now."

"You said you'd stop him from filing for divorce. You said you'd fix it."

"I tried."

"By cutting him off? You can't convince him if you don't talk to him."

"I had no choice. And talking to him made it worse. He doesn't want to hear it from me."

"Give me a break, Justin." She dropped my name like a profanity. I turned in my seat to face the oversize black ovals of her sunglasses. Each lens reflected a tiny me.

"Every time I talked to him, he went to DMZ with what a liar I was."

"You mean the first week?"

"It was hurting me. Between him and Chad and what I did to Shane? Overland was on my ass. Slashdot was twisting my balls. Is it okay with you if I have a career or nah? I gotta be ruined because Gordon didn't trust *you*?"

She flinched.

Too hard, but I'd been bottled up too long to slow myself down.

"It took me months to find a new job because of you," she said.

"Don't even . . ." I waved my hands at her as if that would dispel the ugly lie of what she'd just said. "That's garbage, and you know it."

"You were always jealous."

"Bullshit."

"You climbed from girl to girl, but all you ever wanted was what Gordon and I had. Now you destroyed it." Her lower lip quivered, and her chin got tight. "I hope you're happy."

I'd come to mend fences and wound up building a higher one on top of what was already broken. This was going to turn into a disaster if I didn't chill.

"I'm not," I said. "You don't have to believe me. That's cool. But that doesn't make me happy about it either."

She took her glasses off and dabbed her eyes with a tissue. They were red and swollen. She hadn't worn any mascara, as if she'd known she'd mess it up.

I felt like garbage.

"Heidi. Listen."

"Fuck you, Justin. I don't have to listen. Gordon is my soul mate. He's the only man who can make me happy. And you three assholes? You're all important to him, so you're all important to me. And maybe that's my fault. Maybe I shouldn't have ever cared about keeping you together, but dammit, Justin . . . you put us in this situation. I mean . . ." She sniffed. "You came out of the bathroom naked. You stood there with that monster hanging out. You knew how much I cared, and you made a display of not giving a shit."

"That wasn't why."

"Why, then?" she demanded.

"You busted right in like it was your room. Just right in, accusing me of getting high with Chad so I could bring the entire band down so I could go solo. You accused me of not giving a shit about my friends. That I was going to drag Gordy in next, and then you were going to fuck me up. On and on. What was I supposed to do?"

"Put pants on."

"You should have closed the door behind you."

"You should have locked it."

"You should have been minding your own damn business in the first place."

She put her glasses back on. I should have been satisfied with the fact that she didn't answer for a long time. It meant I won that round. But in the long pause after, I felt worse. What was the point of winning if you felt like crap about making the enemy cry?

Our food came. She didn't pick up her fork. My burger looked like indigestion waiting to happen.

"Eat," I said, dumping a lagoon of ketchup on the side of the plate.

"I'm not hungry."

"Come on. You're too skinny. You look like a model. It's giving me the heebs."

She let go of a little laugh.

"Most women would take that as a compliment," she said.

"Most women aren't you." I plucked a french fry out of my pile and held it out. "Open up. No one resists Pietro's fries and lives."

She bit the fry in the middle, and I let go so she could chew the whole thing.

"Gordon was really hurt," she said, sliding her fork toward her and picking it up as if she had to sneak it. "When you cut him off."

"He thought I was dodging him to fuck you is why."

"No. Two weeks after it happened, he was packing his stuff and . . . well, this is kind of humiliating." She rolled an asparagus spear off the pile and stabbed it with her fork. "I was begging him to stay. That if he wouldn't believe me, he should believe you. And he said, 'He won't take my calls.' The look on his face. He was so hurt, and it made me mad. Just so mad."

The asparagus hovered halfway between the plate and her mouth.

"You posing for a painting?"

"What?"

"Eat it before it goes bad."

I smashed the bun against its contents and picked it up. She bit the flower side without letting her lips touch the stem. I ate my burger and watched as she took a second bite.

"I need a favor," I said.

"No. Forget it."

"You don't even know what it is."

"I'm done with trouble."

"Me too. This is a done-with-trouble favor."

She polished off the last of the asparagus stem.

"I need you to stop calling that number," I said. "I'll give you the new one, and you can yell at me all you want. Day or night. Call me names right to my face, just ditch those digits."

"Why?"

"Just because?"

"Who was the girl you gave the phone to?"

"It's not . . . It doesn't matter." I bit the burger so I'd be forced to shut up.

"Hm." She took a french fry from my plate. "Interesting."

"It's not interesting."

"So, you're asking me to do something by asking me not to do something?"

"Yeah. So?"

She ate the french fry in one bite.

"I can do that."

"Thank you."

"And in exchange—"

"What?" I put the burger down and leaned back. "Don't."

"You talk to Gordon. Explain what happened one last time."

"I can't."

"Why not?"

"Because I'm on career parole."

"Poor you." She pouted. "My husband's writing sad songs no one will look at because without you, there's no band. Shane's trying rock, and he sucks. And Chad? Where is he?"

I wasn't answering that. One, because I didn't know. But also because I wasn't telling anyone I'd broken parole for Chad, or she'd want the same.

"I'll ask her name the next time I call," she said.

Of course she had Kayla's number. I should have shrugged and told her to go ahead, but I didn't. I sat there with a bundle of french fries half-swiped through my lake of ketchup, frozen as if I had stage fright.

"Okay, I get it now." I dropped the fry and wiped my hands. "This is payback. I showed you my ass, and now you know how to fuck it."

"It's your chance to prove *having* a big dick doesn't mean you *are* a big dick."

She couldn't have known how badly I wanted to prove that to Kayla, but I wasn't going to give her any more ammo by admitting it.

"Tell you what. If I do this, and he gets back with you . . ."

I was going to demand a full-page ad in *Billboard* about what an awesome guy I was. Interviews. Essays. She had to tell everyone.

But if I was trying to prove I wasn't an asshole, I should just do what I said I would and let her say what she wanted.

"If he gets back with me, what?" she prodded.

"Invite me for dinner at your house."

"Done."

"And you let my kids in that fancy school you're running."

She forked an asparagus spear and paused before she ate it. "We'll see how many kids you have."

"Fair, fair."

Now all I had to do was reach Gordon without going through my handlers.

~

When Ken called, I was driving. I figured it was too early for him to know I'd agreed to get Gordon on the phone, so I answered.

"Justin. You're done shooting *Pride and Prejudice*?"

"Yeah."

"Good. One thirty tomorrow. My office."

"I'm busy."

"Your assistant says you're open."

"I'm not."

"Good. See you tomorrow."

He hung up.

I did have things to do, but they weren't appointments I could put on a calendar.

My intentions were to get my life in order before talking to Kayla again. Reduce drama 80 percent. Clear my name to prevent new drama. I thought I was doing all that already, but she made me see that the problem wasn't everyone else. To some extent, I had to admit it was me.

So, fine. Me, I could fix.

In four hundred feet, turn left.

On the way to Pietro's, I'd changed the GPS voice to an Australian dude, but on the way home I changed it back to Kayla.

That was a mistake. I didn't need directions to my own house, but I wanted her voice in the car. Hearing her tell me where to go was like having her right there, talking to me with that mouth. She used it like a superstar, and it hadn't been anywhere near my dick. When she'd groaned, I almost lost it right in my shorts. I mean, not really, but metaphorically. Knowing she liked it, too, was gratifying in a way I couldn't explain to myself.

Continue for three-quarters of a mile.

I took the long way home just to hear her voice in surround sound. The car's AI even made her a little snippy. Girl like that under me would feel really good.

141

I shut off the GPS. If I didn't stop obsessing, I was going to do something stupid.

Stupidity was my brand.

Good thing I could find her place without being told where to go.

~

The alley behind the theater was littered with empty beer bottles. The second-floor lights were on, and I could hear girly singer-songwriter music. Mazzy Star, maybe. From below, all I could see were the tops of bookshelves and a movie poster. A shadow moved across the ceiling.

I texted her.

—Hey. I'm downstairs—

No answer. I called, and it went to voice. I texted again.

—Back alley—

—Hello?—

"Kayla!"

I waited. Nothing.

"Kayla!" I shouted even louder.

Nothing.

No pebbles around. I picked up an empty bottle, aimed it for the brick space between windows, and threw it. The glass exploded in a spray that came down on me like rain.

"Shit!" I covered my eyes with my arm.

The music lowered, though. A casement window was cranked open, and she stuck her head out. She was in a pink pajama top with lace around the edges, and her hair was down over her shoulders in a shawl of dark curls.

"What the ever-loving hell are you doing?" she cried.

Man, I liked this girl.

"You should pick up the phone."

"It's off."

"Who turns off their phone?"

"I do. What do you want?"

What did I want? She was supposed to run down the stairs and fall into my arms. What was with the twenty questions?

"Just saying hi."

Really? What the goddamn hell was that dumbass response supposed to get me?

She put her elbows on the windowsill.

"Hi," she said.

"Hi."

"Anything else?"

This game, I knew.

"Nah." I opened the car door, and when I looked back, she was cranking the window shut.

Damn.

"Hey!" I called. "I got something else."

"Okay, what?"

What? Everything's what. How could I play this without telling her everything?

"I'm not supposed to bother you, I know. You said, 'No, thanks,' but I wanted to tell you I told Heidi not to call you."

"Thank you."

She seemed sincere enough, but she was still in the windowsill, where I couldn't reach her.

"Do you like me or nah?"

What a sap I was. What a wuss. Asking this chick if she liked me. She should be begging for it. That was the rule. But no. She just stood up there thinking, "Maybe yes, maybe no," while I waited.

"I like you," she said, final-fucking-ly. "I like you a lot."

"Yeah?" The good feeling of hearing it made me even derpier. And if she did like me? I was okay with it.

"Yeah. I'm glad you're here. I missed you."

"Arright, so . . . uh . . ."

"I'll be right down."

When the window cranked shut, I wished she'd do it faster. It took forever for her to get down, but when she opened the rolling gate in a blue shirt and jeans, I knew she'd taken a minute to get dressed.

Too bad.

"You shouldn't leave that car in the alley," she said, then, with a still-bandaged hand, waved at the narrow space next to her white van. "I think you can fit here."

I pulled the Tesla in, and she rolled down the gate. My plan was to kiss her after she locked it. Just get on her and show her how much I wanted her, but I stopped myself. She knew, and if she didn't, I could tell her again.

"So," she said. "Welcome to the CineSquare Theater, closed ten years over a lack of parking. As you can see."

"Seems nice. Why's the van door open?"

"Couldn't get the bolts out and didn't want to put them back in."

The bolts were a few inches past the edge, on a blue tarp.

"Huh. Well." I climbed into the back, because this I could do. I pointed to the wheeled cart leaning against the open door. "You trying for that dolly?"

"Yeah."

I crouched behind the bolt. "Let's do it."

She put the dolly handles against the edge and took the front end of the cylinder.

"On three," I said. "One. Two." I braced my arms. It was too heavy for her to be on that side. "Wait."

She looked at me quizzically, and I hopped out.

"Let's switch," I said. "The weight's gonna come down on this side."

"You think I'm too weak?"

"You wanna ask that flesh wound you got?"

She held up the hand with the bandage and extended her middle finger.

"Come on, man," I said. "Let me shoot my guns." I made a muscle and kissed my bicep.

She laughed so hard she bent over with her shoulders shaking. When she climbed into the back of the van, she was still giggling, which made me smile a little.

"On three," I said again, bracing my feet on the cart's wheels so it didn't roll away. "One. Two. Three."

She pushed. I pulled, managing the weight so the bolt landed squarely on the dolly.

"Hey!" she cried, hopping down. "I'm mobile!"

"Boom." I swung the dolly away from the van. "Where's this go?"

"Here." She pulled the tarp out and laid it on the floor, in a space against the wall. We maneuvered it into place, and I held the end so it didn't drop too hard.

"I have a ride!" She slapped the van doors closed. "I don't have to leave my only asset in a parking space. Yay!"

She leaped into my arms, and with a whiff of the coconut hair stuff and the feeling of her body against mine, my senses exploded like fireworks. Doing something to make her happy, though . . . that was like a nuclear bomb of unicorns and rainbows in my heart.

Too lame to put in a song. Still true.

"Want to see the theater?" she asked with her dark eyes glittering in the garage light.

"Sure."

~

"Whoa."

The theater part was a little bigger than a gym, with ceilings about the same height. The part that whoa'd me was the floor. It was flat. Front and back—same level.

"Yeah," she said, as if she knew exactly what I was talking about. Then she proved she did. "Being short must've sucked."

"What are you going to do with it?"

"No parking. No money to renovate."

"It's a great space."

"I'm not really interested in owning a movie theater, either, and we can't sell it. So, there's that."

"Denim factory," I said.

"I'm sorry?"

"You got concrete floors and enough ceiling for ventilation. A loading dock. You can do a storefront facing Santa Monica. Cut out the middleman. All profit."

For a second she looked at me and through me at the same time, calculating in her head.

"I never thought of that."

"You don't dream big enough, Kaylacakes."

"I'd need to make sure the water pipes and electric can handle the stonewash machines."

"Doable."

"Yeah," she said. "It is. With money."

The money comment wasn't self-pitying or hopeless. More the definition of an obstacle.

"You'll figure it out."

"Yeah," she said. "I will. Come on. Let me show you the upstairs."

I followed her up to the top floor. It was pretty nice, in an old-guy-lives-here kinda way. Big space with no walls between rooms. The kitchen and the bed were in the back, overlooking the alley where I'd been standing fifteen minutes ago. Couch and chairs in the middle. The other side of the space was just boxes.

Over an old desk, scraps of paper and magazine pages had been stuck to the wall with the same blue tape she'd used on her cut hand. I leaned into them. The white scraps were quick sketches, some were stitch details, others were body shapes for jeans and jackets. She was serious about being a designer, and I didn't know anything about making clothes, but I knew what worked and what didn't. This stuff worked.

"That's not finished," she said. "It's for a meeting Friday."

"Do you mean the outseams to be this long?" I pointed to a sketch with uneven leg openings. "Or is that just a drawing-style thing?"

"They should be that way so when you do cuffs it makes little triangles with the selvedge edge."

"That's cool. Yeah. I get it. You could put a rivet to hold it."

"Oh," she said, grabbing a pencil from a cup. "That's good."

She leaned over the desk and drew a flipped cuff with a rivet on the margin, then quickly erased one cuff on the body and flipped up the edge.

"Yeah," I said, nodding. "Cool. Signature detail."

"Now I want to put it everywhere."

"Take it easy, tiger. Don't go wild with the eraser yet."

"Right." She put the pencil back in the cup. "I have soda in the fridge."

I joined her in the kitchen area. The avocado refrigerator rattled like a diesel engine.

"It's like you're living in a vintage store," I said, coming out with two cans of cola.

"Yeah, like, check this out." She opened a drawer, and I went for the ice, coming out with two handfuls. When I got my head out of the freezer, she was holding up a short fork with fat, hooked tines. "Like what is this?"

Blood soaked through her bandage.

"I got no idea." I put the ice in the glasses and held my hand out for hers. "But you're bleeding."

"I . . ." She saw what I was talking about. "Oh. It must have opened when we moved the bolt. Let me go take care of it."

She headed for the bathroom, and I joined her. She raised an eyebrow at me but unwrapped the blue masking tape around the bandage instead of telling me to get the hell out.

"Nice," I said when the wound started bleeding down her arm. I got the faucet going, and she put her hand under it. "Did you put antibiotics on this or nah?"

"Nah," she said. I opened the medicine cabinet. "Under the sink."

The plastic container I found had gauze and tape from the Dark Ages. I ripped open a brown paper gauze package.

"Apply pressure." I pushed the gauze to the cut, but instead of letting her apply the pressure, I kept my hand there. "I'm getting you a first aid kit. This place is just a bunch of sharp edges and flesh-eating bacteria."

"I got cut on the van."

"That changes nothing." With my free hand I knocked around the box for an old tube of Neosporin and some Brave Soldier. "If you get infected, they have to cut the entire arm off."

"They do not."

"Sure they do."

"Where did you hear that?"

"My mother. You want to tell her she's wrong? I fucking dare you." I pulled the gauze away and aimed the Brave Soldier.

"That might—" I squirted it.

"Ow!" she cried.

"—sting."

"Who taught you how to dress a wound? The Marquis de Sade?"

"The chain-link fence between Gordon's house and Elysian Park." I unscrewed the tube of Neosporin. "This won't hurt. Promise."

She held her hand out, looking at me suspiciously, and relaxed as it turned out I was telling the truth.

"Thank you," she said as I wrapped it back up with fresh blue tape. "I almost didn't let you up here."

"Now you have a ride, and you get to keep your arm." I ripped the tape with my teeth and stuck the edge down. "I feel like that makes us even."

"If I round up. Sure."

"How did you get so hard?"

The words came out before I could think about them. She wasn't hard, and even if she were . . . no one wanted to be called that. My apology was about to follow my insult, but instead of reaming me out, she took the question the way I meant it.

"You want to know?"

"Yeah."

"I'll tell you over flat soda."

She took my hand and drew me into the kitchen, handed me my soda, and went to the living room space, where she sat in a mustard velvet chair. I sat on the matching couch and lifted a foot to put on the coffee table, but stopped myself in time.

"Go ahead," she said. "Take your shoes off first, though."

As I kicked my sneakers off, she sat next to me on the couch where I could reach her.

"I didn't mean to call you hard," I said.

"But I am."

"Still."

"We're close enough for you to make a true observation."

Jeez, when she said we were close, I lost control of my face and smiled so wide I swear my cheeks hurt. I put the cold glass of flat soda against my bottom lip before it split.

"If you're not hard," she said. "You get walked on. Let someone get away with stuff once, and they try again. And the more I have to offer, the more I get screwed. Two hours' free overtime? Make it four. Stick your neck out and your head gets chopped off. Every time. A certain kind of dog can smell weakness. Let them sniff out someone else's butt."

"'Cos you got your hard-ass deodorant on."

"Yup." She laughed a little. "I'm not here to be your doormat. And if that means I'm a bitch sometimes, oh well."

"Did I treat you like a doormat?"

"Until I turned bitchy."

"You were never bitchy. Nasty, yeah."

"What's the difference?"

"Bitchy is fake. Nasty's scary. Bitchy wants you to cry. Nasty wants you to bleed."

"Poor boo-boo," she said, putting her hand over mine and whispering. "Where did I hurt you?"

"Right here." I pointed to my forehead. She shifted closer and kissed the spot.

"Better?"

"And here," I said, indicating my chin. She kissed that too.

"Don't you dare point to your dick next," she said.

"You want to hurt that?"

"No. But someday I might kiss it anyway."

My dick reacted to the possibility. When she let me kiss her, it felt as if it would never go limp again. We stretched out on the couch, attached at the mouth. I got on top of her, and she wrapped her legs around me, groaning that way she did when I pushed my permanent hard-on against her. She arched her back, eyelids fluttering.

"You're so sexy," I said into her ear, pulling up her top to feel the silk of her skin.

No bra. Jesus, no bra. All supple breast and hard nipple that made her gasp when I pinched it. How soft would this hard woman get? How long could I edge her before she lost the last shreds of her hard shell? I had to know.

"I want to make you come," I said, pulling away long enough to look her in the eye. "Let me taste you."

Her hips reacted independently of her mind, jerking forward.

"I can't tonight."

"Why?"

"It's my time of the month. Last day, but still."

"The only thing a period ends is a sentence."

Her smile was all intrigue as she bit her bottom lip.

"You're dangerous," she said. "You keep saying things that make me like you."

"So, yeah?"

"Let's wait."

"You're the dangerous one," I said, getting up. "I need to lay off if I wanna be able to walk tomorrow."

"Fair."

We sat there. She rubbed her hands on her jeans. I scratched the back of my neck, wishing I hadn't just kicked myself out for the night.

"I should let you get to sleep," I said, making a Hail Mary pass for an invitation to hang out.

"Okay. I was just going to watch a movie anyway. So . . ."

"Yeah? What movie?"

She went to a box and flipped the top open. It was filled with hand-labeled black boxes.

"Take your pick."

"Are these . . . movies?"

"The VCR works."

I picked out a random box and handed it to her. It rattled when she cracked it open.

"*A Star Is Born.* Streisand edition," she said. "You want to pick again?"

"Never seen it. I'm down for something new."

The TV was a hundred-pound box on a table at the end of the bed. She turned it on and stuck the tape in a built-in slot. I dived to the end of the bed and grabbed a pillow as I stretched across the width.

"Netflix and chill," I said. "Eighties style."

"You do not," she said, crawling to me.

"Not what? I'm a big guy."

"Move it or lose it."

"There's a chair over there."

I'd been betting on a wrestling match—what I got was her fingers digging into my armpits. I squirmed to get away, but she straddled me.

"Quit it," I laughed.

She was a genius at finding the right spot to tickle.

"Surrender."

"Never."

I kept grabbing her hands, and she kept slipping away to torture me until I had to wiggle off the bed entirely. She snapped up the pillow and hugged it.

"I win."

"Damn. How did you know?"

"You're not the first ticklish person I fit a pair of pants on. You were so cute."

"That's on the DL."

"You surrender?"

I held up my hands.

"White flag."

She sat back against the headboard and patted the spot next to her. I sat, keeping a safe distance through the front-end credits. Then my hand found its way to her lap, and she shifted so she had her head on my chest. We kind of watched the movie. Kind of made out for two hours and then some. I pulled up her shirt and tasted her tits, rolling my tongue and running my teeth over them as she dug her fingers in my hair and pushed up against my dick. I couldn't get enough of her.

She was under me with her legs wrapped around me and her lips puffy and pink from my beard when the tape clicked off.

"That was the best movie, ever," she said.

"I think it won an Oscar." I rolled off her.

"Well deserved." She ran her hand over my chest, and I grabbed it so I could kiss her palm, then her wrist.

"I should get going," I said.

"You should."

"I don't want to." I kissed the inside of her elbow.

"But you still should."

I took my mouth off her arm.

"Yeah?"

"Let's pick this up next time."

"Next time, Kaylacakes." I shifted to the edge of the bed. "Next time you're going to come so hard they're going to give you an Oscar."

"I doubt I'll be acting." She pulled her shirt down.

"Shoot's over. I won't see you on set anymore."

"Now it's a choice," she said, shoving her feet in her shoes. "Seeing each other. I can't hide you or pretend we just passed each other on set."

"Yeah," I said, taking her hand.

Ken had told me to wait, and I hadn't. The movie had been cover, and now it was gone. I had to deal with him, because this girl was going to be mine no matter what he said.

~

After I got home, I lay in bed with aching balls, thinking about her without a single unpleasant thing on my mind.

Then Shane came by. Unlike Ken, he didn't give my cook a hard time, but just like my PR guy, he used how well he knew me to get in.

"I changed my code," I groaned after he slammed the bedroom door open.

"To your mother's birthday." He stood over me, toothpick jammed in the side of his mouth, a corn-kernel-size flavor saver under his lower lip. "I woulda called, but some girl's got your number, right? She's suffered enough."

"What the hell do you want?" I threw the sheets off me and dragged my ass to the bathroom. When I got home from Kayla's, I'd stripped down to my jocks. Not that Shane hadn't seen my dick before, but the last time he had everything had gone down the toilet. Whatever. I had to take a leak. He didn't have to look.

"Gordon don't want to talk to you."

I left the bathroom door half-open and relieved myself.

"You his messenger now?" I shouted over the echo of piss hitting porcelain.

"You're Heidi's?"

"Yeah. I am. Because Gordon's an idiot who won't talk to his wife."

He braced himself in the doorway in ripped-up jeans with a ring of keys on the loop and a Guns N' Roses decal chipping off his black T-shirt.

"That's not your problem since you're the one that started it."

"I told you." I slammed the flusher. "You didn't see what you think you saw."

He crossed his arms and leaned on the jamb as I washed my hands.

"They call that gaslighting. I'm not a 'Beckette,' okay? I'm the guy with the crooked nose."

"You wouldn't listen." I dried off. I'd done a lot of stupid stuff at the Roosevelt Hotel. What I did to Shane was the worst.

"I'm not getting into this." He stood straight. "Just saying leave Gordon alone."

He turned and left. I threw the towel at the hamper. Missed.

How could I feel so good with Kayla a few hours before and like a pile of trash now? Like a minute of relief from guilt was money I hadn't earned. I beat the dog and kept kicking it. Gordon. Heidi. Shane. Chad.

Eighty percent naked, I ran downstairs and caught Shane before he left.

"Hey, Shane."

"We got nothing else to talk about."

"Have you heard from Chad?"

He stopped. Turned.

"No. You?"

"I mean in the last few weeks."

"Not since you left that shit in his room and he split."

I shut my eyes and mouth against everything he got wrong.

"What's going on, Justin? Why you poking at all of us?"

"It's a long story. But he was in Vegas. He contacted me."

"What? You didn't tell us?"

"Stop. Okay. Look, I'm not supposed to talk to you guys. But I did. I talked to him, and he said he was coming back. I haven't heard a word since then."

"What did he say?"

"Not much. He said he was on the 15. Then poof."

"Dude. You shoulda said something."

"You're joking, right?"

He had the nerve to look at me as if I was off my nut, when he hadn't even seen his nuts since the night I broke his nose.

Okay. Whatever. Fine.

I went to the kitchen to get a cup of coffee. Maybe a little caffeine would make my arguments with myself coherent.

Charlotte was nowhere to be seen, but she'd left a pot of coffee for me. I didn't expect Shane to follow me in. He'd already said what he wanted to. He could leave the same way he got in. But there he was.

"You wanna put some clothes on?" he said.

"It's my house."

"You're a biohazard like that."

"You want coffee or nah?"

"Yeah." He sat on a barstool as if he'd been invited. "So, what are you going to do about Chad?"

"What am I gonna do?" I put two mugs on the counter and poured coffee. I took it black, but I got cream out of the fridge for Shane. "I'm going to stop giving a shit. Every time I try and help you guys lately it blows up in my face."

"And I'm supposed to what? Feel sorry?"

"You're supposed to listen when I tell you something. Not threaten me."

"Dude. You were standing over Heidi with your dick hanging out. She was naked. What was I—"

"First of all, she wasn't naked."

"Come on. Give it up already."

"What color was her bikini that day?"

"How should I know?"

Here we were, going over the basics we should have gone over the morning after.

I was done with this.

"Beige." I dropped it like a bomb. "She's white and it was beige, and you saw her through a doorway for half a second before you started yelling like a fool. And when I came outta the bedroom to talk to you? What did you do instead of listen? You ran out with your mouth flapping about going up to the pool and finding Gordon. So, yeah, I chased you into the hall, and, yeah, when you swung at me with your drunk ass, I nailed you."

He poured cream into his cup with his mouth twisted to one side.

"Four times." He slapped the carton down.

"I'm sorry about the extra three."

"Fuck you," he mumbled. He could curse at me all he wanted, as long as he was in my kitchen drinking my coffee out of my cup. I was going to say the shit I hadn't, and he was going to hear me out.

"I was in Chad's room because his dirtbag of a dealer sent me up there. He was freaking out. He was curled up in a corner of the bathroom with his eyes bugging out. The counter had a burn mark and a half-empty bag of powder. I didn't know what to do, because we had recording dates, and he's no good to us in jail. I dragged him into the shower and tried to snap him out of it. He puked on my shorts, so I took them off. He was looking a little better when Heidi comes in with her bikini, all ragey because she saw me talking to the dirtbag dealer. She starts giving me shit for being a bad influence. Me. The one kicking the dealer out. I'm telling her to back it up when who comes in? You. Giving me a hard time about fucking her, which I wasn't even close to doing. Running out to tell her husband a story your drunk ass made up."

Instead of getting more pissed off with every word, I emptied a well of anger I never acknowledged.

"What happened to Chad, then?"

"How many times did he cut out in the middle of geography? And Mrs. Ramirez didn't even notice until the bell."

Shane laughed a little. Good. I'd jammed a wedge in the seam between resentment and friendship. All I had to do was wiggle it enough to split the two apart without breaking everything.

"He's like Houdini, and you know it," I said. "He woke up and slipped out while I was dealing with you."

"You mean breaking my nose?"

"Yeah. Shutting you up before you ruined their marriage. That's the one thing they say I did that night that I actually did. I took the heat for the drugs so Chad wouldn't get arrested again. I got accused of sleeping with Heidi, and you all hate me so much you didn't even believe either of us. So you know what? I cut you off. It was self-preservation, and you can blame me for it but . . ." I picked up my cup so I could prepare for a lie. ". . . I don't care." I drank from it and lied again. "I don't care."

"We don't hate you," Shane said.

"Whatever."

"We just don't trust you."

Fuck the wedge. I could stand their contempt, but the mistrust was bullshit. I thought I deserved it, but nah. I didn't. Not from these guys.

"You know what?" I pushed my cup away as if it mattered where it was. "Get out."

"My pleasure." He stood. "Just do everyone a favor. Let us have a little self-preservation. Stop asking us to listen to your explanations. You're a shitty liar."

He stormed out.

"Fuck you!" I shouted after him. My voice echoed against the walls of my big empty house. I threw my cup against the sink, shattering it. That echoed too.

I put my hands on the edge of the counter and dropped my head. What was I supposed to do? How many times was I supposed to bang my head against the resistance of everyone I loved? They wouldn't let me back in, and they wouldn't let me cut them off. I couldn't make a deal or a gesture that would change their minds. My life was crowded, and my house was empty.

"Give me a break," I said, picking up my head. "Nobody likes someone nobody likes."

Self-pity wasn't going to get me anywhere. Neither was trashy brain poetry. I'd write a few songs about it, clear out my system, and face forward.

I had a past, and I had a future. It was time to start building the one I had control over.

Laying the first brick, I called Ken.

"Yo," I said when he finally picked up. "You finished googling Kayla or nah?"

"We're following up on some things."

"What things?"

"Give me a couple more days."

He was getting zero days, but I didn't tell him that.

CHAPTER 13

KAYLA

Until the day she was hit by a car, walking across Broadway against the light, my mom loved my dad. He wasn't allowed to come to her funeral because, though he loved her as well as he could, in the end, he loved men more. But during their marriage, he got her flowers on her birthday and took her out for their anniversary. He didn't miss a beat until she brought his lunch to the office and caught him getting a blow job from his boss.

She didn't tell me that right off. Not when I was four, obviously. I got that tidbit right before she died, as if she needed to drop that last betrayal to carry me through the years without her so I'd be protected from men like my father.

Mom said, "Trust but verify," but I got only the verify part. I verified a guy didn't write me love notes or buy flowers. I made sure he didn't do anything to prove he loved me. No favors. No sentimental gifts. I thought being loved meant being respected, and respect meant being treated like a piece of furniture.

When I pulled my van into the alley and got out to close the gate, I saw the bolts of denim lying on the tarp in the corner.

Was Justin playing at caring about me with kind acts and gentle words? Was I a conquest and no more?

Did it matter?

It did. How he felt mattered a lot. I believed he was being honest. And why should I? He was a player. An entitled child. He was careless with other people's feelings and protective of his career.

But I enjoyed his attention. He made me feel good, even when he pissed me off. He understood and accepted me the way I was. Maybe that was all fake. Maybe his favors and compliments were tactics in a larger game. Maybe he liked that I was a challenge, and once I wasn't anymore, he'd declare victory and move on.

Probable. He was Justin Beckett, and I was just me. But I was going to see him again. I was going to let him do whatever it was he planned to do, because I was absolutely powerless to protect myself.

I rolled up the gate, letting the light flood in. I needed to sweep the alley. It was mine. The theater was my home, and a friend was coming so I could alter her costume for a Regency ball. The responsibilities I'd chosen proved I was building a new life, and I closed my eyes, turned my face to the sun, and smiled.

Evelyn's car pulled down the alley moments later, and I waved her into the garage. She popped her trunk as I closed the gate and locked it.

"Wow," she said when she got out. "You really live in a theater."

"It's a dump, but it's mine. Kind of."

We gathered the garment bags from her trunk and clapped it shut.

~

I'd set aside a work area with my machine and an ironing board and removed stacks of boxes from the dining room table, revealing a wood surface marked with rings and dark-brown spots.

"I remember these," Evelyn said, rubbing the spots. "My grandmother smoked. The cigarettes were always rolling off the tray."

The spots were clustered in the center, but all over as if the table had been ringed with smokers. The rings were on all sides too. If they'd been caused by one lonely old man, they'd be in his habitual spot.

"Weird," I said. "My grandfather didn't have friends."

"You sure?"

"I guess not? I mean, he was terrible."

Maybe he wasn't? Maybe he had qualities that attracted a small group of confidantes. Maybe he reserved his awfulness for his family or turned inward toward the end. He was lost now. Any chance I had of sitting at that table and asking him was gone.

I had no way of fully knowing the past and had to accept that I'd never correct it. History had left clues but was unchangeable. The marks were mine now.

I draped Evelyn's inside-out dress over the table.

"Okay." I held up my seam ripper. "Close your eyes. This may be painful."

"I want to watch."

"Your funeral." I dug the point into the sideseam and tore the threads.

"You know," Evelyn said. "This big fashion guy puts on this super-exclusive thing during the cocktail hour."

"Oh?"

"In the Toledo Room. It's invitation only, but maybe you can find him in the ballroom after and make friends."

"Who is it?" Having finished the left sideseam, I moved to the right.

"Josef Signorile."

The seam ripper slipped, and I avoided shredding the entire bodice only because my muscles wanted to crawl back inside themselves.

"You've heard of him?" Evelyn asked.

"I used to work for him." I kept my eyes on the loose threads, plucking them like feathers out of a chicken.

"Oh!" She clapped. "Great, so—"

"I'm good!" I said with such a thick dose of saccharine cheer no one would confuse my feelings with actual optimism.

"Kayla?"

"No, really. I'm sorry. Hey. Look. It's complicated. Just . . . Cool. Never mind. Okay?"

"None of that made sense."

"He's not a nice person." I turned the dress right side out. "That's all."

"Well, then I guess don't talk to him?"

Signorile was going to be at the ball. Of course. He took a trip to LA every year before the yarn and fabric shows in Milan. I should have remembered how nice July was in the office.

"Actually, it's not complicated," I said. "He gets his kicks grabbing women who work for him."

"Did he . . . ?"

"Yeah. He has a staff of people to cover it up. It's like a machine, the way it works. Either you play along and take money to keep your mouth shut, or he ruins you. I took door number two."

"I'm sorry that happened."

"It's fine."

"If you don't want to go, I totally understand."

"Los Angeles is my turf now." I held her dress out. "Put this on. Bathroom's over there."

"I'm not shy," she said, pulling her shirt off. "Is that why you came out here?"

"Yes." I rearranged my pins and scissors as if that would focus my energy where it was needed. Evelyn stepped out of her pants. This was supposed to be fun, but I felt as if I'd cut a birthday cake and found worms inside. "Can we change the subject?"

"Sure. Sorry. Hey. Francine's next movie starts in two weeks," Evelyn said from under the skirts as she looked for the armholes. "It's *Treasure Hunt*, and the budget is huge. You coming with us?"

"Not sure." The job offer had gotten buried under all the other stuff I had on my mind, like my meeting with Butter Birds, the smell of Justin Beckett on my sheets, and now my old boss attending an event I promised to go to.

"It'll be low drama," she said brightly after her head popped through the neck. With the sideseams slashed, most everything else hung better on her. Or maybe it was just the way she stood a little squarer and held her head a little higher in period dress.

"Was *Pride and Prejudice* high drama?" I measured the gap where I'd slashed for the size of the side panels.

"Justin was just . . . it was always something."

"How so?" I wrote the numbers down and measured the other side to make sure.

"There were girls when we were shooting in Ireland."

"And? He beat them or something?"

"No just . . . girls. Around. And Gloria freaked whenever he went out. You know there's a thing in his contract where he has to keep his nose clean?"

I liked Evelyn, and I wanted to keep liking her, but her gossipy tone offended me. I had no business getting defensive over Justin. He was a grown man. But I couldn't help wanting to protect him.

"Okay, you can take it off," I said. "So, that's it? Just some vague stuff?"

"And makeup was always complaining that his eyes were puffy," she said as she wrestled out of the dress.

"You know . . ." I paused before continuing, ostensibly because unrolling pattern paper was noisy, but really because I needed to take a moment to decide if my feelings were proportional. They weren't. "Justin's a person."

"Yup," Evelyn answered absently as she got dressed.

"And you're accusing him of . . . well, I don't even know what. But you're doing it by inference. I'm not going to pretend I know what happened that night at the Roosevelt Hotel or in Ireland, but is it possible none of it was as bad as people say?"

"Sure?" She got into her clothes. "Why?"

"He's all right. He's really . . . for an egomaniac, he's not such an asshole."

"Okay, look." Fully dressed now, she leaned over the cutting table. "I'm just going to tell you something that happened that doesn't matter anymore, okay? I'm not trying to make you mad."

"I'm going to drop the armhole three-eighths. And not be mad. So, go ahead."

"There were rumors." She laid her hands flat. "Around set. About you and him."

"You didn't tell me?"

"I didn't believe them."

"Well, thank you for that."

"You're welcome." She straightened. "So you aren't?"

"What if I am?"

"You are?"

"I didn't—"

"Oh my God." Her eyes went big, and she gasped as if she was utterly delighted. "You're having a thing with—"

"It's not a thing!"

"So . . . What is it?"

I smoothed the dress, trying to define what I had with Justin. It was pure, undefined potential for romantic fulfillment or devastating heartbreak. Everything and nothing.

"Never mind," Evelyn said, standing straight. "It's not my business."

"It's just . . ." I drifted off, carefully snipping the seam on a skirt panel.

"I understand." She fussed with the tracing wheel, which was like a half-size pizza cutter with spikes around the disk. "You don't have to say."

Why shouldn't I tell her? The shoot was over. It wasn't as if Justin and I had agreed to secrecy.

"It's a thing. Me and Justin."

"Wow," she whispered.

"Yeah." I chalked out the shape I'd measured. "He's . . ." I laid my hands flat on the table, trying to come up with the right adjectives. "He's the most arrogant man I've ever met. He's got the swagger thing down. But it's self-contained. He's cocky, but it's got nothing to do with me or how he treats me. He's reverential. Respectful. Kind of unsure with me but so confident in himself that he's okay with it." I picked up my shears. "Forget me. I'm not making sense."

"Are you excited for you?" she asked. "Because I'm excited for you."

I was, and it bothered me. Excitement was the lead-up to disappointment.

"Do you want pockets at the sideseam?"

"Duh."

I laid the shears against the flat surface and snipped the panel along the chalk lines.

"I'm sorry about gossiping about him," she said.

"It's his job to be gossiped about." I said it as if to shrug it off, because I didn't believe in magic or spells. I didn't think that speaking something out loud could bring it into being. I told myself the story of his job as a test of my own belief system, asking if I could live with it or not, and deciding I could.

Evelyn wasn't a bad hand sewer, so I had her tack up seams while I used the machine. By lunch, we were almost done, so we ordered in. Over chicken salad and iced coffee, she explained how she'd gotten a history degree at UCLA and—while she was waiting to hear if she was accepted to a master's program—had gotten a job on the set of the historical TV show *Roman Numerals*.

"It was like . . . love," she said, scrolling through her phone. "I was the truck girl, but they let me do a toga. And then I did *Faraway Angels*. This was mine."

She handed me the phone. I wiped my fingers and took it so I could see an actress I didn't recognize wearing full evening dress with lace and a deep-red shawl.

"It's gorgeous," I said, handing the phone back.

"Just an extra, but still." She tapped at her phone with a smile.

I knew the satisfaction she felt very well. Three years into my career wasn't very far, but I was deep enough in to see that I was going to be locked into "design assistant" for a long time. Never entrusted with more than administrative and technical duties, while being thrown a bone here and there. This garment. This group. This update of what sold last year.

Would Evelyn be locked in? Was it okay for me to steal her joy by telling her she should demand more? I'd risked everything to demand . . .

You risked nothing because you had nothing.

"Um," she said, looking at her phone, thumb hovering over the glass. "Kayla? Are you subscribed to DMZ?"

"No." Slowly, I picked up my phone, skin tingling with the anticipation of a physical blow as I navigated to DMZ's alliterative headline.

BECKETT FEEDS FRIES TO FRIEND'S EX.

Justin feeding Heidi—Gordon Daws's wife—a french fry. The woman he'd been caught naked with in a hotel room. Hand-feeding wasn't a habit between adults who weren't romantically involved.

Did the divorce mean he'd stopped caring who saw him?

Was I just a distraction in the meantime?

Or was he just doing what Justin Beckett did?

Frozen in place, I stared at Evelyn's phone, unable to tear my eyes away from the intimacy of his posture, her parted lips, the way the hand that had touched me the night before braced against the table so he could lean forward.

"You all right?" Evelyn asked from a million miles away.

"I'm fine."

The article under the picture was short and full of words that stabbed my heart. It was a "tête-à-tête" on a "private patio" at a restaurant known for its "discreet staff." Justin and Heidi were "bosom buddies" who were the subject of "whispers by those in the know" to be "trysting" while her husband filed for divorce over "rumored infidelity."

I wasn't stupid. The article was written to titillate and shame. But I wasn't immune to getting hurt either. All I could imagine was them going back to his place—wherever that was—and . . .

Wait. Was the picture time-stamped?

The picture wasn't date-stamped, but I scanned the squib of an article again and found the time.

Last night, about seven p.m.

He'd texted me right after, and by seven thirty he was in my alley, smacking glass bottles against the side of my building. Sure, he could have had a quick thing with Heidi in between, but it didn't seem likely. I didn't want to say a word or expose my immediate horror. If I ignored it, maybe it would be all right. Maybe I could steer clear of his reputation and think he wasn't half the douche he was rumored to be.

But based on past history and the tone of the captions, I was sure Evelyn assumed Justin had slept with Heidi, and though her opinion of him didn't matter, her opinion of me did.

I weighed my choices. Was she a friend, or a potential antagonist?

I put the phone down.

"Kayla?" As if she'd intuited that I was deciding how much to trust her, my name was a question.

"He came here last night. Right after dinner."

"Oh."

She was going to think ill of him. I wasn't ready to draw conclusions from the clues I had, and I didn't want her to either.

"And it was nice," I said. "We had a good time. We found a tape of *A Star Is Born*."

"Like, on a VCR?"

"Yeah. He helped me figure out how to rewind it when it was done."

"Cool," she said. "He sounds pretty cool."

"We'll see." I closed my food container. "Let's get back to work."

~

Evelyn left in the afternoon with a smile and a dress she loved. I'd convinced her and myself the pictures of Justin and Heidi were nothing, because I believed it. He'd fed her a french fry across the dinner table. I really didn't care. As a matter of fact, I hoped they could be friends again.

But I hadn't shared my worry that my relationship with him was going to be defined by garbage headlines. It nagged me as I cleaned up loose threads and scraps of fabric, and went in for the kill when I looked at my phone again.

As if the universe was suddenly aware that I was vulnerable, a red BREAKING NEWZ! banner appeared, and since it seemed like the quickest way to get away from the picture of Justin hand-feeding Heidi, I tapped it.

As it loaded, a black Buick parked and idled in the alley below.

The big "newz" was that Justin Beckett had been spotted behind a defunct movie theater with a mysterious young woman. The pictures were blurry and shot from the second floor of the building across the alley, but it was him throwing a bottle. Me leaning out the window with my face blurred. Me opening the back gate with the same blur. Us talking. Him pulling his car in. The gate closing with his Tesla inside.

The pictures of us the following morning had better lighting.

"Christmas on a cracker," I said softly, scrolling to the end. I was a "lovely lady" and a "mysterious maiden" who was having a "secret meeting" with the "notorious" musician and—quotes theirs—"actor." Going through the pictures again, the license plate on the back of my van was blurred, but a white van with a blue stripe was a white van with a blue stripe.

The black Buick was still idling. The rear window was rolled down.

I closed the windows and called Talia.

"Hey," she said. "What's happening?"

"I don't know," I said.

"Okay?"

"You're a lawyer."

"Yes?"

"Can anyone publish my picture just because?"

"Why would anyone do that?"

"Like if they saw me with Justin Beckett?"

"Come to my office right now."

Not wanting whoever was in the Buick to see me, I called an Uber and met the car in the front.

~

The receptionist at the law firm had gotten me a cup of water that shook so hard in my hand I had to gulp it before it splashed out. When Talia met me in the reception area, I was still shaking, but at least I was hydrated.

"Come," she said, and led me behind the double doors. No one was looking at me, but I kept my gaze on my sister's back so I wouldn't make eye contact with anyone.

Talia took me to a conference room and closed the glass door behind her. I sat, and she sat catty-corner at the head of the long table.

"I saw," she said before I had to explain. "Are you okay?"

"I feel weird. Like outside myself."

"Normal. Do you want water?"

"No. I'm good. Is it legal? What they did?"

"Well, you're not a known commodity. You didn't seek attention. So they're limited in what they can do. But your face is blurred. They don't give the location, so your privacy is nominally protected. They never say you're having sex with him or anything negative about you, so it's not libel."

"But they found me. There were paparazzi hanging around the alley."

"That's their job."

"Is everyone going to know who I am? Who I was in New York?"

"Probably."

I covered my face with my hands and bent forward as if I could hide from the truth.

So much for the new life with new friends and a clean-slate career. Starting over was going to be impossible with the past nipping at my heels.

Talia rubbed my back.

"We'll figure it out," she said.

"How?" I asked into my palms.

"First, I need to know what's going on with you and him."

I sat straight, with a sweaty face and hair coming out of my ponytail.

"It's a disaster," I said. "I don't even know. We hung out a few times. Last night he came over, and he left at five in the morning, but nothing happened. No. Things happened but not *the* thing, not that it's anyone's business."

"So, if you're going to be together, that complicates things."

"But then I saw the pictures of him and Heidi. His bandmate's wife, right? And I don't know if I'm more hurt about that or the guys with the cameras. Because I like him, Talia. I like him so much. He's sweet and funny and don't look at me when I say . . . he's smart. He's attentive and cares about people in his life. And I thought I could be one of those people. But there's this Heidi picture all over the place, and it was all lies. He wasn't being sweet. He was manipulating me for a thrill, and I got all turned around. I fell for him when I wasn't looking." I couldn't see Talia's expression through a fog of self-abasement. "I have crappy taste in men and zero professional instinct. How could I be so stupid?"

"You're not stupid." She handed me a tissue that I crumpled in my sweaty fist.

"I am." I pounded the table. "I packed myself up, drove a few thousand miles, and left my brains behind. I'm two days away from my first meeting. Now I'm going to have to move to the moon if I want to start fresh. Everyone's going to know why I was blackballed out of New York, and they're going to blackball me out of LA too."

I opened the tissue and rubbed my eyes even though they were dry.

"If you don't see him again, they'll lose interest." Talia put the tissue box in front of me.

"Do you think?"

"Yeah." She stretched for a black plastic garbage pail and put it at my feet. "You're not clickbait without him."

I tossed the dry tissue and snapped up another one.

"That should make me feel better."

"But you like him."

"Yeah. I do."

"Why?"

I laughed to myself and balled up the tissue, lodging it at the base of my palm.

"Remember the Christmas Mom didn't have money for paper, so she wrapped everything in those annoying PennySaver flyers that got left at the door? No ribbons. No tags. Just pictures of pink meat at bargain prices? Our names were written in the white parts with ballpoint pen. I knew there was no Santa Claus that year, and that was the year I knew we were poor. And I thought, 'Wow, I should be sad about that,' but . . ." I wiped my nose with the tissue ball. "But I wasn't. That was the year she got me a sewing machine and a whole kit. She wrapped up each spool of thread separately so I'd have more things to open. And for you, the tackle box, right?"

"The line weights were separate. Took all day to unwrap."

"That's Justin. He's wrapped in gross paper, but inside it's not so bad. Maybe not a Singer with all the attachments, but something really cool. He loves his friends. He sticks his neck out for them. He's generous and honest. Of course he's egotistical and entitled, but not when it comes to me. And there's always another piece of him I uncover that's part of the present I asked for but never thought I deserved."

She sat back in her chair and crossed her legs.

"That's not what I expected you to say."

"What did you expect?"

She shrugged. "I thought he was exciting for you."

"I mean . . . sure. But he's exciting because he surprises me. This stuff—me—on the internet isn't exciting. It's scary. I don't want to be scared, but I don't want DMZ to make choices for me either."

"Okay. So. I didn't want to tell Mom I was a lesbian because of Dad, right?"

"Yes, and she surprised you, I know, but it's not like you had a choice to be gay."

"Can you let me finish?"

"Sorry."

"The only thing she worried about was other people not giving me a fair shake. She was right. It sucks sometimes because people suck. But I have to be true to myself, and so do you. Now I'm not advocating that, of all the guys in the world, you stay with Justin Beckett. I know the last thing you want is everyone's eyes on you for the wrong reasons."

"I don't."

"And he's a real piece of work."

It sounded as if she was going to tell me to drop him, and maybe that was what I needed to hear, so I nodded as if I agreed.

"Maybe," Talia said. "You should give him a chance to make you happy until he doesn't."

Her quick turnaround pulled a surprised laugh out of me. My relief was a bright, blinking sign that she was right.

"You got all the sense," I said.

"You got all the talent."

"Whatever." I sniffed. "I need some good news. World peace or a sale at Nordstrom's. Anything."

"Anything?" She smiled and slid her phone from her pocket. "Even if it doesn't help you at all?"

"Yes. Show me now."

She handed me her phone, and I gasped when I saw the sonogram. "No way!"

"Shh. It's not three months yet. So . . ."

"You or Soley?"

"Soley. My egg. The sperm donor's anonymous."

"This is why you can't keep up the theater."

"It's expensive all around. So, yeah."

"I'm so happy for you."

She looked at the sonogram with an involuntary grin, as if seeing it for the first time. Her pride was infectious, and though it changed nothing about my situation, the light of her joy chased away the shadows of my life's unknowns.

Justin was too complicated to make me smile like that. Or maybe I was too complicated.

CHAPTER 14

JUSTIN

"Oh, no. Yeah, no," I said, scrolling through the pictures of Heidi. My trainer, Dina, leaned on one foot, granite-muscled arms crossed. She didn't appreciate the interruption, but when Ken texted with 911 and a link, what was I supposed to do?

When the second link came through, she snapped the phone out of my hands.

"Give it to me." I held my hand out, but she pocketed it.

"You committed to an eight-pack," she said. "And I committed to giving you one. Star plank. Now."

Fine. Kayla didn't seem like a constant consumer of celebrity gossip. No one was sending her links of me feeding Heidi. She could wait an hour while Dina tortured me.

On my eightieth star plank, Kayla's reaction to the pictures faded into the background, and I thought about Gordon. He'd served her divorce papers, but there was a 100 percent chance he was a mess about it.

I should be there to help him out. Instead, I was making it worse, giving the media every reason to follow me around, showing up in public with his wife and feeding her like a dumbass. Cutting him off made me feel as if he were in some other universe, but that wasn't the deal. We were connected by an entire industry that bought and sold our lives. I was too stupid to see it.

Dina yelled for a hundred crunches, and I leaned into the burn in my muscles, hardening the ones just under my heart.

Stupid. Just dumb.

I couldn't even call him and explain again. He wouldn't believe me, even if he picked up. Knowing Gordon Daws like I did, he was leaning into his own burn.

"Another set," Dina barked, standing over me.

"Please." I dropped onto my back and reached up. "Phone."

"Do it."

Giving her the set did nothing to break up the frustration.

"Walk it off," she said.

I paced and bounced. My gym overlooked the pool where Sunset Boys had partied for days on end. There were nights I'd never remember and mornings I woke up naked on the living room carpet with a full condom crusted to my dick. Chad had stood on the edge of the pool and pissed right in it. Everyone got out as if the water had turned to acid. I'd laughed so hard my abs hurt almost as much as they did after a hundred crunches.

Dina handed me the phone.

"Good work today," she said.

"Yeah." I opened Ken's link. "Thanks."

"See you Tuesday."

The alley. Kayla's blurred face. A buzz rose in my ears. Pure, vibrating tension.

"Sure."

The Tesla pulling up next to her white van. The early morning exit in the previous night's clothes.

Kayla wasn't used to this. She didn't know it would go away. She didn't know what to expect, and I wasn't there to tell her it would all be all right. She hadn't asked for this, but I'd brought it on her. I used to think success was easy. Every path I walked turned to gold as soon as I stepped onto it. I must have used up whatever grace I'd been born with. Now I ruined everything I touched.

The pressure of the buzzing was so loud I didn't hear Dina leave.

I started to call Kayla but stopped myself when I imagined every dumb thing that could come out of my mouth.

I texted.

—Hey—

Three running dots appeared where she'd answer. Her phone was on. She hadn't blocked me, but it took forever for her to reply. Ken's office called, and I dismissed it. He probably wanted to talk to me about the pictures. That could wait.

I went outside, and when she still hadn't replied, my skin got hot to tap out a demand that would backfire.

Instead, I stripped my shirt and dropped it at the edge of the pool.

I checked my phone. Still nothing from her. I put my phone facedown on top of that and dived into the water wearing my gym shorts.

The tense buzz was replaced with the whoosh of water, and the burn of the workout was cooled, though the tightness of broken muscle was still there. By the time I popped up and reached over the edge for my phone, she'd answered.

—Hey—

In three letters, she told me I was going to have to bring up the pictures. Did she know about Heidi? The alley? Both? Neither? Would she have been wordier under normal circumstances, or was she just busy?

—I'm not going to beat around the bush. Did u see the pics in DMZ or no?—

My wet fingers left domes of water on my screen. I wiped it on my shirt.

—Which ones?—

Indirect conflict was my kryptonite. I called her and put her on speaker.

"Where are you?" I said when she picked up.

"On my way home."

"What did you see?"

She sighed as if she was the most exhausted person in LA and the person responsible for her exhaustion was the person on the other side of the phone.

I lifted myself out of the pool.

"I'll meet you at your place."

Standing over the phone as it nested in my shirt, I waited for her to answer.

"Kayla?"

"No."

No? I felt a jolt of surprise and a flash of frustration that I squashed like a bug. Then I was just bummed out.

"All right—"

"The people across the alley," she continued. "I can't tell if they're home, and you can't come in the front because you can't walk the streets, so . . ."

"Come here."

She sighed again. What was that about? Resignation? Frustration? Irritation? It wasn't like her to breathe hard instead of saying what was on her mind.

"Please," I continued, "or I'll meet you anywhere you want. A coffee shop. Paris. The moon. The—" I tried to think of someplace impossibly far away but came up with a closer option. "Louise's. Meet me at my grandmother's if you don't want to meet me alone. You know where it is."

"Your place is fine, I guess."

I sent her the address and got ready.

~

Standing in my house with her thumb hooked over the strap of her bag, she looked around without trying to make a big deal about it. Her yellow dress crossed over in the front, and the blue flowers completed each other at the seams. Her denim espadrilles matched the dress, and her makeup made her skin glow. I couldn't tell if she'd spent thirty seconds getting ready to see me, or if she'd stressed over every decision.

"So," she said. "This is your house."

"Yeah."

I was suddenly embarrassed by how I lived. She was judging every piece of furniture my decorator had picked. She could spot the things that came with the house and didn't quite go. The art on the walls was trash. She knew exactly how much every piece cost, and she knew that I didn't.

We should have met at Louise's. I wouldn't have to explain that I was never home when I'd bought this house, or that I hadn't had the time or energy to make the place my own.

She was perfect and I wasn't. She was a nutrient and I was a toxin.

"You look good," she said.

"I got that going for me."

She tilted her head to one side as if I wasn't making sense, which I wasn't, because she hadn't heard any of the trash I was talking about myself.

"Wanna sit outside?" I asked.

"I have a meeting, and I need to work on my portfolio."

"Right. That's cool. Who are you meeting with?"

She jammed her tongue between her teeth and cheek, as if she didn't want to say anything.

Was she waiting for me to bring it up?

Fine. I'd bring it up. I had nothing to hide.

"I can explain," I said.

"I don't want you to explain."

"What do you want?" I sounded put upon and annoyed, which wasn't how I felt. "Just tell me and I'll make it happen."

She cleared her throat, looking inward for a moment before she spoke.

"You're going to say Heidi is just a friend, and it wasn't anything, and yada yada. The pictures of us from the other night? I don't know. You'll say anything from . . . you won't come by me anymore to you'll buy the building across the alley."

My phone buzzed like I had a beehive in my pocket.

"That's not a bad idea," I said, pulling it out. Ken. I shut the damn thing off and tossed it onto the cushions.

"I'm just trying to give you the benefit of whatever explanation absolves you or takes care of whatever doubts you think I have so that we can get to the bottom of this."

If she was getting to the core of something, I was sitting down for it. I dropped onto my couch, got comfortable, and held my hands out to my sides.

"Go ahead. Take me down."

She sat on the arm of the couch, still hugging her bag as if she wanted to split. The neck of her yellow dress gapped with the twist of her body . . . and yeah, she was fully covered and all, but that little imperfection was all I could see. Like the first cut into fruit that bled sweet juice. When I touched her there, I'd lick my fingers clean.

"It's not a new bottom," she said.

"Is it the one where I take over your life and you have nothing?"

"Yeah."

"And it's my fault this goes on?"

"It's not your fault, but it's because of you."

"Right. So, you want to pick up and move to, like, Madagascar or something? Because this is what it is. If I quit music and acting tomorrow, nothing would change. I could live in a monastery in the Himalayas, and they'd find me. And, man, sometimes it's like I don't know how this happened. People need entertainment, and I want to do that. I love my job, but it's not about my job anymore, is it?"

"No." She slid off the arm of the couch and onto the cushions. She needed a reason to be with me, my past, my reputation, and my career, and I couldn't give her a single one. I wanted to put my arms around her so bad, just to ground me enough to say the right words, but everything in her body language said "nope." I was on my own with my conflicting motives clenched in a fist of fear.

If I was going to explain it, I had to loosen the fist and toss the motives on the table.

"I was just having fun with my friends. Then I was making money. Then traveling and fucking around and somewhere in there it stopped being about entertaining anyone. It was about me. What I did. How I did it. Who I did it with."

She looked away as if she had a choice between that and telling me I was being a baby.

"I know," I continued. "I brought some of it on myself, but not all of it. To them . . . the websites and the gossip sites . . . I was gonna either be an altar boy or a scumbag, and I ain't no altar boy. So I just did what I wanted. Then the whole world became my parents, and I was a rebellious kid trying to separate. And now . . ."

Now this perfect woman was sitting in a corner of my couch clutching her bag as if it were a life preserver and I was a shark.

Had I scared her? She didn't have fear on her face. More an anticipation of an emotional gut punch I had no intention of delivering.

I gently took hold of her bag. She let it go, and I put it on the table.

"And now," I said. "I'm sitting here, on my couch in a big house, with this girl I'm crazy about. I'm wondering if she'll let me touch her. Where she'll let me kiss her. What I have to say to make her accept me when I'm a grown man, but the world still thinks they're my parents. I'd love to tell her that's gonna change, but it's not. And I can't think of a reason she should have to deal with that."

Her hands were folded in her lap as her thumbs circled each other.

"That's very honest," she said.

I shifted over until my arm stretched over the couch behind her and let my hand hover over hers, waiting for a sign it was okay to lower it.

She raised her hands until they touched my palm, and they fell back into her lap.

"I'll do the best I can to protect you," I said. "That's all I got."

She extended her thumb to stroke my index finger.

"I believe . . ." She filled her lungs and let it go. "I believe you'll try."

"Yeah?"

"I do. I'm out of my mind to believe a word you say, but something about you, Justin. There's something the cameras don't catch, and I can see it. When you're close to me like this, I can see the part of you worth trusting."

"Kaylacakes." I kissed her cheek and went down the length of her neck. She smelled like coconut oil.

"So we're clear . . ." She faced me. "After the next kiss, before we go any further, I expect monogamy."

"So do I."

I kissed her that promise.

"After we kiss again . . ." She twisted to face me and laid her fingertips on my lips. I'll never know why that was such a turn-on. "No slipups. No excuses. I'll drop you no matter how much I like you."

"So, you like me?"

"Enough to let this get further than the next kiss."

My hand left hers and drifted to her knee.

"How much further?"

She bit her lip, then took my wrist and pushed my hand up her skirt. The inside of her thigh was warm and soft.

"I should kiss you first," I said, brushing my lips across hers. "Seal the deal."

"Seal it," she said.

So I kissed her.

CHAPTER 15

KAYLA

I went to his place to gauge my own feelings. Was he messing with me? Did he like me enough to make the feelings of vulnerability worth it? More importantly, did I like him enough? Was I just fooling myself? Was I falling for a brand image, or a human?

When I first came in and moved my gaze to him from his living room walls, I caught sight of him in an unguarded moment. He was a checkered floor that always looked black on white unless you saw it out of the corner of your eye. For that split second, it became white on black until you looked right at it again.

For the first time, he didn't take up more space than he should. He didn't exude magnetism and charm. In that moment, he was a kid in a grown-up house.

Then the Justin I knew returned, until he told me his story, and I could look that kid in the face. He was that kid, and the man he became, and everything in between that was more than the tabloids and less than what was expected of him.

A fully human man with all the beautiful trappings of a god, who was still riddled with flaws and insecurities, looked at me—with my incompleteness and deficits and as if I were a goddess.

I'd never known how much I needed to be looked at like that, because no one ever had. His veneration lifted me, and his acceptance grounded me.

"Seal the deal," he said.

"Seal it." I opened my mouth for his tongue and my legs for his hand. He brushed the damp cotton of my underwear where I was swollen and sensitive.

"I bet," he said with a husky vocal fry, "if I got under there, I'd feel how wet you are already."

"Better check."

"Open your legs wider."

I shuddered so hard my eyes closed, and then slowly I spread my knees.

My permission granted him the leisure to take his time; he ran his finger along the edge of my underwear, then behind it, where he touched more fabric than skin.

"Soaked," he said between kisses. "Did you finish your period?"

"Yes."

He slid his finger inside me, and my whole body turned into a whirlpool around it.

"What are you like when you come?" He ran his lips along the center of my chest, and his free hand moved the neck of my dress away, exposing my breast. Not waiting for an answer, he kissed my nipple, sucking on the hard whorl.

"You're going to find out if you don't stop," I gasped.

"You want me to stop?"

"No, I'm just . . ." Pushing deep inside, he put his thumb on my clit, and I couldn't finish.

"Tell me how this feels."

Two fingers. More thumb.

"Like a bomb's gonna go off. Justin. I . . ." I grunted like an animal, opening my legs, lifting my hips to make him press harder.

"Come for me."

"I don't want to . . ."

"Want to what?"

"Waste it. I want to fuck and . . ."

"Who says you can't come twice?"

With that, he rolled his thumb quickly against my clit, and I exploded, jerking and moaning with my skirt around my waist and my bodice half-off, pulsing around his fingers, gripping the couch cushions as if they could save me from falling down an endless abyss of pleasure.

When I was done, he removed his slick, sticky hand and put his fingers in his mouth.

"Perfect."

In my adult life, no man had ever licked my juices off his fingers. I had no idea I needed to know he was into every single part of me, nor had I realized how hot that was.

"I can't even think about how you got me off so fast," I said.

"It's more fun if you don't."

He stood over me. He peeled his shirt off, revealing the taut perfection that made girls scream, but all I could see was the impossibly large tent at the crotch of his sweatpants.

"I have rubbers upstairs," he said.

"My bag." I held my hand out for it. He reached behind him and placed it in my lap. I dug the foil pack out of my wallet, and when I looked up, his erection lay bare before me in all its glory.

"Jesus," I said. "Will this fit?"

"Yeah." He sat next to me and took the packet. "Tight, but fine."

I peeled my dress off, and as he unwrapped, I kissed his chest, his abs, and finally licked the bead of precum from the tip of his erection.

"Oh yeah," he groaned. With my mouth on him, I reached up and took the condom, unrolling it over his length. "I have a bedroom," he said as I straddled him.

"I figured."

He lined himself up, and I lowered myself onto his dick, stretching for him as he watched my face.

"Slow," he said. "That's it, Kaylacakes. Nice and easy."

Every inch demanded more of my body, and every stroke found more pleasure. When we were joined, he shifted my hips and his along an acute angle that put my clit against his shaft as we moved. He got quicker, and when he threw his head back and growled from deep in his throat, I knew he'd been right. I could come again.

～

"Don't you have to work on your portfolio or something?" Justin asked with his body curled against mine. We'd moved to the bedroom to have another go at it. The sun was low in the sky. I was pleasantly sore and so relaxed I could barely move.

"Yeah. And I bet your phone's been ringing."

"That phone's too demanding. I'm breaking up with it."

"You better. We agreed on monogamy, player."

He flipped on top of me and pinned me with his hips.

"You calling me a what?"

I reached for the sensitive skin on his waist and tickled him. He erupted in spasms of laughter, rolling over to get away, but I straddled him and kept up the torture until we were both laughing so hard we couldn't breathe.

CHAPTER 16

JUSTIN

Kayla called while I was driving. I put her on the car speakers.

"Wish me luck," she said.

"You gotta tell me what for," I said, getting off the 110.

"My meeting's today."

"Nah, you don't need luck."

"I do. There could be traffic. I could fall into the mud. I could projectile—"

"Okay, okay."

"I could be perfect, and they could say no anyway, which would be the worst."

I couldn't imagine it, but she could, so I waved the white flag and did what she wanted me to.

"Good luck." I stopped in the red right outside the high-rise where Ken had his office. "So, about yesterday."

"Yeah?"

"You cool?"

"Totally."

I smiled and nodded. I figured she was feeling good about it, but it never hurt to check in. The confirmation made it like we were in it as a team. Which was cool. I had teams of people, but they were all focused on me. I liked being her support.

"You wanna get together tomorrow?" I asked. "You can come hang in the studio."

"Sure."

A car behind me honked. I couldn't stay in the red much longer without being seen.

"You're all right. You know that?"

"If you say so."

"I say so." I put the car in drive and headed into the parking lot. "Gotta roll."

"Bye, player."

The connection dropped before I could tell her not to call me that.

~

Ken's office was all windows and shining metal, perched in the corner of the top floor, overlooking Wilshire Boulevard. Everything about it said control, which was what Ken Braque LLP sold to the out of control.

I was showered and my hair was brushed, but next to his snazzy suit I was a precision-crafted slob. His aesthetic needed a touch of chaos.

Instead of sitting across from his desk, I threw myself in an upholstered chair in the living room section every executive had in their office. He got up and came to me.

"So, Justin," he said, unbuttoning his jacket before sitting on the couch.

"I told you I was busy."

"Yet here you are."

"You're welcome."

"I have some news."

"I saw it all. I'll say it again for the people in the back. I'm not banging Heidi. She wasn't eating, so I fed her a fry. I'm done explaining myself."

"And?"

"My dad's sailing around the world with my mom, and I don't need a surrogate father. I do what I want, and you manage it. That's all."

A flicker of a smile flashed across his mouth and disappeared.

"Do you know who she is, really?"

"A nice girl. Period."

"Did she tell you why she left New York?"

He was going to tell me. I knew as well as I knew my own songs that I didn't want to hear it.

"We did a show at Madison Square Garden for *Cherry Girl*. We shook our security to go to an after-hours. It was in some warehouse in The Bronx." I took my feet off the desk and leaned forward. "Shane and I met these girls and went back to their place."

"Spare me the details."

"It was cool. They were cool. So we figured we'd get a cab back to our hotel. You couldn't throw a rock without hitting a yellow car, right? But the girls laughed, 'cos no. Cabs don't hang around The Bronx. My girl . . . Imani was her name. She had a car, but she was gonna be late for work if she took us back. She said it took an hour to go five miles. I thought she was lying. You know, maybe it was her boyfriend's car or something. Or I said something to piss her off. So, fine. We took the train to the airport. The train, man. And a bus. You never seen people packed in a little box like this. Like pomegranate seeds. Guess how long it took?"

"I don't really care."

"Two and a half hours."

"Is there a point to this story?"

"I didn't ask why she left New York, because you don't need a reason to get outta hell, okay?" I leaned back and put my foot back on the table, realizing I couldn't stall anymore. He was going to tell me something I didn't want to know. "Some of the streets are still made of flat little rocks. Rattle like hell. Bad enough to give you a headache. And everything's packed. There are people every-fucking-where. Nobody notices the smells either. Like vinegar and rotten hot dogs."

I'd been there all of two days, and I still had a couple of things left to complain about.

"She ran away," Ken said.

"Car alarms day and night."

"Did you hear me?"

"Yeah, I heard you. Her sister's here. She was born here. She inherited a theater. That's not running away. That's running toward, okay?"

"You know Josef Signorile?"

"Yeah, sure. I don't do preppy, but I know the stuff. You got any water?"

I didn't wait for an answer but got up and opened the little fridge under the bookcase.

"The *New Yorker* ran an article on him," Ken continued behind me. "Accusing him of groping one of his employees, and two others came forward with the same story. His backers pulled out. Stores pulled his stock off the racks. His wife came forward with proof the initial allegation was completely made up. The rest recanted."

"Bummer." I cracked the bottle open. I could see Ken in the reflection of a picture frame. "But good he didn't grope anyone."

I drank the entire bottle of Fiji down in three gulps.

"His accuser's name wasn't public," Ken said. "And she shut her social media. But Seventh Avenue's a small community. Everyone knew who she was."

"Gossip mills are always right." I finally turned and held up the empty bottle. "You got recycling in here, or does the blue clash?"

"Under the counter."

Finding it, I tossed the bottle and let the cabinet door slap shut. I couldn't stall or deflect anymore. Ken was going to earn his retainer whether I liked it or not.

"Why would she lie?" I said. "Did she try and blackmail him?"

I was joking, but I should have taken this seriously.

"According to him? Yes. When he said he wouldn't promote her to creative director, she went to the *New Yorker*. The other two were just in it for reasons I'll never understand."

"So, just let me get this straight." I stayed standing. No way I was sitting for this. "Kayla worked for Josef Signorile and made up a story about getting groped. Tried to blackmail him and when he said, 'Yeah, no,' she told a reporter. Stayed anonymous though everyone knew who she was. The reporter found two other girls to lie using their names until his wife proved Kayla was a liar and the other two said nah. I got this right?"

"You got it right."

"Yeah, nah. I'm going to ask her."

"No," Ken said, standing so straight he looked like an exclamation point. "You won't. The days of you being too young to know better are over. The bad boy image doesn't translate into a bad man image. There's a recording date that's still dependent on you keeping on the straight and narrow. You just wrapped your feature debut, and I don't want you to let this go to your head, but the word is your performance was . . . and I'm quoting here . . . phenomenal."

"Who said that?"

"Everyone at Overland. They're adding marketing dollars for a damn period piece everyone knows the ending of. But you pushed it with Heidi."

"It was a french fry!"

"She's still married, and the climate isn't right for maybe-he-is-maybe-he-isn't. If you step over the edge, your record deal is canceled, and getting you on a film set's going to be a pain in the ass, even for Gene Testarossa."

My feet kept shifting back and forth as if they wanted to bolt the hell out of there, and my eyes went to the view of the Hills, where I'd started my house, back to the stack of scripts on the desk, to the photos of Ken with half of Hollywood. The carpet. The doorknob. My Gucci sneakers. Every bone in my body fought to wander in a different direction.

"Look, she seems . . ." Ken waved his hand, forfeiting the challenge of finding the right word. "I can tell you like her, but you committed to cleaning up. People are talking about your talent, not your escapades. Not the model you're fucking or what happened in some hotel somewhere. We have Hollywood laser focused on your gifts. It's what we wanted for you. It's what we worked for. It's here. Right now. You're so close to winning it all. Is she worth losing it?"

Ken's question missed the point.

Why walk through fire if there's just the same old shit at the end?

Why finish if the girl on the other side of the flames—the one who made you walk faster and want it more because when she beckoned you realized the fire was an illusion—lived in the same fake world?

Nah. She was hotter than the fire. More important than Ken's issues.

Before that could filter down into words, then a businesslike explanation, Ken opened his fucking mouth and answered before I could.

"You have a responsibility to your talent."

I'd said I didn't need a surrogate father, but that was exactly what my dad would have said. The whole speech was pure Beckett. I could run the neighborhood until my shoes had holes as long as I took care of my responsibilities. The boundaries were wide but indestructible.

He clapped me on the shoulder and looked me in the eye.

"I know you," he said. "You'll do what's right."

Ending it like that was why Ken Braque had houses in Malibu and Como. He made me want to see it his way, but I couldn't just cut Kayla out. She was part of this, too, and I wanted the story from her gorgeous mouth. I needed to make her want to tell me her side of it instead of coming at her like a bull running at a red cape.

That wouldn't matter to Ken. For him it was all about what powerful people thought fans would think. They underestimated fans like it was their job. Which, I figured, it was, more or less.

As I drove down Wilshire, I passed the Signorile store with its boring preppy argyles and flat-front trousers. I whipped around the corner to get to the back entrance.

I knew how this had to go down.

I couldn't force her to tell me anything, but I could wear something to remind her that she trusted me.

CHAPTER 17

KAYLA

Butter Birds occupied a warehouse space deep in Downtown Los Angeles, where Alameda Street turned into a right-of-way for freight trains, and the density of the graffiti had its own abstract logic.

After the guard waved me into a parking spot, I crossed the lot, where a dozen women and men in blue pocket aprons lined up for a taco truck, and went into the building.

The smell of old leather and cut cotton met the sight of matte-sanded raw wood and blackened, industrial steel. Behind the reception desk, where I signed in on an iPad, a burly man in a blue apron opened the door to a cutting room with the white noise of fabric saws and unintelligible voices. It closed behind him, but I'd seen all I needed to.

I wouldn't say it felt like home, but as the leather couch squeaked under me, it was a space I understood. Clutching my portfolio, I realized how out of my element I'd been since I'd driven my newly purchased white van onto I-80.

No. I'd felt cut off since the head of Signorile's HR came to my desk with two security guards behind her and asked me to pack my things. With her manicure and blowout to match an insincere look of compassion, she'd cut a cord that had been fraying over months of whispers and glances.

This was what I was meant to do.

A handsome guy my age wearing a lanyard with an ID card at the end and his shirt tucked into his jeans just so came through the cutting room doors. He was short and slim, with a little scruff on his olive skin.

"Kayla?" he said with his hand out. I stood and shook it. "Dale. Dale DiMineo."

"Thanks for meeting me."

"Come on in."

There may have been a shorter way to our destination, but I was glad to see the sample floor and industrial washers. The banging embroidery and rivet machines were links in a chain of activity I found thrilling in its tedious repetition. Design, trace, wash, fit, sell, repeat, repeat, produce, pack, ship.

By the time Dale showed me into the design room, which was a warehouse-size open space of its own, I was buzzing with love for an industry that had rejected me.

"This is an awesome setup," I said, passing glassed-in offices.

"It is. We have ten proprietary laser machines I'd love to show you. Ralph saw them at Prima Cosa last year and bought the entire company. Just like that." He snapped his fingers.

"Wow."

"So," he said with a hint of juicy gossip he wasn't supposed to say out loud. "Your father says you're friends with Justin Beckett."

Friends? Had Justin and I risen to the level of friends? Or had we whizzed by it on our way to more than friends?

"I know him."

"We've been trying to get him in our fall ads."

"Huh." I didn't know how I was supposed to respond.

"So, he's not a total ass, then?"

"Oh, he's an ass, all right."

Dale laughed and led me into his office, holding his hand out for my portfolio before taking the seat behind his desk.

"I understand you're looking for backing. Not a job."

"Right." I sat across from him. "I have a head start on some selvedge for sampling, but I'm looking for facilities to make protos and thought . . . well, I read somewhere Ralph . . ." I cringed. Companies changed hands all the time, and I hadn't looked at the trades in months. "Ralph Cardello? He still owns you guys, right?"

"Until the day he dies," Dale said with a charming smile.

"Cool. I understand he does some investing in designers he believes in. Didn't he let Larry Falk use the facilities here to get his start?"

"I brought Larry in," he said proudly. "He still owes me a favor."

"I'm sure he's in a position to pay you back now."

"Do you have a business plan?"

"It's in the front pocket. I'm really looking for help with a first proto run, then for production I can get a letter of credit against orders."

"Let's see what you have here." He opened my portfolio and skipped the business plan, going right to the sketches I'd cleaned up in the days since Justin had seen them.

"This is nice." He indicated a fringe detail. "So your résumé says you worked at Josef Signorile?"

"Yeah."

"How was that?"

"I learned a lot." I shoved past all the things I'd learned about people. "How a denim business runs from concept to delivery, mostly. Putting out production fires."

"Inevitable, right?"

"Oh, absolutely!" I sounded like a cheerleader, so I took it down a notch. "There was this one time we had shade bands—"

"Do you have contacts in New York you could have hit up?"

Why were my nerves and hopes sitting in my throat? I could barely talk around it.

"LA is about denim," I said.

"This is a fantastic detail." He tapped the pointed cuff and closed the portfolio before getting to the section of things I'd done at past employers. "You seem really talented."

"Thank you."

"There's . . . uh." He cleared his throat as if he had something sitting there too. "I made some calls, and . . . maybe this isn't true, but there are people saying you were the one who made allegations against Josef Signorile?"

The sweat glands in my palms opened like spigots, and the lump in my throat expanded into a sticky balloon.

"Are you allowed to ask me that?"

"You're not seeking employment, so . . ." He shrugged. "Yes."

Was I supposed to lie? Was I supposed to explain the entire story? I didn't owe him anything, but I wanted to get in to see Ralph so that I could find a way into his debt.

If I was telling the truth, I was going to hold my head high and say what I needed to.

"It was me," I said, ready to tell him all the reasons and excuses for why it went down like it did. But he spoke first.

"That's fine," he said, poking a slow leak in my voice balloon. "They're so uptight in New York, don't you think?"

"Yeah." I laughed nervously.

"It's different here. It's not all about money and business. There aren't a bunch of finance guys in three-piece suits telling us what to do. We don't work for the banks, we work for the customer." He put his elbows on the desk and folded his hands together. "Los Angeles is about entertainment. Influence. Our currency is *access*."

I was trying to figure out if that was any better than being run by the banks, because I lacked both credit and connections, when it hit me why he was staring right at me as if he was waiting for me to offer what he couldn't ask for.

I had access to something they wanted. Some*one* they wanted. In exchange, they'd overlook all the reasons I left New York. Maybe. None of this would be stated explicitly.

"If marketing wants Justin Beckett's ass in your jeans, why am I meeting the creative director?"

He smirked.

"This is how it works. I mean, why did you stay anonymous? Sometimes there's not a straight line between your job and what the company needs. Right?"

"I . . ." Some functioning filter in my head stopped the rest of the sentence, because there was an apology inside it. I'd already made an apology to the one person who deserved it. "I'll think about it."

"Excellent." He took a business card from his pocket and gave it to me. "Give me a call, and we'll set up a meeting with Ralph."

"Sure." I hugged the portfolio to my chest.

"I look forward to working with you." Dale stuck his hand out. I shook it.

~

When I got back to the theater, I threw my portfolio on the floor and kicked it so hard it slid the length of the space until it tapped the far wall.

Access.

Talent was fine, but it was access to Justin that made me valuable.

I shouldn't have been surprised. In one way or another, this happened all the time. So-and-so's parents mortgaged their house to get him started, or they were big in the club scene, or they were an actor's kid. It would all be played off as an advantage the universe gave only the most talented. Twenty years down the line it would play differently. Putting Justin Beckett in Butter Birds jeans would be a cute genesis story.

It wouldn't be a big deal.

That wasn't going to happen.

Maybe I could mention it to him.

He probably got requests like that all the time.

Which didn't mean he liked them.

I went back and forth, swinging between doing what it seemed everyone else did and the moral high ground. In between those two states, as the pendulum swung low, I remembered Signorile was a part of the equation. It made me feel as if Dale had the right to ask. If he hadn't shifted my mask of anonymity, he would have just taken the meeting, but asking for a favor would have given me too much of an upper hand.

I couldn't go anywhere. I just sat on the couch, mesmerized by the pendulum and the regular intervals where Signorile laughed.

A text from Justin snapped me out of it.

—You coming to the studio tomorrow?—

I'd told him I would, but I couldn't imagine it would make a difference if I didn't.

—I'll be in the way—

—Nah—

Not exactly enthusiastic. Did I want him to beg? That was childish, and nah was nah. If I wanted to wiggle out of it, all I had to do was say I didn't want to go.

And I kind of wanted to. He'd be behind glass with a microphone in front of his face, but as I thought about it, sitting around and sulking seemed less appealing.

—Do you want me to bring you something?—

—Yeah. Your sweet ass—

Gross and so the opposite of gross at the same time. Context was everything.

—I'll see you at around six—

—Cool—

He sent the address, parking, and how to get through security. Then a kiss-face emoji next to a fist-bump.

Maybe I could bring it up with him.

~

The studio was in the Valley. Justin had sent a password.

Literally, a password. I had to say "tangerine" to get through security.

I rolled my eyes, but when I saw the crowd outside the building and the scrum of paparazzi, I understood the necessity. Once I got out of the van and handed the valet my keys, a woman in a pantsuit approached.

"Kayla Montgomery."

"Yeah."

"I'm Coralee. Nice to meet you. This way, please."

Beside me, her heels clicked on the parking lot pavement. She nodded to a guard, who opened the door to an empty waiting area.

"Snacks in here," Coralee said. "Bathrooms here. Also restrooms on every floor. Justin's on six. I'll take you up."

Another guard at the elevator let us in. The doors closed, and it rose to six with a flash of numbered lights.

"Is there always this much security?" I asked.

"For Justin Beckett? Yes." She smiled, not unkindly or without a trace of sincerity. "He rented out the entire facility since last time."

"Last time?"

"A very disturbed man was convinced Justin was the reason his girlfriend left him. He rented out the studio just below and caused some problems."

"What kind of—"

"We're here!" she said right before the elevator dinged. "Which is where I'll leave you. Just to the left."

"Thank you." With a smile and a wave, she was gone.

The hallway was carpeted, with rows of doors. Two set close, one with a red light, then ten feet and another pair. It looked like a horror movie. Carter stood in front of a door with an illuminated red light.

"Hello, Kayla."

"Hi. How's it going?"

"I have no idea," he said, opening the door without the light.

The engineering room had a glass wall, couches, a table of food, and a soundboard with a hundred little knobs being adjusted by a skinny guy with long fingers and headphones. A man I didn't recognize had his leg slung over the arm of the couch, his phone in his face, and a doughnut in his mouth. A balding executive with a sports jacket leaned into the mic. I was studiously ignored, catching the balding guy midsentence.

"—need to rework the bridge."

Justin was alone in the sound booth with his back to me, erasing from a sheet of paper that rested on the grand piano. The room was huge, with racks of guitars and a drum kit. When he turned, my heart tightened as if he'd unintentionally grabbed it.

That hand tightened. It wasn't love. It was what he was wearing. White jeans with a pink-and-yellow argyle sweater that was a size too small. It had been a cardigan that—when your sailboat got midday hot—could be worn over the shoulders with the sleeves tied in a knot. I should know—I'd designed it for Josef Signorile.

Justin had turned the sweater into a vest by cutting the sleeves off. He'd fastened the wrong buttons to the wrong holes as if he'd run out the door without looking in the mirror, making the hem end at a point on one side. It should have been atrocious, but it was perfect. He'd turned basic preppy wear into douchecore excellence.

Looking down, he brushed eraser nuggets away with the side of his hand.

"Nah. It's not the bridge." His voice came from everywhere. "I got it."

Balding turned to me, looking me up and down.

"And you are?"

"Uh, Kayla . . . I'm—"

"She's with me," Justin said.

"We had an agreement," Balding said into the mic.

"Yeah. No fans or entourage. She's neither." Through the glass, he directed his attention to me, and I melted like a groupie. "Kayla, this is Trevor from Slashdot. He's not an asshole, no matter what everyone says."

Trevor held out his hand, and I shook it.

"Gotta keep this guy in line," he said.

"Good luck."

"Have a seat, Kayla." He said my name with deep appreciation, as if he knew something I didn't. "We're five minutes to break."

I sat next to doughnut-face, who nodded at me before moving his feet.

"All right," Trevor said into the mic. "Let me hear it from 'breakneck.'"

"I'm changing keys."

"It's not a show tune," the bald guy said.

Instead of answering, Justin started singing. There were no instruments, just the voice everyone could recognize behind layers of production. With nothing to back him, he had a casual, jazzy cool that was still infused with rough emotion. He sang about speed, the wind in his ears, the changing landscape, the high of forward motion. Then he stopped.

"Blah blah, chorus," he sang.

"And you want strings with this one?"

"Full string section," Justin replied, writing something down. "Badass. It's the single."

"We'll pitch that to marketing."

"You do that." He slid the earphones off. "We'll be on the roof."

Trevor winked at me. "Have him back here by seven."

~

He put his arm around me as we followed Carter down the hall and into the elevator. The bodyguard stood silently between us and the doors, over six feet and built like an inverted triangle in a tailored suit.

"Strong silent type," I whispered to Justin.

He nuzzled my ear and spoke in breaths. "I'm not supposed to tell you who he's dating."

"Why not?"

"I can hear you," Carter said as the elevator bounced to a stop.

Busted like a kid talking in class, I elbowed Justin away. He wrapped his arm around my neck and tightened it until my temple was close enough to kiss.

The doors opened. Carter kept his finger on the "Door Open" button, leaned out to check the hall, looking left, then right, and stepped out to let us through. When the doors closed, he led us down the hall to a short flight of steps. Justin kept his arm around me, and I put mine around his waist. Ours wasn't a casual arm-in-arm stroll, but a purposeful walk forward while we held each other tightly to feel the movement of our bodies against each other.

"When did the novelty wear off?" I said while Carter opened the door at the top of the stairs and checked around. "Of the security detail?"

"I hate it," he said. "You hear that, Kincaid?"

"Yep," Carter said, indicating we could move forward. "I'm not here to be liked."

"This bunch of Beckettes literally rented the house down the street from mine. Carter rang their doorbell and laid down the law. They hate him."

The rooftop patio had an awning draped with strings of white lights. The sky was dark blue in the east, and the wind was cooling by the minute.

"As I said," Carter added. "Not here to be liked. Knock when you're ready to go back down."

He closed the door behind him. As soon as the lock clicked, we were on each other, connected at the mouth, my hands in his hair, his fingers clutching my ass.

"Fucking missed you," he said as he caught his breath, pushing me against the brick wall.

"Mi—" I couldn't tell him I felt the same with his tongue in my mouth. We were crawling all over each other, pushing and grinding like high schoolers in the back seat of a car, all breath and fingers. The only sounds were our gasps and grunts, the traffic and the crowd of Beckettes on the street below; the rumble of a bus fading in the distance, creating a sonic gap for the rumble of Justin's stomach.

"You're hungry," I said.

"For you." His face was buried in my neck. I gently pushed him away, but not too far to lean my elbows on his shoulders.

"I'm on a no-cliché diet, player."

His stomach replied for him, and we laughed as we walked to the table hand in hand, then he picked me up in his arms. I squealed, then let him drop me on the bench.

A table of a dinner of grilled chicken and vegetables had been set up.

"I gotta eat light when I'm working." He sat opposite, manspreading as if he owned the joint. "That's okay?"

"I like chicken." I laid the paper napkin across my lap.

"Big meals slow me down. Shane, though . . ." He laughed to himself. "Slab of raw beef and a potato the size of a football." He stabbed a piece of chicken and a carrot. "Light or dark meat?"

"Dark."

"Attagirl." He filled my plate, then his own.

"Do you miss them?" I asked. He ripped meat from the bone, lips pressed together in silence. "Sorry," I said. "I shouldn't ask that."

"Nah," he said, stabbing meat and a carrot. "It's cool. If you get just the right size carrot with a piece of chicken, it's perfect in your mouth. Try it."

He leaned over the table to feed me.

"Is this a habit?" I asked.

"One of my better ones."

I opened up and let him give me just the right size carrot with the chicken.

"It's good."

"Charlotte puts brown sugar on the carrots."

"Your voice sounded really good," I said. "Not that I know anything."

He made a verbal shrug that came out as a *tsk*. "It's out of shape."

"How late will you go?" I asked.

"Until I dry up. I start tearing shit up after midnight, but I've never . . ." He stopped talking to jab at his food. "The guys are usually working with me. So whatever. I don't know how long I'll go. Yeah. I miss them. A lot. Being in the studio without those assholes is . . . I don't know. Like invitations went out but I'm the only one who showed up to the party."

"Did you really send invitations out?"

"What's that mean?"

"Do they know you miss them?"

Another shrug. Another pause as he chewed, staring at his plate like an adolescent.

"Nah." His leg bounced under the table. "Once they started believing our own PR, that was it. It was a long time coming. I'm not saying I've never done drugs when it was fun. But Chad's problem is a problem, and they blame me. Maybe they're right. But then Gordon got his claws out whenever I said two words to Heidi like . . ." He dropped his fork. "Like I'd ever. And Shane had a bug up his ass from day one about the music. It was my fault, my voice that made us a pop band, which . . . hello . . . he doesn't have enough hours left in his life to spend the money our pop band made." He glanced up at me. "Sorry."

"Don't be. Here." I held up a forkful of chicken with a crescent of squash on top. "Open up."

He let me feed him, then he fed me. We ate dinner for each other, which probably looked ridiculous from the outside. From inside we were making a promise to show up for each other; to give of ourselves what the other needed; to allow ourselves to be tenderly cared for. I'd never experienced something so intimate with a man, and that was probably as good an explanation as any for what happened next.

I'd forgotten about the Signorile sweater until he stood, and I could see all three argyle diamonds from the top to the bottom rib. I was reminded of the fitting room. My boss's hands on me and the hundreds of humiliations that followed.

Stop.

I wouldn't let it ruin the night. I looked at the sky instead, smiling at the moon.

We were walking back to the door with our pinkies hooked when a little nagging voice reminded me that I'd had a meeting that afternoon, and it had been an unpleasant negotiation over both my value and my values.

I didn't want to break what we'd made over dinner.

We'd shared without being transactional.

If I could just ask him without asking . . .

"I like what you did with my sweater," I said.

"Your sweater?"

"It's a Signorile. I designed it for them."

"Huh." He made the sound as if realizing that for the first time.

"When you wear something, people notice."

"Yeah. There's always someone trying to get me to wear something, then getting pissed when I cut off the sleeves."

"I'm not pissed."

"Cool."

"I kind of love it."

If I was going to mention it, that was the time, but he ran me off the road.

"You were the creative director at Josef Signorile or something?"

"Just a design grunt. Sketches for days. Fittings."

"Didn't like it?"

"No, I . . . I just had to go."

"Messed up—what happened to him."

"Yeah."

"That's like a nightmare for every guy."

"Really?"

"Getting falsely accused like that? And you can't do anything? Messed up. I mean, what kind of person would do that shit?"

I pulled my hand away from his. "Your nightmare is a false accusation?"

"He almost lost everything."

He was doing that thing where he slouched as if he actively, aggressively, didn't care about anything. Righteous anger pushed against my filters, squeezing through.

"A woman's nightmare is getting raped or killed," I said. "And it happens every day."

"Sure, sure, but—"

"Shut up, Justin. Just stop talking."

"Hey there. That's not cool."

He was going to push me into punching his face. I had to get out of there, but he grabbed my arm as I passed.

"Kayla?"

"He did it." I flung his hand off me and leaned into his offensively casual bearing, pointing an inch from his face as if I wanted to inject the truth. "He fucking did it."

"Whoa, Kaylacakes."

"He let the model go, and when we were alone, he put his hand up my dress. He breathed in my ear and *squeezed* between my legs like he owned it." I jabbed my finger at Justin with every recitation of fact. "He did it. He did it. He did it." I counted off on my hand. "He abused me once in the fitting room and again when he said it was nothing because it was just a little feel. He did it when he fired me. His wife did it to me when she gave him an alibi. Then he did it again when he called me a liar, and the entire industry did it to me when they believed him. I was assaulted so many times I ran away. He did it, and I'm not hearing that he didn't. And I'm not. Seeing. That. Fucking. Sweater. On. You."

I ran for the door, but he caught my arm. I swung at him, and he held his hands up when he let me go.

"I'm sorry." He peeled the sweater off, leaving him in a plain white T-shirt. "I shouldn't have touched you." He tossed the sweater in the trash. "It's gone."

"I knew what he was, and I was still surprised. But why did I deserve better? He did it to me, and I didn't say shit because I figured

I'd get over it. Then he did it to Brenda, and that was it. He broke her. She was so strong, and he broke her, but even after that I stayed there and used my talent to make money for him. Of course he thought he owned me. I sold him my ass. Nothing I did made up for it. Telling what happened blew up in my face, and he's probably still grabbing whatever he can, but now he's better at it. Good enough to get away with it and scrubbed clean by my, quote, unquote, 'lies.' He's got a billboard on Santa Monica Boulevard. Right in my face, because he wins and I crawl away. He still owns my ass. Still."

"He doesn't."

"When you come here with your little dance-around asking about it, it's not you I'm reacting to. It's Signorile yanking the chain." For the first time since I started throwing around the truth, he looked away. "You're not subtle, Justin."

"Listen, I believe you."

"Do you?"

"A hundred percent. But okay, I'm going to be honest. I got pulled into my PR guy's office over this. I'm trying to keep my nose clean for the label and the studio, and I'm already up a creek because of Heidi. Now this?"

"This?"

"It looks bad."

"Wait, wait. I'm making you look bad?"

"No. No, you're not. But you could . . . we want to just . . . all I'm saying is . . ."

"I *could*?"

"It's not you. It's just a bad . . . it's because of my past . . ."

"Spit it out."

"I think . . ." He put his hands over his face and rubbed his eyes, speaking with his sight covered. "Maybe we should just cool it until I'm on my feet?"

Before he moved his hands away, I went to the table and picked up my things.

"You're mad," he said.

"I'm disappointed." I slung my bag over my shoulder, looking at the multicolored sky at the horizon, the food, the strings of lights arcing under the pergola. Anywhere but at him.

"I know but—"

"In you," I said, heading for the door, eyes on my shoes. "I'm disappointed in you."

"Kayla."

He didn't touch me as I left, and lucky for him. I would have taken his arm off.

~

The rumors about my lies had gone on without me. I had no control over what people said, and the more I defended myself, the worse they got. Lies turned into revenge. Revenge turned into blackmail. My résumé went from calling card to indictment.

With the emotional depth of a slice of pizza, Zack had shrugged my ruination off as a temporary setback, hailing the fact that I didn't once inconvenience him with a single tear.

In his own way, my boyfriend had turned his back on me just like everyone else and still managed to make me feel guilty for moving out.

I hadn't cried for him either.

But Justin?

The party boy in his douchecore getups, flashing his middle finger on the DMZ alerts?

The dudebro known for his immaturity and sense of entitlement?

That guy?

As soon as I closed the van door behind me, I cried like a loser. My face was full of snot, and my tear ducts couldn't release the pressure behind them fast enough. I cried so hard I had to pull over on the 101 because I couldn't see a foot in front of me.

I didn't have a tissue in the glove compartment or the center panel. I went to wipe on my cuff, but I was wearing a sleeveless dress.

And still I couldn't get control of my blubbering. I cried over that asshole and every asshole before him, too alone to care about my running nose or hitched breath, wailing as if I were at a funeral, because the possibility of getting away from my past was dead and buried.

I couldn't even stop when there was a knock on the window, and when I cranked it down, the cop who waited on the other side got a full view of my stupid, useless bawling.

"Miss?" she said, flashing her light in my empty van. "You all right?"

"Yes!" I shouted, because my breath wouldn't come out otherwise.

"What's going on?"

Snot had traveled over my lips, and if I spoke again, I was going to get a mouthful of it. I picked up the hem of my skirt and blew my nose into it.

"Nothing," I said.

"Doesn't look like nothing."

"Just give me a ticket, okay?"

"License and registration, please." She took out her pad and pen. I wiped my nose on my skirt and reached for my bag.

"Miss," she said. "Do you want a tissue?"

"I'm fine." I got my wallet out.

"Did he hurt you?"

"Of course he did." I riffled through for my license. "But not in a way that's illegal."

She put away her ticket book.

"Are you sure?"

"There's no law against broken hearts, Officer." I handed her my license, and she glanced at it before giving it back.

"You shouldn't drive when you're like this," she said. "Do you have someone nearby you can stay with?"

"I'm new here so . . . not sure?"

"You're near the Hollywood Hills. I can let you go if you take the next exit. Highland."

"Yeah. My father's off Gower. On Park Oak?"

"Good. Follow me."

"Okay."

"Don't let the bastard know you cried," she said. "Or make it the last thing he ever finds out."

~

The lights were on in Dad's house, which was encouraging. The driveway was full of cars, which was less so. Once I gave the cop a thumbs-up, she coasted away with a wave.

I parked half a block away, and as soon as I headed up the front stairs, I could hear voices. He was having some kind of party or something.

Figuring I was fine to drive home, I turned around to leave, but the door opened.

"Kayla?" Dad's voice came from behind me. Getaway thwarted, I faced him.

"Yeah, I was just stopping by, but it looks like a bad time."

"What happened to your dress?"

I looked down. The front of my skirt was wrinkled into a snot-encrusted pucker.

"I didn't have any tissues."

A tall, skinny man holding a drink came up behind Dad.

"Who's . . . is that your daughter? Oh my God, Raymond, she's your clone."

a

He brushed past Dad and with an outstretched hand came into the light, where I could see his red beard, brown hair, and big smile.

"Terry. You're Kayla?"

"I was just—"

"Everyone's been dying to meet you."

The outstretched hand wasn't for a shake but so he could pull me inside. The day had skinned and spit-roasted my resistance, so I let him.

Five men around my father's age sat at the dining room table, surrounded by bunched-up cloth napkins, glasses of wine, phones set glass-down, and a large platter of crumbs. They were talking and laughing in the rhythm of people who had known each other a long time. I recognized Adam and Darren, but no one else.

"Everyone!" Terry cried.

"Terrence," Dad said, laying his hand on my back. "Embarrass her and I'll burn you alive."

"Shut up. Hey!" Terry snapped his fingers, and the guys at the table hushed. "Guess who this is?" He presented me like Vanna White turning a letter.

"Hi." My voice cracked.

"What happened?" Adam asked.

"Kayla," Dad said. "This is—"

"I knew it!" A guy with a goatee slammed his hand down.

"The minute you walked in," a professor type said as he stood and came toward me. They were all up in the next second, shaking my hand, kissing my cheeks, telling me how pretty I was and being so nice I burst into tears all over again.

They led me to a chair at the head of the table and fussed over me with tissues, cloth hankies, and wine. The crumby platter was reloaded with cookies and put in front of me like a steak dinner. When I could breathe, I took a bright-yellow one but couldn't find the appetite to bite into it.

"Ice pack," Terry said, handing me a blue cloth bundle.

"Thank you."

"Over your eyes, honey." I pressed the cool pack to my swollen face, shutting out the kind voices as they went back to their conversation. I was grateful for their carefully orchestrated disinterest. By the time I took the pack away, my ducts had closed, and my throat was dry and sore. My cookie was on a clean plate, and my wineglass was full. I took a bite of the soft cookie, and my mouth exploded in a bright sweetness.

"This is good. What is it?"

"Ali calls them Lemon Shits."

Ali had a wedge of a nose, a thick black beard, and a smile as unexpectedly blinding as a full eclipse.

"They go good with the Chocolate Fucks."

It wasn't that funny, but I was raw and vulnerable to suggestion, laughing so hard I almost spit my cookie.

"Kid," Dad said, crouching down beside me. "Do you want to talk about it? We can go upstairs."

"No." I took a gulp of white wine and shook my habits right out of my head. "Yep. Yep I do. Right here."

Dad went to his seat at the other side of the table. After another gulp, I put my glass down with deliberation.

"Besides Adam and Darren, I don't even remember all your names, but you're the nicest people I've ever met."

"You don't know Boris yet," Terry joked.

"Neither do you, obviously."

That must be Boris. Frameless glasses. Professorial. A thick, eastern European accent that made a simple phrase quite funny.

"Well," I said, draining my glass. "Let me give you some background. What has my father told you about me?"

"Everything," Terry and Ali said at the same time. "Jinx!"

"Nothing," Dad said, reaching for the wine bottle so he could pour me another.

"He says you're brilliant," a guy in a tie said. I was never going to remember these names. "Talented. Ambitious. Tough. What else?"

"Nothing specific," my father said with a wink. "If you know what I mean."

"Oh good. I control the narrative for a change. So. Nutshell version. I was run out of New York on a rail."

I told the entire story, getting up to pantomime or pace, leaving out nothing except the details of the sex, up until the moment the lady cop gave me a piece of advice and an escort off the 101 instead of a ticket. My wineglass was as bottomless as their attention.

"And that, gentlemen, is why there's snot on my skirt."

"Who do we beat up first?" Ali asked.

"Dale DiMineo," said the guy in the tie, whose name I'd forgotten.

"Steve," Dad said, his voice low and serious.

Steve ignored him and addressed me.

"I'm the CFO of Butter Birds, and I got you that meeting."

"It's going down . . . ," Darren sang under his breath.

Maybe I shouldn't have exposed everything. Common sense should have told me Dad's friend from Butter Birds would be at the table, but common sense had taken a nap.

"I'm sorry," I said. "I wasn't trying to give you a hard time."

"No." He shook his head to underline the denial. "I'm the one who's sorry. He was supposed to meet with you and assess the likelihood you'd make us money. He wasn't supposed to try to get access to your relationship. And using what happened to you as a threat? Unacceptable. Absolutely unacceptable."

In the shift from funny/sad story to the actual consequences of it, the table had gone silent.

Boris started to tip more wine into my glass, but I covered it.

"I'm drunk enough."

"Chocolate Shit?" Ali held the tray out to me, and I picked out a brown cookie. "What are you going to do about Douchey McDoucherson? You going to wait?"

"She. Is. Not." Adam threw a napkin at him.

The room swam. My mouth tasted like roofing materials. I put my elbow on the arm of the chair and held up my head with it as the guys argued about whether waiting for Justin's PR team to give us the go was an option. Or if I could see Justin casually and maintain my self-respect. They didn't know it wasn't about self-respect or how it all looked. It wasn't about getting laid on occasion or anything like that.

It was something else, and I let the thought come into my mind with clarity and volume.

"I'm in love with him," I heard myself say, then bounced up so hard my stomach flipped.

Dad crouched by my chair in an instant.

"You need to get to bed," he said. "Come on. I have a guest room." He stood and helped me up. The act of standing made me trip on my own feet. Dad caught me.

"Good night, all you guys!" I said. "You're all beautiful people, and I love you."

They chanted good-nights and blew kisses. Dad put his arm around my waist and helped me up the stairs.

"I have some pajamas," he said. "They may be big on you."

"I want to sleep in snot."

"Not in my house."

He led me to a neat bedroom with a balcony, grabbing a set of pajamas from the dresser as I went into the private bathroom.

"Fresh toothbrushes are in the drawer," he said.

"Cool."

I closed the door behind me and got ready for bed, drinking a quart of water right from the faucet. The cotton seersucker pajamas were huge but comforting. When I left the bathroom, Dad was already sitting in the bedroom chair, poking at his phone.

"That's a look," he said when he saw me.

"I hope I don't puke on them."

"I have a washing machine." He turned down the covers. "In you go."

I slid between the sheets.

"I'm sorry, Dad," I said. "I ruined your party."

He sat on the edge of the bed and patted my leg.

"You were a marked improvement."

"I'm sorry about not speaking to you all those years. I didn't think of it when I was a kid and when I was grown up . . . and Talia found you? Mom was so upset. It felt like a betrayal, and I didn't want to do that. I didn't want to hurt her."

"Your mother had a way of holding on to her pain."

"But it was stupid. I hurt you instead of her. I always hurt someone. Even Justin I hurt by risking what he worked for. And Brenda by not saying anything right away."

"Who's Brenda?"

Had I missed that part of the story? Or had I just left it out because I didn't want anyone to know how awful I was?

"Dad?"

"Yeah?"

"I didn't know you were so nice."

"Sometimes I am. Are you going to be okay here by yourself?"

"I was wondering something." I sat up a little and let the room settle before continuing. "You're a handsome guy. Successful. You have good friends. And I don't want you to take this the wrong way, but you might."

"I won't."

"Have you been in love since Mom?"

He laughed. "Oh, Kayla. It's such a long story."

"Will you tell me sometime? I mean, unless you don't want to relive the past, then . . ."

"His name was Jacob. He was perfect and I screwed up. I'll tell you everything when you're sober."

"You don't have to if you don't want."

"Sweet girl, we have to talk about the past or it eats our future."

"I hate it."

"I know. When you were in preschool and you got in trouble . . . I think you were rooting around someone else's lunchbox for candy . . . you went into a fit the likes of which . . . let's just say it wasn't like you. You didn't throw tantrums because you didn't get a cookie. You could take no for an answer. But getting caught doing something? You flipped, then you froze us out. Wouldn't look at either me or your mother. You wouldn't let us talk to you about it. We figured you were punishing yourself so much we didn't have to."

"How old was I?"

"Three."

I slid back down between the sheets, ashamed of my toddler self, because my adult self wasn't that much different.

"I'll bring some water." He stood up.

"M'kay."

He shut off the light, and I fell asleep to the sounds of good men talking and laughing downstairs.

CHAPTER 18

JUSTIN

After Kayla left the studio I cut the session short. I couldn't think about music, knowing I'd been such an ass. Ken had asked me to hold off, but I didn't. Couldn't. And I'd had sex with her. Promised monogamy. Led her on, knowing there was this dumb vetting process happening behind her back. Then, because taking it all the way was the Justin Beckett brand, I punished her for getting molested by her boss.

And that stupid sweater. I'd worn it to give her the chance to just tell me what happened, but what I'd really done was stick her nose in a steaming pile of shit.

So, obviously I didn't sleep, which was why I got Louise's text at six in the morning.

—*Ned is dead*—

She didn't reply when I texted back, so I drove over there.

"Weezy!" I called as I got in with my key.

"Coming!"

I went into the kitchen. The coffee was cold, so I made a fresh pot. She blew in wearing jeans, Crocs, and a cardigan, while the coffee maker dripped. I gathered her up in a hug.

"I'm so sorry, Gram."

"Oh please." She pushed me off. "He had it coming."

"What?"

"Yesterday, the plumber came." She took the pot off the burner while it was still dripping, leaving a sizzling pool behind.

"Weeze! Are you serious?"

"Yes. I am." She put the pot back. "The plumber left the garage door open so his van could stick out. I came back from lunch with the girls, and there was Ned . . ."

"Oh man. You found him?"

"Going through the Baby Justin containers your parents left. And I said to him . . ."

"Hang on."

"I said, 'You motherfucker, what the hell are you doing?' And he stands there with your second-grade report card in one hand and that folder of songs you wrote when you were thirteen in the other, and he says, 'I was just curious, baby.'" She shook her head and sipped her coffee. I waited for her to tell me about Ned's heart attack.

"Baby," she sneered. "Can you even believe the nerve? If your grandfather ever called me that when he was caught red-handed—which, believe me, he was, and not with ephemera, either—I would have—"

"Weeze. What happened to Ned?"

"Well." She put her cup down. "His hands were full, so I reached into his pocket and took his phone. Guess what was on there. Right there, pretty as you please, an eBay account with your baby pictures. The ones from my goddamned closet. He was getting good money, too, that's the truth."

"Did you . . ." I paused before saying something I'd regret, then said it anyway. "Did you hurt him?"

"You bet I did. He started giving me some story about his pension checks, and I got so mad. I punched him right in the chest and told him where to stuff his big, fat dick."

She punched a guy who just had a heart attack in the chest. Ned had gone from plain dead to murdered by my grandmother.

"And?"

"And what? He started crying and begging blah blah. Then the plumber came downstairs to get something from the van and asked me if I needed him to remove the gentleman." Another sip of coffee. "Naturally, I said yes. Couldn't refuse an offer like that."

"And?"

"And the plumber left this morning right before I texted you. You look hungry. I can make you some . . ." She opened the fridge. ". . . eggs all right?"

"So, Ned is dead or nah?"

She put the carton on the counter. "Dead to me. The sink is fixed, though."

I pressed my forehead against the cool granite. This woman was going to cause my death before Ned's.

"I hope you like scrambled." She cracked eggs into a bowl.

"Sure." I got up and grabbed a loaf of bread. Might as well make toast, seeing as no one was dead and my grandmother wasn't going to prison.

"Have you thought about your birthday?" she asked.

"Nah."

"Coming up. I can throw you a little something here."

"I have a wrap party that night."

"I don't know how many more of your birthdays I'll be around for, but all right."

"I'll take you out to dinner, okay? I'm not up for a thing."

"Why not? You're always up for a—"

"I'm just not!" I didn't mean to shout, but my voice echoed. I snapped the bread down in the toaster. "Sorry."

"For what?"

"Yelling at you."

"I'm not made of sugar."

I thought she was going to let it go, but no. Not my grandmother.

"Though," she said, "*why* you yelled is another story."

"It's nothing."

"Is it because you're getting old?" She put her hand on my back. "It only gets better, you know. Older you get . . ."

"I'm turning twenty-six."

"And such a handsome man," she said, grabbing my jaw in one hand. "Your beard's growing in."

Facial hair had been a reality since I was twelve, and she knew it. She released her grip and stirred the eggs.

"I didn't shave this morning."

"In some cultures, men wear beards when they get married. I think you'd look nice. It's the style now."

"I'm not getting married." The toast popped.

"Obviously." She turned off the gas under the eggs. "Whoever this girl is, let her go if she makes you this cranky."

"Weeze, please."

"I'm just saying. Your grandfather made me miserable, and it wasn't worth it. Happy and single is better than married and cranky."

"There's no girl." I lied because I'd convinced myself I didn't want to talk about it.

"Good. You made the right choice."

"I didn't make a choice! And she doesn't make me cranky!"

"Is this the girl with the roses? With your number?"

"Can I have my eggs now, please?"

She pursed her lips and prepared two plates of toast and eggs, silently sliding my breakfast to me over the bar.

"Okay, look," I said. "You know all I ever loved is doing my thing. The music. Okay? And acting is so cool, it's next best. That's all I ever wanted, and I worked hard. I know I had it easy, and I had it all early, but I worked. I earned it. I'm not throwing it all away for someone who thinks I'm some kind of douchebag asshole."

"Why would anyone think that?"

"Because I'm a douchebag asshole, okay? And whatever. I did stuff, and until the day I put it behind me, my career comes first."

Anyone with emotional sense would have advised me to follow my heart and let my career take care of itself. But my dad didn't come from nowhere. Professional urgency was baked into our genes.

"Oh, I agree," she said. "Not about the douchebag asshole part. Your grandfather had a corner on that, and trust me, you aren't anything like him."

I shoved my eggs onto the toast.

"I know."

"So, no birthday party?"

"Nope."

"Where are you taking me for dinner?"

I rooted around my brain for the nicest restaurants in Los Angeles, when I should have been wondering why she'd given up so easily.

CHAPTER 19

KAYLA

The difference between an industrial sewing machine and your grand-mother's home Singer was power. The cute motor of the home unit hisses and hums. The factory machine pounds like a pile driver.

The headache I woke with in Dad's guest room was a steady indus-trial thump hammering a seam that started somewhere around my waist and ended a few inches below the ceiling. The Advil and water by the bed turned the beating pain down enough to lie in bed and really give myself the lashing I deserved.

It was out. People knew. Everything I'd done and had failed to do had followed me thousands of miles like an empty can tied to my ankle on a long string.

I'd been happy at Josef Signorile. That was the worst part. I'd felt valued for my creativity and talent. I'd been so happy that when a position in outerwear opened up, I pushed for Brenda to fill it. When Signorile put his hands on me, I told myself I was too happy there to rock the boat. I didn't want to get fired, so I didn't tell Brenda. I didn't tell anyone. I barely even reminded myself of what had happened.

Then he did it to her. It was my fault twice over. I'd gotten her the job, then I didn't warn her.

I'd spoken up too late. Brenda had moved already, so she couldn't vouch. Signorile's wife had changed his schedule for that day, planting a meeting with her across town that never happened. I was now a liar. I would always be what men feared and women resented. Even Dara Signorile—the wife—resented me. I didn't know how she held resentment and guilt in her head at the same time. A week later, I knew she wasn't. The guilt must have been taking the oomph out of her resentment, so she got rid of it. She called me to the fourth floor late in the afternoon to give me denim overages. She begrudged me my truth, because she lied and I hadn't, so she paid off her culpability in protecting a first-order scumbag. She gave me the selvedge and said she hoped I "learned from this experience."

I learned all right.

My lesson was that you can't win against power. Not outright. The only thing you could do was keep your head down, take the Japanese denim given to you, and bust your ass to become the power that tried to break you.

So I'd left. I turned my back because so many backs had been turned on me.

What a selfish brat.

The headache didn't abate as much as move to my chest, squeezing it sharply with a drawstring of guilt.

Who was he grabbing now?

Brenda hadn't wanted that job at Signorile, where the sample size was a six and the fit model was five eleven. She wanted to work on her sizes, but she needed money. I told her to stay for a year. Learn the ropes. Wait for something more suitable to appear. I gave her the most mature advice I could, then acted like a child over and over again.

From somewhere under my father's clean white sheets, my phone vibrated against my hip.

When would a phone ringing not make me think of Justin Beckett?

I dug it out on the third ring. A number in Redondo Beach, California. I had no idea where that was and answered it anyway.

"Hello?" a woman said. Middle-aged husky with a gentle singsong quality.

"Who is this?" I asked with the phone between my ear and the pillow.

"This is Wanda." Big dogs barked in the background. "Aunt Wanda. Is this Justin's number?"

I sighed. She seemed too nice to snap at.

"You have the right number, but the wrong number."

"Oh?" she said as a little yippy dog joined in. It sounded just like Zack's dog, Buster. "Muffin! Down!"

"This is his old number."

"Hold on. Let me get the babies a treat." A box shook, and she cooed about what good dogs she had. They went utterly silent. "Now sit."

"Is that a Chihuahua?" I asked.

"Yes, and she's the alpha around here, aren't you, sweet girl? So, okay, so I'm sorry to bother you, but Louise told me to call about the surprise party?"

"Surprise party?"

"For Justin's surprise birthday. Saturday? She said to RSVP with his assistant. She said you were very nice."

I got myself up on my elbow. My empty stomach did a half twist, but my head didn't object too much.

"That's very generous of her, but I don't know anything about it."

"Right. I know. You're trying to protect the guest list."

"No, it's not—"

"And I'm supposed to tell you something so you know I'm really his aunt."

"I believe you. Really."

"When Justin was seventeen, he was playing this big stadium in Beijing. The one they used for the Olympics? Well, he was such a big deal, but he found out Marcie died . . ."

"Who's Marcie?"

"Our Great Dane. Lived sixteen years, but the cancer treatments were too much for her old heart. Justin paid for them, by the way, and when he found out she didn't make it, he flew all the way back here right after the concert so he could be at the funeral with us."

"Wow." I gave her the answer she was hoping for, and maybe if I wasn't feeling like a pile of Marcie's steaming poop I would have had more feeling behind it.

"Then," she continued, "he flew all those hours back for his show in Tokyo. Now if that's not Justin, I don't know what is . . . right, Minnie?" She paused for licking noises. "So, it's me. I'll be there."

"Aunt Wanda." I repeated her name and dropped back to the pillow.

"And Uncle Herb too." One of the big dogs belted out a couple of woofs.

"Got it."

"See you there!"

"Bye," I said.

She hung up. I sighed and found Louise's number. I hadn't known her last name, so Louise was right next to Annie Loranda . . . Brenda's mother in Houston. We'd spent our last spring break in Houston so we could work on our projects without social distractions.

I tapped Louise's number before I got caught up in a depressing whirlpool of guilt, and was sent to voice mail.

"Hey, Louise. This is Kayla. The girl who brought Ned's roses. Listen. You gave Justin's aunt Wanda the wrong number. She and Herb are coming to the party, by the way. But if you could make sure to give the right number out, that would be great. Thanks."

When I hung up, the contacts came back on the screen.

Annie would know where Brenda was. I knew her, and she was a decent person who would be nice to me even if she hated me for what had happened.

I could just get her number and call Brenda when I was ready. Maybe in a few months. A year. Never, even.

With the promise to myself that I wasn't doing anything more than gathering information I didn't have to act on until I was ready, I tapped Annie's number.

"Hello?"

It wasn't Annie. Right away, I knew that voice.

"Hi," I said. "Uh, I was calling for Annie, but—"

"Kayla?"

"Brenda?"

"Oh my God."

"Brenda, I'm so sorry!" The rest came out in an unpunctuated stream. "It was all my fault I was a coward and I put you in a terrible position it wasn't fair I understand if you never forgive me but I miss you."

I put my hand over my eyes to block both the sun coming through the window and the rebuke I was sure I deserved.

"No!" she cried. "I left you there holding the bag. I knew what was happening, and I ran away and hid."

"But you had to."

"I didn't. But I was so scared and I just . . . for the first time in my life I hated this body."

"You're beautiful."

"I miss you so much. How are you?"

"Terrible. I'm in LA. There's this guy? And he found out what happened. Now he hates me."

"Fuck him."

"Yeah. Fuck him."

"Fuck him with a serving spoon."

229

Even though it made my head hurt, I laughed.

"Tell me how you are," I said.

"A little stuck."

"Oh no."

"For a long time, I felt his hands on me whenever I closed my eyes. I couldn't sleep. I almost flew back to New York to defend you a hundred times, but I couldn't. I was in the airport once, and I had a panic attack at the gate."

"Jesus."

"I was a bad friend, and I'd understand if you hate me."

"I don't," I said. "I thought you hated me. And you should. I should have warned you."

"We all knew, Kayla. Remember Winnie? Who he paid off? And there was this NDA?"

I sat up all the way, brow furrowed, remembering the atmosphere at Josef Signorile Inc. I'd pushed the toxicity to the back of my memory and propped up his support to block the view.

"Right," I said. "I forgot about that. There were lawyers everywhere for a week."

"We all went out for drinks when she resigned. She bought us all rounds, but it was like her mouth was sewn shut."

"And Alicia."

"Same. Right?" Brenda said. In my mind I could see her pacing with her pointer finger waving in accusation. "She went on that LA trip with him and came back a different person."

"I asked her, but she said everything was fine." Of all my failures, the ones that hurt the women right in front of me weighed the most. "I should have pressed harder. I should have made her tell me."

"We all knew there were roaches behind the cabinets, but we kept cooking supper."

"We stayed. It's our—"

"Don't you say it!" She cut me off. "My mother spent thousands on therapy so I'd stop telling myself it was my fault. I'll save you the money. Josef Signorile worked really hard to make sure we didn't know anything for sure. He groomed us with compliments and creative freedom. We gave him the benefit of the doubt, and he used it against us so he could . . ." Her deep swallow was audible. "So he could assault us. Use us. Treat us like meat when we felt most confident. You know what you did? You made it harder for him to get away with it."

I swung my legs over the side of the bed. The cuffs of my father's pajamas hung past my feet.

"I'm going to a ball here. A costume dance. The same one he took Alicia to, and he's going to be there. I shouldn't go."

"Will seeing him make you feel unsafe?"

He was never going to touch me again, but I couldn't guarantee I'd return the favor.

"I'm going to want to punch him if I see him. But . . ." I thought for a moment and decided this could be my chance to unload guilt. I didn't even have to do anything but be visible as a reminder that I knew who he was and what he did.

"Kayla?"

"I want him to be uncomfortable."

"I understand."

I cradled the phone against my cheek as I looked out the window. It was a beautiful day.

"I want him to feel unsafe."

"I wish I could see you. I'd know if you had that look on your face."

"What look?"

"Like your brain's on fire."

"I'm not sure what I'm cooking, but yeah. Something." My white van was parked in the driveway of my father's house. I was safe here. I was valued.

"Did I tell you I missed you?" I said.

"You don't have to anymore."

"We can be friends again? Do you think?"

"Girl. Yes."

Relief practically knocked my legs from under me. The loss of my friend had been like a picture I'd placed over a window. Until it was removed, it was easy to forget how much light wasn't coming in.

"Thank God," I said. "And thank you for letting me come home."

~

Dad had gone to work, and I puttered around his kitchen. He'd left me a note with his work number and the location of the eggs and bread.

I couldn't get the idea out of my head. If I was safe and supported, I could make sure Signorile didn't feel the same.

All I had to do was tell the story. The truth could clear the path for me to be with Justin. I could rewrite my story. It played itself out like background music as I made breakfast.

Butter was sizzling in the pan and I was scrambling the eggs when a call came in. Florida. It was either a garbage spam call or—

"Hello?" a kid who sounded about five said. "Is Uncle Justin home?"

"You're calling to RSVP."

Breathing.

"Hello?" I could barely hear him. I turned the gas off.

"I want to go to the party," he said.

"Okay. What's your name?"

"Teddy."

"Hi, Teddy."

"Will there be karaoke?"

"I don't know."

"I can bring my karaoke machine. It has all his songs on it."

"That sounds like fun."

"Uncle Justin likes to sing with me."

A man's voice came from the other side. "Give me the phone, kiddo."

Rustling as the transfer was completed.

"Hello?" He sounded almost exactly like Justin. "This is Justice Beckett."

"Oh, hi. I'm Kayla, and this is Justin's old number." I turned the stove back on.

"Ah," he said as if he'd put together a string of clues to solve a puzzle. "Louise is being Louise."

"It's fine. I'm used to it."

"Teddy was all set to tell a heartwarming story."

"I can give her the message."

"Can you confirm the time and place? Roof of the Line Hotel? Saturday at eight?"

"I can't. And I'm not sure about the karaoke machine either."

"I'm sorry to bother you. I'll call Louise."

"Not a problem."

We hung up, and I stirred my eggs. When the phone buzzed again, the call was coming from Beverly Hills. Assuming it was another RSVP to a party I wasn't invited to, I picked it up.

"Kayla Montgomery?" Male. Older.

"Who is this?"

"This is Ken Braque. I manage Justin Beckett's public relations. Do you have a moment?"

CHAPTER 20

JUSTIN

Kayla was mad at me, and she was right to be. I could live with her being mad, but I couldn't stand not knowing what to do about it. I felt the world looking over my shoulder, judging my every move, waiting to cancel me. That was my reality. It nailed my feet to the ground in a way that had been helpful. Not anymore. Now I wanted to fly and couldn't.

Kayla took up space in my head, which should have been uncomfortable. It wasn't. I wanted more—and had no idea how to get it without ruining everything. Even though I knew the way to the studio, I used her voice to guide every turn.

In four hundred feet, turn left.

"Kayla," I said as I turned. "Where are you?"

Coldwater Canyon Avenue and Moorpark Street.

The GPS told me where the car was. What else had I expected?

"Where am I going?"

Ten thirty recording session at Slashdot Studios.

"I miss you."

I miss you too.

The voice was so real my entire brain lit up like a Christmas tree. I slammed on the brakes, nearly getting an ass full of honking Range Rover. I pulled over.

Of course the software had been pumped full of Easter eggs. If I asked it how many roads a man had to walk down before he became a man, Kayla's voice would reply that the answer was blowing in the wind. If I asked why the chicken crossed the road, Kayla would make any one of seventeen preprogrammed jokes.

What would it say if I told it what I was really feeling? Would it make another stupid crack? Did it matter? Wasn't the point that I was just spitting out what needed to be said? Did I just need to say it to an AI version of her so it was out of my mouth and into the world?

"Kayla?"

I am here.

That was almost comforting, even if it was a provable lie.

"I love you."

I love you too.

A computer loved me, but her voice sounded so real I got this warm tingle all over me.

"I'm sorry."

Love means never having to say you're sorry.

Cups up to Elon Musk for stringing together two answers, but no. That wasn't true. Love meant saying you were sorry all the time. Being sorry meant you were learning how to not be careless. Love meant you weren't afraid of being wrong, because the person you loved made you a better person. And in that circle of logic, right in the center, was Kayla.

What if it was too late?

What if I lost her?

What if Kayla made me a better person for the benefit of some other girl?

No. There was no one else. I was talking crazy to myself. I could have just about any girl I wanted on four continents, but I wanted only her. Not like a car or a house. Not like my publishing rights or creative control. I wanted all that, sure. Some of it I'd demand.

But I wasn't terrified of losing things I wanted. The thought of not getting that stuff didn't make my blood run cold in the front seat of my car or turn my future a dull gray, like a morning fog that was so dense you couldn't see five feet in front of you.

I knew I was being weird. I knew this wasn't normal. I was over-reacting. I was putting my entire future on a woman who had her own life to think about. It wasn't fair, but I didn't feel like a fair, rational person. Everyone thought I was an impulsive, immature, entitled prick, and now I knew exactly what that meant.

It meant this feeling. Right here. Right now. Like I'd stop existing if I didn't take care of this immediately.

"Call Kayla Montgomery."

Calling Kayla.

The screen flipped to her name and number. It rang once, then again. By the third ring my palms were sweating like I was in grade school, trying to act cool enough to sit next to Harmony Davis at recess.

"Just pick up, all right?"

As if she heard me, she picked up.

"Justin," she said flatly.

"Hey. I just wanted to make sure you got home all right."

"You're not in the alley, are you?"

"No. I'm on the way to the studio. I want to . . . I want to see you. We should talk."

She sighed as if she was resigned to something. Whatever it was, it wasn't a good sign.

"I don't think it's going to change anything," she said.

"Ten minutes."

Stupid. As if promising less would make her mine again.

"Don't you have to go to the studio?" she asked.

"I'm Justin Beckett. They'll wait."

"Fame has its privileges."

"Yeah, it also has limits."

It can't make you forgive me.

Nothing would, but I wasn't even close to giving up. My next tactic was flat-out begging, but she saved my knees from the scabs.

"Okay," she said. "I'm at my father's house."

"Cool, text me."

"Ten minutes, Justin. I have things to do."

"Sure, sure."

She texted me the address, and her voice guided me there.

~

The house wasn't far into the Hills. A couple of turns off the 101 onto a curved street with intermittent sidewalks. Her van was in the driveway. I parked behind it, letting the ass of the Tesla stick into the street.

She was sitting on the front steps of a sharp, modern house in the same clothes she'd worn the night before. Her hair was pulled back, and the waves flattened against her scalp looked like the wet sand after a swell retreated back to the sea.

"Hey," I said, sitting next to her. She shifted to give me room. "This is your dad's place, huh? Pretty nice."

"Yeah."

"So you came here?" I asked. "After you left the studio?"

She shrugged. "I needed to be around people."

"Yeah. I left the session early. Needed to be alone."

She smiled so briefly I would have missed it if I could have taken my eyes off her, which I couldn't. Not for a moment. She seemed so permanent in my life right there, with the morning sun coming through the trees, that I had to remind myself that she might not see herself that way.

"I'm sorry I flipped out on you." She drew her knees up and wrapped her arms around her legs.

"Nah. It's cool. I was kind of a dick."

She shrugged again. "I should have told you."

"I understand why you didn't."

"I wanted to just be me. Without all that stuff. I thought coming all the way here . . . to LA . . . would wash it all off me. It doesn't work like that."

"It's no big for me."

"It should be. I put you in danger. Your career. You worked hard, and I just came along thinking my past didn't matter. But it does. I'm poison for you, and it's not fair."

Poison?

Was that what she thought? Had I said anything like that? Implied it? Or was that what she'd gotten from the situation?

"Them's strong words, lady," I said.

"I'm trying to not dance around the facts."

"They're not the only facts."

"They're the ones that matter. I'm not going to sabotage you because I . . ." She faced me. "It doesn't matter how I feel. I'm not even a blip for you. I'll never own you. You don't even own you. Justin Beckett belongs to a big chunk of the world."

"Fuck the chunk."

"No. Your fans pay your bills. They're a part of you. It's just how it is, and neither of us can change it. You need someone who belongs to the world as much as you do or someone so anonymous she's a vacation from it. I'm just this in-between person who can drag you down. Even if we wait until Ken gives us the go-ahead, it's going to be the same. I'll never be able to pull you up."

Something was off with what she'd just said, and I was so lost in her meaning and her brown eyes it took me a second to pinpoint it.

"Ken?" I said.

"Your PR guy."

"Did I tell you his name? Ever?"

"He called me."

"That son of a—" My hands were balled into fists, and if I opened them, a hundred profanities were going to fly out. "What did he say?"

"That you have a habit of getting in your own way, and that I'm just the latest iteration of that."

"No. That is fucked up and a lie."

"He didn't say exactly that. I inferred it. But . . ." She looked away again. "He's right in a way. It's just the way it is. Look what happened to Gordon and Heidi. If you just scrape away the particulars, the problem was that she's a regular person who wasn't regular enough. She isn't owned by the world. She's halfway in and halfway out, and she got dragged into a situation she didn't have the resources to manage. Look what happened. Not just to her but to Gordon. To their marriage."

Through her whole speech, I was jumping out of my skin to contradict. I scoffed. I ran my fingers through my hair. I shrugged as if the clouds had me on puppet strings.

"Are you done?" I asked.

"I'm done."

"Heidi's problem wasn't her job with famous people's kids. Her problem was that she came into my room to give me shit for talking to Chad's dealer, when she shoulda stayed by the damn pool minding her own business."

"Still."

"Still, nothing. I already have a nice house, paid in cash. If I can't finish the new one, so what? What am I going to do with a house like that if I can't put who I want in it? I am sick of this. So sick of it. I want to do what I want. I know half the world owns me. I feel that on me every day from the minute I wake up. But there's a piece of me I don't show them. It's the piece with all the stuff I can't say out loud. It's where the songs come from. I didn't know what I was saving it for until now, but it was for you. I want you to own that part of me."

"Justin—"

"Nope." I cut her off, because the look on her face wasn't all happy and grateful. It was full of apologies, and I didn't want them. Love meant never having to say you're sorry.

"You already own me," I said. "So you might as well just take me."

"This is so confusing."

"What's confusing? The movie's shot, and either I sucked or I was good. I can fire Ken right now. I can tell Slashdot to suck it and finance my own album. Or not. I don't care. I don't need permission to make music, and I don't need permission to love you."

Ah shit.

That was what I meant, but it wasn't meant to be said out loud before I replaced "love" with something less heavy.

"All I'm saying," I added as a distraction. "Ken shouldn't have called you. My life isn't up to him. He's had a bug up his ass to get me solo ever since . . ."

Ever since Gene brought me the Slashdot deal.

"You're not going to drag me down," I said. "If that's your real reason."

"It is."

"Okay, good. It's settled then."

"And it's still a good reason. For now." She stretched her legs down to the next step. Two straightened knees closer to walking away. "I didn't think I'd respect you the way I do. I want to be something good in your life."

"You are."

I heard those words as if I were a different person watching them on a screen. I sounded like a whiny bitch, and once I realized that, a wall went up. I'd told her I loved her when I shouldn't have, and she'd thrown the word *respect* back at me. I'd handed her my heart on a platter, and she was gearing up to tell me thanks but no. That wall was my ego, and it was there to protect me.

So, cool. Fine. Cool.

No problem.

I couldn't push myself on her. Signorile had done that, and I didn't want to be that guy. And yeah, I was as human as the next man. I felt like staying there and taking up her time until she understood. Yelling my needs in definite terms. Forcing facts into her brain. I could make an argument that if I didn't touch her, I was better than Signorile, but nah. Forcing myself on her wasn't a sin of degree or proportion. You were either doing it or you weren't. And yeah, I wanted her, but not enough to hurt her.

"You know what?" I said. "Fine. You're right."

"If we wait a little while . . . I need to unload some stuff. And if it all goes well, then Ken's going to love me."

"This vague shit's not giving me a good feeling."

"Trust me."

"Yeah," I said, standing up. "Sure. Whatever."

She stood too. A step above me, she was closer to eye level. I looked away.

"Can I call you?" she asked.

"You have my number."

I waved and went to the car, tapping the remote to open the door. I got under its wing and closed it, pulling out into the narrow street without looking back at her.

When I turned onto Gower, I switched the GPS voice to a generic female that Tesla had named Tammy and shut it off. Tammy couldn't guide me where I wanted to go.

CHAPTER 21

KAYLA

I could call Justin. I *would* call him.

When I did, I'd feel better. Lighter. Exonerated. Unencumbered by other people's lies and my own silence. I'd be a strong person who acted from conviction, not fear.

Six days before, on my dad's front steps, he didn't seem to get it, but he would. Tomorrow, after his surprise party, I'd call him and explain it fully, with details. We'd laugh about the dozens of RSVP phone calls I'd gotten that week, some with stories about the favors and good deeds he'd done. I'd tell him how every story proved he was worth loving a little more. We'd belabor the fact that the Regency ball where I threw off my chains was his birthday.

"So, you're doing it?" Brenda asked over the Bluetooth speakers.

"My dad got me a shark of a lawyer. She talked to Alicia and Winnie. She's ready to rip off a limb and I love her for it."

My lawyer's name was Shawna Jackson. She had sable skin and amber eyes that could simultaneously transmit rage at a situation and compassion for those suffering through it.

I pulled up in front of Evelyn's house in Highland Park. She shared a four-bedroom house with seven other film industry people.

"Are you going to say anything?"

"Lawyer says I shouldn't yet." I put the van into park and reached into the back for my stuff.

"She's probably right," Brenda said. "You can just ignore him."

"He's been let off the hook too long."

"He has."

"And so have I."

"Kayla," Brenda said sternly. "We talked about this."

"I know."

"Try to have a good time."

"It's going to be the time of my life."

~

We took a cab to the ball, draping the back seat with a few yards of fabric and lace.

Subcultures I didn't know about always hid in the corners of New York City. Los Angeles wasn't any different. On that particular day in July, a crowd of ladies in parasols and bonnets stood on Orange Drive, off Hollywood Boulevard, with gentlemen wearing tailcoats and breeches. The line meandered around a brass side door to the hotel. Tourists and natives in jeans and sneakers stopped to gawk as the guests slowly filed up the marble steps.

"Kayla," Evelyn said when we were stopped at the light right before the hotel.

"Yeah?"

"Are you nervous?"

I hadn't mentioned Signorile again or told her about my new lawyer because I wanted her to have a good time. But she was right. I was sweating, and my mind had gone blank. I had too much riding on this. Not just vengeance or exoneration. I'd resigned myself to living without either of those. But I wasn't resigned to living without Justin.

All I could think about was how close I was to calling him and telling him I couldn't be accused of being a liar anymore.

"You're nervous too." I squeezed her hand.

"A little."

"Eddie likes you."

"Maybe," she said.

"He does. You'll see."

"I can get a glass of Madeira in me before he arrives."

"You don't need it. When you're in costume, you have the confidence of a supermodel."

"I don't feel different."

"Maybe, but something happens. You'll be fine."

The cab stopped, and we got out to face the men we loved and hated.

CHAPTER 22

JUSTIN

I need to unload some stuff.

When I went to dinner with Louise, I still had no idea what Kayla was talking about. Stuff? What the hell was *stuff*?

"You sure you made the reservation for the roof?" I asked Louise after Carter joined us in the elevator. "Because Vic told me they don't take roof reservations."

"When your dead husband supplied all the furniture for the guest rooms, and your grandson is a household name, you get a reservation anywhere you want."

And if it all goes well, then Ken's going to love me.

This part worried me to fucking distraction.

"Fine," I mumbled. I didn't even hear what she'd said over the questions in my head.

I need to unload some stuff.

"I don't know why you have to look so grumpy," Louise said, hugging her bag and looking at the lights flip from floor to floor.

"I'm not grumpy." I was worse than grumpy. I was exhausted from trying to ignore the week that had passed without Kayla. I'd spent my nights not sleeping and my days not being all the way awake.

"Birthdays aren't for sour faces," Louise chimed.

"This face? This is a sour face? This face is my birthday face, and it's sweet as cake with sprinkles, okay?"

She scoffed. "Who broke your heart, I don't know."

She said it as if she knew damn well.

The elevator dinged on the top floor. Carter would get out first, make sure I was clear of both Beckettes and real dangers, then escort us through. But when the doors started to open, he shifted to the side with his hands folded in front of him and a suppressed grin.

"Cart—?"

"Surprise!"

~

Someone put a beer in my hand, and I used the other to shake hands, hug, and backslap.

Thirty people were on the roof, and I loved all of them as much as I hated surprise parties.

But not Kayla.

My brother and his wife and kids.

Everyone else you care about is here.

My aunts and uncles from everywhere.

Why do you feel entitled to her?

A bouquet of flowers from my parents, who were somewhere between Indonesia and Papua New Guinea.

I need to unload some stuff.

The party was small, so it was manageable, but the intimacy didn't make it easier. I watched myself have a good time and thought, *You really got this acting thing down.*

"What are you wearing?" I asked Eddie, tipping my beer bottle at a jacket straight outta the movie we had just finished.

"Long story. Happy birthday."

I slapped his back when we hugged, and as we separated, Louise came between us, facing Eddie.

"I'm Louise. Justin's grandmother."

"Ah. Thank you for inviting me."

"I'm your biggest fan. I mean you must hear that all the time."

"Not really."

"Can we do a selfie?"

"Of course."

Louise shoved her phone into my chest, and I took about ten pictures of them.

"Thank you!" She kissed his cheek. "You're staying for the cake, right? It's from Jacquard Jacques."

"I—"

"Strawberries. I mean the thing is just covered in strawberries."

"I'd love to," Eddie said. "But I have something else."

"What?"

"Weeze," I said. "Come on."

Eddie waved away my warning.

"There's a dance . . . more a costume ball. I promised someone I'd go."

"Oh, are you taking a lady?"

"Weeze!"

Eddie was a little too happy with my grandmother's attention. She had a way of making people think rude comments were cute questions.

"Two, actually." He looked up at me. "Ev and Kayla."

When he said her name, I went cold. Not because there was anything wrong with her going to a ball or whatever, but because I was making a real effort to not think about her, and he'd just shaken a can of soda and popped it open. Fizzy emotions got everywhere. The party got really far away, and all I could think about was how much I needed to make sure she knew how much I wanted her.

"Oh," Louise gasped and put her hands over her mouth, then shot me a glance.

"What?" I sounded angry, but I was just surprised and busy trying to stuff the thought of her back in the box.

"Oh, Justin," she said, putting her hand on my arm. "I boo-booed."

Eddie laughed, but Louise looked panicked.

"What?"

"Well. So. You've had a face on from here to Jerusalem, and my intuition told me it was because of that girl. The one with your phone number? Who brought me the roses?"

"Kayla?"

"And so, I wanted her to come, but I couldn't just ask her so . . ." She glanced at Eddie, then back to me. "Well, all these people had the old number, so when I told them to RSVP I just said to call you and your assistant would pick up."

"And so . . . they all called her?"

"Well . . . yes."

"Aw, Weeze, what the . . . ?" I threw my hands up.

"I said they had to tell a nice story about you to prove . . . oh, I don't even know now. But the idea was I wanted to give her the chance to come. Because after hearing all the nice things your family had to say about you . . . what woman in her right mind wouldn't come?"

I had no words. None. One, Kayla hated being my damned secretary. Two, she still hadn't come to the party. I wasn't sure if I blamed her or not.

No, I couldn't blame her. I didn't know what *stuff* she was up to, but she'd been clear.

"I'm sorry, sweetheart," Louise said. "For interfering."

"I love you, Grandma, but damn. Goddamn."

Eddie cleared his throat. At first I thought he was trying to be polite by reminding us that he was there.

"If you wanted to come where she is, to the ball," he said, "I could take you."

I wanted to go so bad, and I wanted to prove I could leave her alone even more.

"Thanks, but nah," I said.

"No," Louise said. "You have to go."

My grandmother was the last person I wanted to explain this to, since I could barely explain it to myself.

"Yeah." I shrugged. "But the cake."

Trying to make it look like a casual decision backfired.

"To hell with the cake!" she said. "I can take a picture. You go. Come back by ten."

I'd never make it back by ten, and I was about to say that when Louise jumped back in. "Everyone from far away's going to be here tomorrow. I'll have a thing at my house, so you can catch up all you want."

She pushed me by the shoulders so hard it was borderline assault.

"Weeze, really?"

"Just go," she demanded. "I put a ton of work into this girl already, so don't you suddenly get manners and ruin it."

I glanced around. Aunt Wanda was showing my cousin Ron a picture on her phone. Uncle Charlie was looking over at us from the buffet, where he was talking to Irma, an old family friend from the neighborhood.

I could go. I really could. Seeing Kayla meant I could apologize for Louise's RSVP strategy and maybe put a lid on the boiling pot of anxiety.

"Get out," Louise said. "I mean it."

My phone buzzed. I looked at it for no other reason than to distract from this garbage situation. It was a text from Shane.

—We found Chad—

Holy shit. I didn't forget Kayla, but she became my second-most-urgent problem.

"Hold on," I said so I could text.

—Where? And who's we?—

—We're downstairs. On Ardmore.
Gordon and me—

"I'll be right back," I said. Louise kissed my cheek, thinking I'd agreed to go, and Eddie gave her a hug before following me to the elevator.

"I have to stop home anyway," Eddie said. "I have something that might fit."

"I'm just going down for a minute."

"Your call."

~

Shane's 1967 Mustang was parked in the red. I walked with my head down, hoping no one recognized me. He cranked down the window when I got there.

Next to him, Gordon looked like a guy who hadn't had a decent meal in a week.

"Where is he?" I asked, leaning in.

"A facility in Pomona," Shane said. "We're heading out there."

"I'm coming."

"No." Gordon spoke without looking at me.

"He doesn't want to see you," Shane added. "He found out about Slashdot and Ken."

"What about Slashdot and Ken?"

They looked at me as if I'd forgotten the lyrics to "Get the Girl" in Yankee Stadium.

"You didn't know?" Shane said. "About his two-year noncompete? The bonus if they could release your solo without a Sunset Boys album release?"

I bent lower, leaning my forehead on my arm. I could hear people shouting and talking in the background of my own thoughts, which shouted, *Of course, of course, you dumb asshole.*

"You guys," I said, eyes on the pavement. "I'm sorry I flipped out on you, Shane. I never shoulda hit you, but I didn't do any of the other shit you're blaming me for, and you know it."

"We know." Gordon's voice cut through the street noise. I picked my head off my arm to see Gordon looking at me. A flash went off.

"You know?"

"This asshole . . ." He jerked his thumb at Shane. "He told me what you said about that night and, you know . . . I had to kind of entertain the notion that you didn't sleep with Heidi, and once I got out of my own way, that made the most sense. So . . . I guess I'm the one with the sorries."

His words freed me from a prison I didn't even realize I was in. I felt like a man given a new lease on life. I took him by both sides of his face and kissed him, and the night was lit with flashes and shouts.

"Thank you," I said.

"Get off me," he replied with a half smile.

"Dude," Shane said. "How are we going to get out of here?"

Looking up, I saw how hemmed in we were. Paparazzi with big lenses. Fans with phones. Dozens of people crowded around the car, trying to get our attention. Carter was holding them back while cops cleared the way for traffic, but the mob was growing. Getting back upstairs would be a pain in the ass. I could do it, but now that I was out of the party, the way to Kayla seemed like a bright line. The police let Eddie's Lexus crawl through the crowd, and that was it. I made my decision.

"Call me when you're there," I said and leaped over the Mustang's hood, ass sliding on the warm steel as flashes popped and my name filled the night. I landed on the other side and knocked on Eddie's window. He popped the lock, and I got in.

"Nice crowd," he said as I waved to a girl in her teens.

"Yeah. So, I can come to this thing with you?"

"You bet."

"Where is it?"

"The Roosevelt Hotel."

"Well, shit."

CHAPTER 23

KAYLA

The ballroom was art deco, making it an anachronism by a hundred years, but it was still gorgeous. Evelyn and I sipped our drinks and admired the costumes. Evelyn accepted a dance, and I memorized how she moved in case I decided to take to the floor.

The Madeira went right to my head.

"Hey," I asked a waiter as I put my empty glass on his tray. "Where are the bathrooms?"

"There's one right there, but if you go up to the mezzanine, they're less crowded."

I thanked him and found the stairway up. The bathrooms were indeed less crowded, and I was done in no time.

As I was about to push through the door to the stairs, I noticed a small crowd in costume near the elevators and heard a voice that was burned into my mind.

"Do you have your dance card?" Josef Signorile asked an older woman who stood near him.

"Monsieur!" she said, handing it over. "I'd be honored." She was Vanda Winthorpe, the lead editor of British *Elle*.

As he signed for his dance, I held my breath. They were all masked, but I knew them. Winthorpe's husband stood next to her, joking with the creative director of Jeremy St. James and the six-foot model Thomasina Wente.

So. Now was as good a time as any.

I let the stairway door go, flicked open my fan to cover the bottom half of my face, and—with my chin high and my shoulders back—joined the crowd to wait for the elevator.

The blue eyes under Signorile's mask landed on me as he handed Vanda Winthorpe's card back. His white cravat had a red pin in the center, and the collar of his cream waistcoat was at attention. His dark-brown hair was carefully brushed over the ribbon of his mask.

The elevator opened and people filed in.

He nodded to me with a little bow. "Madame."

I nodded back and knew I wasn't going to do it. I was going to go back downstairs, have another glass of Madeira, and dance.

"Room for one more," someone said.

"Please," he said, indicating that I should take the space. I could have. I should have. But the other elevator dinged, and that seemed like an opportunity to breathe through my panic.

"I'll take this one," I said from behind the fan.

"I'll accompany you," he said, as if he were a gentleman protector, not a predator.

The crowded elevator door slid shut before I could insist he stay with his friends.

"Your shawl is lovely," he said. He wasn't leering. He wasn't gross or creepy. If a girl didn't know any better, she'd think he was just a nice guy.

"Thank you." The doors of the second elevator opened. It was empty.

Signorile let me in first. Naturally. He pushed the button for the ballroom and the doors closed. We were alone. Our reflections in the polished brass stood shoulder to shoulder. The flesh between my legs wanted to crawl up into my body.

One floor. I could make it one floor without ripping his face off.

"Do I know you?" he asked.

"Maybe."

"Well, then you'll join us downstairs for a drink while we figure it out."

Yeah. Patience was looking less and less virtuous.

"You're so kind," I said, fan fluttering. "But you misunderstand."

"How so?"

I snapped the fan down so he could see my chin and lips—the ones he'd covered with his hand months ago. In the reflection, Signorile went into profile as he turned. I couldn't look back or I'd either panic, cry, or kill him. I kept my gaze on the numbers.

"You're Kayla Montgomery," he said, pushing his mask up. "The liar."

Casually, as if choosing another floor, I pressed the red emergency button. The alarm went off, and I turned my back to the panel to block it and to face him.

"That's me. I lied when I let you railroad me. I lied when I ran away." I flipped the fan closed, the tucked end against my palm, then shoved up my mask. "I lied to myself, but that's over. I can still feel your hands on me. I still hear you chuckling in my ear while I cried, you sadistic fuck. What you did . . . what you do to any woman who threatens you? That's over. I'm standing between you and any other woman you want to attack. I will never, ever stay silent again."

He smiled as if he found the whole thing amusing.

"You have no proof, my dear." He didn't look scared. Not one bit. I doubted myself for a moment, then remembered how he'd put his hand over my mouth. How it had smelled of the soap in the office bathroom, and how I couldn't bear the smell of eucalyptus afterward.

"Lawyer up, asshole."

I jabbed my elbow into the red button. The alarm went quiet, and the elevator lurched to life.

"I hope you like mud," he said. "Because you'll be dragged through it."

We were locked in a stare until the doors slid open. He nodded with a smirk and—as if nothing had happened—walked out to meet the crowd of friends waiting for him.

I pushed my mask down and flipped open my fan. My hands shook. My composure collapsed into a pounding heart and sweating palms, lost in the moment of verbal violence that had just passed. I'd done it. Something. Declared war. Fought a battle with no winner that left my confidence shredded.

I wanted to run, but from what?

My focus narrowed to what was directly in front of me, the path back to the ballroom.

And in that narrow path, looking at me with a smile, stood a beautiful man in a period suit and mask.

When I saw him, my vision widened, my heart quieted, and my step quickened. I ran into his arms.

"Whoa," Justin said.

"I'm so happy you're here." I slipped off him to look into the shelter of his gorgeous, wonderful face.

"Yeah, I heard the elevator alarm."

"No, it's . . ."

"What's wrong?"

"I did something stupid."

"How stupid?"

"Not stupid like an accident." I lowered my voice when Signorile's crowd passed. "Something I thought would be easy and satisfying, but it wasn't."

Taking both my hands in his, he led me to a couch and sat down with me.

"Talk to me."

I turned my gaze down to our interwoven hands. No matter how I told it, he was going to have a strong reaction.

"I set off that elevator alarm. That was me." I looked back up at him. We hadn't bothered to take off our masks, and maybe that was for the best. "I was in there alone with Signorile."

"What did he do?" Justin's body was coiled in tension as if he wanted to launch out of his seat.

"Nothing."

"He didn't touch you?"

"No." I squeezed his hands when I said it, and a little of the tension released.

"Lucky for him."

"I set it off because I wanted to tell him something, and we only had one floor."

"Tell him what?"

"That I'm coming for him. I won't be quiet anymore. I won't let him call me a liar and . . ." I took a deep breath. "I'm doing it for me, but it has a side effect for us. If I clear my name, maybe I won't be a liability for you."

A quick laugh escaped him as he looked away, then back.

"I should have asked you first," I continued, "but I was so tired of this. Ken, and your contracts, and I realized you weren't the only one with problems that interfered. I had to take care of it. So I got a lawyer, but I might have just made it worse."

"Not as bad as I'm gonna make it when I go in there and kill him."

"Justin."

"It's gonna hurt my career, but it's gonna feel so good."

I couldn't tell if he was joking.

"No, you're not."

"Who's stopping me?"

257

Did he want me to beg for mercy? Petition his sense of self-preservation?

I wouldn't do either.

"He's mine," I growled. "You understand?"

Justin bit his bottom lip, clear blue eyes narrowing under his mask.

"That's so hot," he said. "Say it again."

I leaned into him and deepened my voice.

"You leave him alone. He's mine. I'm going to be the one to destroy him."

"You're making me want to destroy you," Justin answered, running his hand up my thigh.

"Later," I said. "I want to have fun. Ask me to dance."

He stood up and held out his hand. "You wanna dance or nah?"

I took him up on it, and we strolled to the ballroom together.

"I didn't ask what you were doing here," I whispered.

"Making sure no one else dances with you."

On the ballroom floor, couples stepped and twirled with a cohesiveness that looked practiced. I didn't think I could ever be part of something so seamless, not the way I felt right then, with my heart ready for war and my body's desire for Justin.

"Didn't you have a birthday party?" I asked.

"Louise kicked me out when she found out you weren't coming." We got on the floor. He placed a hand at my waist, and I put my arm on his shoulder. "What was I supposed to do? Say no?"

"Happy birthday, by the way."

"Thank you." He took my right hand in his left.

"I'm warning you ahead," I said. "I don't know how to waltz."

"Follow my lead."

He swung me to one side. I almost fell over, and he laughed.

"Don't make me tickle you," I said, craning my neck for Evelyn but only catching sight of my old boss. Signorile was dancing with a woman in a white gown. I followed his gaze to Evelyn and Eddie.

"It's one-two-three, one-two-three. Follow."

I let him take me, following his steps as if I were in clown shoes.

"Where did you learn how to waltz?" I asked.

"Had to be a triple threat. Singing, acting, dancing. You're getting it. There you go." He tightened his grip around my waist. "Stop looking at that guy or I'm going to punch him."

I turned back to his expressive lips and the half-hidden eyes. I'd seen him in costume a hundred times, but at the ball, his willingness to be there made him more handsome than ever.

"You look gorgeous," he said.

"I'm glad you're here," I said. I hadn't noticed the tension in his shoulders until I felt them relax. "Even though I specifically told you to fuck off for your own good."

"I'm not good at my own good."

"Yeah," I said. "You should get better at letting people take care of you."

"Here's the thing." We spun with the room. "My whole life started with me and my people. I had my buddies and my family. Me and them. We said it wouldn't change, but it did. Everything got distorted. What happened with us started going through this filter of what fans thought. Or what our team thought fans would think and how the label would react. Then it was just straight-up 'How's Ken gonna be?' I stopped thinking for myself. I hired it all out, and I gotta say, once you hire out your brain, your heart's right behind."

The room spun behind him, and I surrendered completely to the music and the way he moved.

"I'm done," he continued. "I want to be the guy you can trust, because I trust you. I don't want any filters. It's you and me. Nobody else is telling me who you are. Not the public or my PR guy or fucking DMZ. Fuck all of them. I can't control what they think. And if they want to think I'm a fuckup? Let them. As long as you don't."

"What if I'm the fuckup?"

"You're not." He pulled me as close as the dance allowed. "It's not that I don't care. I care. I don't want you to fuck up, because I want you to be happy. And you're not a fuckup at all. You're the balls."

I laughed.

"And I'll tell you what else," he added.

"What else?" I caressed the back of his neck.

"I'm not a dick. I got a lot going for me. I'm not entitled to you or nothing, but if you want me, I think that's a pretty good choice on your part."

"Is it?"

His steps stopped when the music paused, but we stayed in each other's arms.

"Yeah," he said. "You could do a lot worse."

He wasn't bragging. His confidence came from a place I hadn't seen through the filters of who I thought he was. Maybe the mask made him more visible, or maybe he'd changed. Maybe I'd broken past the need to harness my love to my expectations.

The music started again, but we didn't dance. We were locked in a moment only the truth could break.

"I've loved men who were worse," I said. "But I've never loved a man as much as I love you."

We bent toward each other, collapsing the waltz-appropriate distance between us into a soft kiss made of sighs. He pulled me so close only my toes touched the floor—and flicked his tongue on my lips until my mouth opened and our kiss went from gentle dance to passionate embrace. The music was miles away until a twirling body brushed against us.

Signorile was now dancing with a woman in a gold dress, and I didn't even care.

"Upstairs," Justin said into my ear. "There's a conference room. I want to pull that fancy dress up and show you how much I love you back."

Every word went right from my ear to the fast-melting throb between my legs, bypassing my brain altogether and angling my hips to brush against the outline of his erection.

Another couple bumped us, so we moved off the floor.

Evelyn stood with Eddie. Signorile didn't matter. The throb in my vintage undergarments was very present and very insistent.

"Let's go," I said.

Justin pulled me into a narrow wooden door behind the bar. When he was stopped by security, he pulled up his mask and was let through. Through another door, and halfway up the back stairs, we stopped to kiss. My back to the plaster wall, I gasped at the feel of his cock through our clothes and his hand on the bodice of the gown.

I was sure we weren't going to make it to the second floor, but a door opened above us, and we got our hands off each other just as a waiter skittered down the steps.

"No more stopping," I said, taking his hand.

A door. A carpeted hall. We passed the Toledo Room to another door that opened to an empty room with a long shiny table and six chairs. Windows with closed blinds. A door on the other side of the room. Justin snapped both locks shut and stepped close enough to push up my mask.

"Beautiful," he said, running his hand down my face and along my collarbone, where his lips took over. I bent backward over the table, and he hitched me up by the waist to sit on it, wrestling with my skirt and slip until he hit bare skin.

"I hate to ask now," I said when he laid his hands on my thighs.

"In my wallet." He opened my legs. "Lie back."

The hard wood was uncomfortable, but smooth enough to let him pull me forward. He took my panties off and stuffed them in his back pocket, then spread me wide again. His gaze on me was enough to send a wave of arousal down my spine, and, when he ran his tongue inside my thigh, I didn't think I'd be able to keep the orgasm down long enough for his mouth to get to its destination.

As if he knew how to torture me, he went slowly and methodically, prying me open with his tongue and teasing me with the point, kissing my clit so gently I barely felt it and almost came anyway.

"You're really close," he said, easing two fingers inside me.

"Master of the obvious."

"I'm going to make you come." He took his fingers out and laid them on my lips. "Be quiet or someone's going to think I'm killing you."

"You won't even know."

"I'll know." He dipped his head down and ran his tongue where I was wettest, then up to the core of my pleasure, slowly flicking, then sucking until my hips jerked against him and it was hard to keep my lips locked around his fingers.

When the orgasm burst through, my mouth opened, and I let out a silent howl into the sparkling blackness.

Justin removed his fingers and stood between my open legs with a glistening smile.

"Thank you," I gasped, dropping my head back to stare at the ceiling.

"No problem."

I heard him get out his wallet and open the condom. He undid his trousers and pulled out his dick. I wondered if there would ever come a day when it didn't look monstrously huge.

"You comfortable?" he asked.

"Yes."

He slid the condom on.

"You still love me?"

I got up on my elbows.

"Yes."

"That's good." He got between my legs, shifting them open so he could slide the head of his dick along me. "I never made it with a girl

I could say that to before." He pushed against me, and I pushed back until he was in. He laid his hands on my knees and thrust again, stretching me open.

"God. Damn," I said through gritted teeth.

"You okay?"

"I think I can come again."

A few more thrusts and he was all the way in. I opened his shirt to feel his skin. We wrapped our arms around each other and he took me, owned me, and cared for me with kisses and sweet, true words, bringing me to another silent orgasm as he buried his face in my neck for his own, and I wondered how I'd gotten here, to this strange city thousands of miles away, only to find myself home.

"Damn, I love you, Kaylacakes."

Maybe I should have been surprised, but nothing seemed more natural, more true, or more obvious than those words.

"Good. You oughta."

We kissed, and it was lovely and sweet until we heard a bang from the adjoining room and a half grunt, half squeal. Justin raised himself a few inches from me, turning to face the doorway we hadn't come through.

"Stop it!" a woman's voice came through from the adjacent room.

"Is that—" I started but couldn't finish as he went to the door, taking the air with him. I got up on the heels of my hands and dropped my legs over the side of the table while Justin turned the lock with his shirt open, his waistband halfway down his ass and his condom-wrapped dick hanging out like packaged kielbasa.

"Justin!" I shout-whispered, sliding onto my feet. "Your pants!"

He opened the door in that state, which showed an impressive prioritization of heroism over shame, and he leaped for Josef Signorile, pulling him by the collar and dragging him to the floor.

The first thing I saw was Evelyn, with her mask pulled down over her chin. Her eyes were kohl with running mascara, wide with shock as she stared to my left.

Justin was straddling Signorile, dick still out, fist pulled back.

"Justin!" I shouted. "Stop!" As if woken from a nightmare, Evelyn ran into my arms.

Justin's right arm was frozen by his ear. The left was pushing my old boss down by the throat.

"Please," I said, holding my friend. "Don't make it worse."

As if he had to do it before he changed his mind, Justin shot up, standing with a foot on each side of Signorile's hips.

"You—"

"Get off me!" Signorile growled. I remembered that voice. The way he'd groomed us with snarls of dissatisfaction and complimentary cooing.

"God, I want to fuck you up so bad," Justin said with his fists at his sides.

"Put your dick in your pants." Signorile tried to shove Justin's leg away.

"Nah." From behind, I could see his hips bend forward.

"Are you okay?" I asked Evelyn. Before she could answer, the door to the hallway opened, and a security guy came in, closely followed by Eddie.

When Evelyn saw him, she ran into his arms.

"Step away," the security guy said to Justin.

Justin put away his assets before turning around, thank God. I didn't want everyone looking at what was mine.

~

The cops came and took statements. Evelyn had been in line for the bathroom when Signorile said he knew of one that was less crowded. He made her laugh in the elevator. Eddie thought she was gone too long and came up after her. He heard a scuffle on the other side of the door and called security.

Signorile had never gotten caught in the act before, but he had his story. Evelyn repeated it to me when she was out of the room. He'd said she'd wanted him to stick his hand up her skirt, and when he saw that Evelyn and I were friends, it turned into entrapment.

When the cops called me into the little room, I stormed in like an angry, Regency-era goddess.

The cop was in her twenties, dark skinned with exacting care to her hair and makeup. You could tell a details person.

"You don't have to say anything if you want a lawyer," she said. "And I can't detain you, if you want to go."

"I have a lawyer." I looked at the clock, because we were all supposed to be in the ballroom—a public space—not the hotel's administrative offices with beige industrial carpet, blinds, no-frills paintings that looked as if they belonged in the rooms upstairs. "He has a history of this."

"So does Justin Beckett."

"Signorile assaulted my friend."

"Oh, we know that."

"How?"

"The hotel has a new security system," she said. "All the event spaces have cameras."

My cheeks tingled. If there were cameras in the Toledo Room, there were cameras in the adjoining room. Which meant there was video of Justin and me screwing on the conference table, and security had seen it.

Justin.

If the sex video leaked, I'd be seen, and it would be terrible, but I'd get over it. Justin wouldn't be able to shut the internet off. He'd be a dog who was inappropriate for young fans. This was going to be a problem for him.

I tilted my chin up haughtily—a woman incapable of shame.

"Are we done?" I asked.

"All done."

My phone buzzed. My lawyer.

—Now—

~

Evelyn and Eddie were in the waiting room, still in their finery. My stay was starting to pinch, and I'd stepped on the hem of my skirt so many times it was gray.

"Kayla," Evelyn said when she saw me. Eddie put his arm on her back as if letting her know he was there.

Yes. It was just lovely, and I wanted to hear all about it, but not right then.

"Where's Signorile?"

"He just left," Evelyn said, indicating the door out to the lobby, as if that was the one to avoid.

"Perfect."

Before they could ask why, I texted my shark.

—Lobby—

—They're on it—

"Where's Justin?" I asked.

"Ken Braque came just as you went in," Eddie said. "They went into an office down the hall. That way."

"Thanks." Before heading in that direction, I kissed Evelyn. "Are you okay?"

"I'm fine."

"You sure?"

"I called the *New Yorker* like you suggested. I'm telling them everything."

She was so brave. I wanted to be like her.

"I'll come," I said.

"Really?"

"Totally."

She hugged me. "Thank you."

"He's not getting away with this anymore, sister." I let her go. We nodded to each other, and I went down the narrow hall in my swooshing skirt, peeking past the open doors and into the little windows.

I found them in the last office. Justin sat in a black chair with wheels, feet spread apart and elbows on his knees as if he were really listening to the guy in the tailored suit sitting at the head of the table. He glanced up and noticed me through the glass.

When he got up to come to me, I felt cared for, protected. In two steps, he made me feel so alive that when he opened the door, I threw my arms around him.

"Whoa, Kayla," he said, holding me tight. I rested my head on his shoulder and closed my eyes, extending the moment as long as I could.

"Let's talk," Ken said from the other side of the world. Justin and I loosened our embrace. He kissed me and held me in his gaze.

"I'm not going to stop seeing him," I said, lost in frost-blue eyes. His temple was scratched. Signorile must have gotten a good swipe in.

"Yeah," Ken said. "I get that. Fine. But can we try to not end his career?"

With my body still toward Justin, I faced Ken.

"Nobody wants that."

"You're standing in the Roosevelt Hotel, where this guy, just a few months ago, was fully naked when he punched his bandmate. Today, he was only half-naked."

"I didn't punch him," Justin said. "They got video."

"Of that and more, apparently."

"Him assaulting Evelyn is all you need," I said.

"That's not going to work." Ken wagged his finger twice. "Our friend here burst in from the adjoining room, ass all over the place. That requires an explanation. One needs the other to make sense. So we're suppressing all of it. You're welcome."

"No," I said, then snapped my mouth closed. Did I want to give Justin grief? Ruin his career with a sex video? Just so I could have easy vengeance?

I took a few deep breaths in a stretched stay, shaking my head slowly. Evelyn. Justin. Evelyn. Justin.

"Kaylacakes," Justin whispered. "What?"

"It's . . ." If I explained, I'd be putting it all on him, but if I didn't? That was as good as not trusting him. "The video could finally prove what Signorile does. But I know that if it comes out, you'll lose your contracts—"

"Good!" Ken stood. "You get it."

Having decided we agreed, he started to walk out.

"Yo," Justin called. "Kenny?"

Ken spun. "I have an appointment."

"Yeah, cool. It ain't gonna take a second for me to fire you."

"To what?" He was back to us in two steps.

"I don't need you. I got this."

"We have a contract."

"And we both have lawyers. They'll figure it out. But you don't tell me what to do anymore, and you don't call my girl ever again."

"Justin . . ." Ken glanced at me as if he wanted me to disappear, then back at his client.

"Get off my work. Get off my life. Get your hands outta my pockets."

"Without me, you'll burn it all. You know that, right?"

"It's mine to burn, bro. Been a good run. Sorry about your bonus, but not sorry."

I didn't know what he was talking about, but Ken did. A flash of surprise crossed his face, then disappeared as if it never happened.

"I never steered you wrong," Ken said in his defense.

"You tell yourself your story." Justin stuck out his hand. "I'll tell mine."

Reluctantly, Ken shook his hand. "This is going to be expensive."

"If you say so." Their hands separated, and Ken strode down the hall and disappeared.

"Asshole," Justin muttered, squeezing my hand.

"I hope that wasn't a mistake."

"Nah."

"You sure?"

"You know where you said you didn't want all my shit becoming all your shit?"

"Yeah?"

"Now it won't. Because that guy was never gonna let you be."

He kissed me tenderly with a brush of the lips and his palm on my cheek, sealing a promise that my life was my life, and he'd do whatever it took to make sure our common problems were shared equally.

Our kiss was interrupted by a text from my lawyer.

—*Where are you?*—

"Crap." I pulled Justin's hand. "Come on."

"Where—?"

I yanked him down the hall, through the door, around a table with a huge vase of flowers, through another door, and out to the lobby, where a half dozen guys in suits, another half dozen in police uniform, and a handful of reporters were filing past the revolving doors.

My gaze followed their path, and I was rewarded with a sight grander than Mount Rushmore, more delicious than a Lemon Shit, and finer than hundred-dollar-a-yard French lace.

Signorile was bent over halfway with his hands behind his back as a uniformed police officer snapped cuffs on him.

"Wait," Justin said. "This happened like half an hour ago . . ."

"All week." I pulled him forward with me so I'd be right in my old employer's path. "I got a lawyer to file a civil suit. She called some contacts she had in New York and found out they were already pursuing him. When she told them he was leaving the country to go to Milan, they were all, 'No he's not,' and coordinated with LAPD to meet him here. Look!"

Signorile was being led out under the bright camera lights, and I just stood there smiling like a clown, willing him to see me, just for a moment. But he held his head low as he was pushed out, and, as he passed, I figured it could wait for the courtroom.

Just as he was almost gone, one of the cops said something, and Signorile turned to answer, looking up just enough to catch my eye and know from my smile that I was free.

And like that, he was gone, leaving a crowd of onlookers posting their videos. A girl no older than sixteen looked at Justin, put her hand over her mouth, and screamed.

"Where's Carter?" I asked.

"My grandmother's party."

A flash went off. The crowd's faces ranged from excited to ecstatic as pens, pencils, notebooks, and little slips of paper were extracted from bags and pockets.

"You're going to need him," I said.

"Nah," he said. "I got this."

"They love you."

"Just like the old days," he said, taking a pen.

CHAPTER 24

JUSTIN

After half an hour of selfies and signatures, hotel security eventually got me behind the counter where Kayla was waiting for me. I kissed her, putting my arm around her as we walked down the back hall, side by side.

"That was intense," she said.

"Yeah." I pulled her close. "Sorry."

Her makeup had worn off. Mascara left gray shadows around her eyes, and her smile had only a little pink at the edges. She was a knock-out, even half-done.

"I took over your life again," I said.

"Comes with the package, I guess."

"Victor's sending a limo. Where am I taking you?"

"I should get home."

"I'm taking you at your house," I said, texting Victor the deets. "Got it."

She smiled with a raised eyebrow, as if she got my meaning but hadn't decided whether it was cool or not.

"What?" I asked, ready to type her address in.

"Don't you have a birthday party?"

"It's over."

"You missed it?"

"No sweat. I can still eat cake tonight."

She rolled her eyes, and taking that as an okay, I sent Vic the info.

The car was already waiting in the valet. The two of us piled in the back as if we'd climbed a mountain in costume. When the doors closed, we were safe behind tinted windows on both sides. The driver knew where to go, so as soon as I felt us moving, I closed the window between us.

"We should talk about the video," she said.

I pulled her onto my lap, hitching up her skirt so she could straddle me.

"Why?"

"We haven't even seen it."

My hands moved from behind her knees to cupping her bare butt. I was hard before I was halfway there.

"My guys won't do anything until you and Evelyn give the thumbs-up."

"Maybe you should see how it looks for you."

I slid my fingertips between her legs and slid down enough to push my dick against her. She bowed, eyelids flicking like butterfly wings.

"You like that?" I asked, pushing harder. "You're wet already."

"I don't want to ruin your life," she groaned into my neck, reaching for my waistband button.

"Then stay mine."

She didn't say anything. She just released my dick and lined herself against its length, moving her body so we slid together without me getting inside her.

"That's very serious, Justin," she said with her nose against mine.

"What is?" I moved her in a rhythm along me.

"Saying that I can ruin your life. You shouldn't say it if you don't mean it."

"I mean it. Everything got taken away, and I tried to grab it back. But I grabbed the wrong things. I let my friends go so I could hold my career. I'm not doing it again. Not with you. Say you'll let me hold on to you. If I have to let go of that future, say you'll let me be part of yours."

"Yes, but . . ." She was lost in a groan as I slid her along the shaft of my cock.

"But what?"

"I don't have a future."

"Yeah, you do. You're coming in this limo."

Her hands on my shoulders, she let me guide the pace and pressure. The best moments with her were feeling her submit to me, and that pleasure went right from the base of my skull to the base of my balls, adding to the pressure behind them.

"You know what I mean," she whispered. "Your future is . . . Oh . . ."

Fisting the hair in the back of her head, I made her look at me. Her face was slack. Eyes half-closed.

She made a noise that wasn't a vowel or consonant and couldn't keep her eyes open. I felt her pussy twitch against me, and I couldn't hold it.

"Watch me come," I said from deep in my throat.

I pushed away so her clit was at the base of my cock and my explosion landed on me, not her. She reached down and took me in her fist, expanding the friction into a new dimension. My neck arched involuntarily, and when I opened my eyes, I saw the moon steady in the flowing roll of the night sky.

She collapsed against me, and I held her.

"Your phone's buzzing," she said. "I can feel it on my leg."

"Nah. Fuck them."

"We're almost there." She rolled off me. "I have a cramp in my calf anyway."

"Fine." The mess on my shirt was exposed. I'd have to get it dry-cleaned before I returned it to Eddie, for sure.

I dug the phone out of my pocket. Shane.

"You going to answer it?"

I slid the answer button, but I was half a second too late. The connection cut just as the car stopped. Kayla tipped her head to see out the back window.

"We're in the alley," she said.

"Yeah, I—" My phone dinged in my hand.

—Chad wants to see you if you're around—

The text was followed by the address of the place.

"That them?" Kayla asked.

"Yeah. He's in Pomona." I put the phone in my jacket pocket and got my dick in my pants before the driver came around.

"Is that far?"

"Too far."

"You were just talking about choosing the wrong things," Kayla said. Behind her, the door opened. "Going to see him is a right thing."

"You're forward. You. This is getting pulled backward."

"No." She kissed me. "It's pulling him forward."

I walked her to the door, but she wouldn't let me in.

"I'm gonna call you," I said.

"Go." She pushed my chest. "I'll be here."

"Promise?" I stepped back.

"Promise." She looked up as if she'd heard something. The blinds on a second-floor window swayed.

As if we'd practiced this dance a hundred times, she and I simultaneously flipped the person behind the window two fat birds. Our middle fingers would end up on DMZ by morning, and we laughed, because it didn't matter.

~

I stopped home to change my clothes and pick up my other car—a Mercedes without Kayla on the GPS—then I shot over to Pomona Mental Health Associates. Sunset Boys had done a show at the college years back, but I hadn't been out there since. The main drags were all parking lots, floodlights, and box stores. The houses had three-car garages behind wide white doors with windows spaced like movie reel notches.

The facility looked like a strip mall where everyone lost their lease.

The waiting room was small with mismatched furniture that had old copies of *Us* and *Star* piled on the tables. A receptionist had a land-line wedged between her shoulder and ear as she typed on an ancient computer with clacky keys. Shane and Gordon were sitting across from each other, talking. They stood up when they saw me, as if I were some kind of foreign dignitary.

"Yo," I said, flipping my car key ring around my index finger. "What up?"

"Kathy and George are in with him," Shane said, jerking his thumb to a set of swinging double doors that Chad's parents had gone through. His gray Elysian Park Elementary sweatshirt was open to show his Black Flag T-shirt, and his purple Converse were shredded. It had always been a pain in the ass to get him to pay attention to his clothes.

"Cool, cool." I flipped my keys in Gordon's general direction. "Hey."

"Hey." Gordon sat down. His shirt fit, and his shoes weren't doodled on, but he looked more tired than he had a few hours before.

Shane and I sat. We were all at opposite angles. A triangle in what should have been a square.

"How's he doing?" I asked.

"You know." Gordon ran his fingers through his hair. "Stress messes him up. So they make him sleep and take it easy. No access to drugs." He snapped his fingers. "Miracle cure."

"Hardly." I lodged my foot on the table and slid down the seat with my hands draped over the armrests. "He been here the whole time?"

"A week, give or take," Gordon said. "They're releasing him tonight. You heard from him on the way outta Vegas?"

"Yeah. Then . . . poof . . . he ghosted me. I didn't know crap from shit. Was he using again? Or another breakdown?"

"Using, then a breakdown," Shane said. "Living on the street, talking to parking meters."

"Damn." I shook my head.

"He wasn't cut out for this," Gordon said. "You guys want a soda or something?"

"Something with caffeine," Shane said, reaching for his wallet.

"I got it." Gordon pointed at me. "You?"

"Water."

"Cool." Gordon went through a door next to reception where I could see a vending machine through the glass.

"Thanks for calling me," I said.

Shane shrugged. "Felt weird not to."

"Excuse me, sir?" the receptionist said, looking right at me. "No feet on the table."

"Sorry." I took my foot off. She was the right age group to be an original Sunset Boys fan, but either she didn't recognize us, or she didn't care. That was cool.

"How's the music coming?" I asked Shane. Behind the door, vending machine bottles thumped.

"Great."

"Yeah?"

"Nah." He twisted a silver skull ring around his middle finger. "I like listening to the harder stuff, but making it's a different story. When I go all out with the drop tuning and crank the gains, it sounds like a cat getting killed with a buzz saw."

"It all sounds like that."

"Ignorant much?"

"Get out of harmonic minor if you want to go broad."

"When I try to make it more commercial, I sound like one-quarter of a boy band."

"You got any on you? Let me check it out."

Gordon came back. He dropped an energy drink in Shane's lap and tossed me a bottle of water before flopping back in his chair with a container of juice.

"Justin thinks he wants to hear my new stuff," Shane said.

"Nah." Gordon cracked the top of his juice. "You don't. Dude. It's a wreck."

"Bet all together we could make it good," I said without thinking. Getting us back together wasn't exactly on my radar, but I was too tired to deny what I wanted most. So though I'd braced myself for blowback and dismissive laughter, I got neither. I took it as a cue to continue. "It's not as marketable, but maybe smaller's okay, you know? Better for Chad."

"Chad had the best hooks," Shane mumbled into his energy drink.

"Justin doesn't do vocal fry," Gordon said without looking at me.

"Kinda do," I said. "New thing."

The first level of obstacles had been casually overcome. In the silence that followed, the air-conditioning droned like a truck idling on the side of the road, and the receptionist's typing clickety-clacked like a long-nailed puppy running on a tile floor.

"Talked to Chad," Gordon said, looking at me for the first time since I got there. "He remembers that night. At the Roosevelt. Says you weren't in bed with Heidi when I came in. He thinks I should know you better."

"Gave him an earful," Shane added, scrolling on his phone. "It was ugly. If he said, 'Justin's your brother,' one more fucking time."

"Broken fucking record." Gordon tilted his head back to drink his juice. "I promised him I'd apologize to you."

"Forget it," I said. "I needed a break from you anyway. You're a pain in the ass."

As hurtful as the last few months had been, a lot had changed. I was a different man in ways I couldn't explain to myself. And there was Kayla, who made it all possible.

"I screwed up with Heidi," Gordon said. "I love her too much for my own good."

"Tell her you believe her."

"Then what?"

"Fucked if I know. I've never been with a girl more than . . ." I shrugged the rest off. How long had I been with Kayla? Officially? Unofficially? We couldn't have met more than a few weeks ago, but she was already a harmony in my life. The melody would be the same without her, but the music wouldn't have the same depth.

"This girl?" Shane held up his phone to a photo of Kayla and me in her alley, giving a set of blinds the one-finger salute.

"That girl. You should see the video coming out. Gonna ruin both of us or turn us into porn stars."

I'd tell them about it before it was released. Maybe tomorrow, but soon, because I had the feeling we were going to be responsible for each other again. Just like the old days, but better.

"Pretty free with the fuck-you finger," Gordon said. "She's like your soul mate."

"You got that right." I nodded to both of them as they stared, wide-eyed at my admission.

"To this girl." Shane held up his energy drink. "For proving this asshole has a soul."

We tapped our bottles and cans and drank to Kaylacakes Montgomery.

CHAPTER 25

KAYLA

Evelyn and I sat on the side of the conference room table facing the windows. Talia and my Shawna—my personal and now-beloved shark—were on the other side with notetakers and associates. Together they'd reduced the cost of billing for Evelyn.

A wood panel had been peeled back to show the previous night's video. Evelyn had left the room for it, and I couldn't blame her. Signorile hadn't gotten far up her skirt, thank God, but the attempt was ordeal enough.

"So," Talia said when Evelyn returned. "You knew who he was, but not his face?"

"Right," Evelyn said.

"Then, when you were in line for the bathroom, he approached you, put his hand on your arm, and whispered in your ear."

"So no one else in line would hear. Which made sense if he was telling me about a secret bathroom with no line."

"And he said he'd let you into the bathroom in the private room."

"I really had to go."

Talia let the yellow sheets of her notepad drop closed and folded her hands in front of her. I'd never seen her look so lawyerly.

"He's usually more careful," I said. "I think I sent him off the rails a little."

"Here's what I'm going to tell you," Talia said. "It's not open and shut. He's going to say you signaled, and you let him touch you and get close enough to whisper."

Evelyn's face dropped and her shoulders hunched. When her posture changed, she straightened, becoming the bold, confident woman she was in Regency clothing.

I'd convinced her to wear stays under her jacket, and at that moment, I knew it had been the right thing.

"There was no consent," Evelyn stated.

"Oh, I know." My sister glanced in my direction. "I know how he is."

"We're together on this," I said. "I'm coming out. Name. History. Everything."

"Are you sure?" Talia asked.

"Yeah." I looked over at Evelyn, who had been willing to go at it herself if I'd let her. I wouldn't. "We're in this together."

Shawna finally spoke.

"Good, because you'll need each other. It's more fun to watch justice served with a friend." The relish in her eyes was infectious. I couldn't wait. "No guarantees, except this one . . . none of this is going to be easy for him."

~

In the underground lot beneath Talia's offices, Eddie waited at the parking lot entrance. Valets in white shirts and black clip-on bow ties scuttled everywhere, giving up car keys and taking cash. Car doors slammed and locks chirped in a song that echoed against concrete walls, but when he bent at the waist and kissed Evelyn's hand, we were transported back to a time when a woman's value was gauged by her ability to marry above her station.

I handed the valet my ticket.

"How was it?" Eddie asked.

"Awful," she said, then looked at me. "But doable."

"You're a brave woman," he said, taking her hand before addressing me. "Do you need a lift?"

"My car's here." I pointed to my white van with its blue stripe. We said goodbye, reassuring each other that it was all going to be all right because we weren't alone.

"Kayla!" Evelyn called as I was taking my keys. "Fittings for *Treasure Hunt* start next week. Will I see you?"

"No," I said, getting into the driver's seat. "I have other plans."

She gave me the thumbs-up and the valet closed the door.

I was driving west on Wilshire when my phone buzzed. Hoping it was Justin, whom I hadn't heard from since he left me at my door, I hit the Bluetooth.

"Hey, sweetheart," Dad said from the little speaker. "You out of Talia's?"

Not Justin. Okay. That was fine, but I was getting worried.

"Just a few minutes ago."

"How'd it go?"

"We're going to rip him a new asshole and feed him Ex-Lax."

"Attagirl."

"I'm terrified."

"Sensible. Listen. Steve. You remember him? From Butter Birds?"

"Handsome guy in the tie?"

"He is cute, isn't he?"

"Duh."

"Well. Because Dale did what he did, Steve passed your name to an Italian company that specifically finances fashion brands."

"If it's not Vasto, I'm not interested, ha ha . . ."

"It is."

Even with Bluetooth, I almost hit a Chevy.

"How?"

"Ask him. He said he'd call you. Just pick up the phone."

Easy.

Picking up the phone was what I was all about.

~

Covered in sweat and dust, I took another box of old reels to the loading bay and dropped it into the back of the van. I had room for a couple more. I'd found an archive that would take them as well as a nonprofit in the memorabilia business. If the theater was mine, it was going to be mine. Not Grandpa's.

I checked my phone.

Nothing.

Twenty-four hours after he left me at my door, Justin still hadn't called. I'd told him how I felt, sealed it with an orgasm in the back of a limo, and now began the ever-speeding slide into getting taken for granted. He'd call me when he got to it, and when I was mad about being ignored, he'd ask me if I was on my period.

Isn't that how it went every time?

I'd known it was going to get bad, and I'd allowed it.

Not this time.

Justin didn't take me for granted. Chad was back, and he needed space to deal with it. When I looked for a call from him, it was because I was curious to know how it had gone in Pomona.

Even the voice that gave me a hard time for being a romantic doormat didn't believe it was true.

Picking up a box, I heard a *pop* from the other side of the loft, where the windows overlooked the alley. I put the box down and ran over, cranking the window open just as another pop came from the wall near the window and green bottle glass sprayed like glitter.

"Oh shit!" A voice from below.

I leaned out the window with a smile that could have cracked my cheeks. Justin and three guys stood in the alley. I didn't recognize all of them in the hard glare of the Tesla's headlights, but I knew who they were, and I knew how it had gone in Pomona.

"You're cleaning this up this time," I said.

"Sorry!" he called up.

"You could text me," I said. "Or nah?"

"He thought this was more romantic," the stocky one with the goatee said. By process of elimination, that had to be Chad.

"You ready?" Justin said.

"Yeah." I leaned my elbows on the windowsill.

They huddled. Chad snapped his fingers in time. The skinny one, Gordon, hummed a note, and they all looked up and sang. By the second verse, I recognized it as "The Long and Winding Road," the first song they ever sang together between Justin's front windows and the porch. Justin led with a raspy take on the verses, holding his arms out to me as he sang of loneliness and all the unexpected roads that led him to me. Without the distraction of a huge production, I heard the beauty and power of his voice, shaping every word for me. Only me.

The window across the alley opened, and a guy held a phone out to video the surprise reunion of Sunset Boys.

Let him. He was documenting the reknotting of old bonds and the tying of a new one.

The building across the street emptied into the alley, and a dozen people stood in their sleepwear, holding up phones.

They sang in harmony, nodding to each other, letting Justin take the bridge for all it was worth. They were so good, with Chad, Gordon, and Shane humming the string section as Justin begged not to be left standing there, waiting.

Never, never would I make him wait at my door. Not as long as I had a breath in me. Not as long as he wanted me with this kind of honesty.

When they finished, they clapped each other on the back, and I couldn't wait another moment. I ran downstairs, taking the steps two at a time, unlocking the loading bay gate and yanking it up like a rattling steel curtain. Since I'd lived there, the alley had never held so many people.

But Justin wasn't lost in the crowd. He would always be just a little bigger, shine just a little brighter. That was for the world, but for me? He'd always be the man my eyes sought out and my heart expanded for.

I ran into his arms.

"That was beautiful," I said.

"Wait." He looked at me with curiosity. "Is that . . . are you *crying?*"

"Only a little."

His face flashed stark white on one side.

"I want to kiss you," he whispered. "But I didn't expect a crowd."

I leaned my arms on his shoulders and leaped into him, wrapping my arms around his neck. He laughed and held me up.

"Kiss me," I said. "Show the world who you are."

"I'm yours," he said.

Then he kissed me, sealing a promise to always be the man I loved.

EPILOGUE

KAYLA

Justin had offered Kaylacakes Denim enough investment money to launch, but I wouldn't take it. Even though I was stretched for a while, I wanted to do it without him. I wasn't quite ready to combine business ventures with my famous boyfriend. I was his and he was mine, but I was still my own. We did move in together, though. I'm no dummy. It got hot in September, and he had a pool.

Vasto came through just before I had to take another costume job, then everything went crazy. I had to hire staff and a contractor. Justin and the guys started writing new songs together while deals were being broken and rewritten. He was so confident in the music, he restarted building the house in the Hills. I was having the seats ripped out of the theater when the last of the papers for *Sunset Men* were signed and tour dates set. Heidi brought sparkling cider so Chad could drink it. I pulled crystal glasses out of an old box. When we clinked them together, the sound echoed in the rubble.

We built two individual lives connected by shared goals, mutual attention, and trust. I read the scripts his agent sent and listened to his music. He tried on my jeans and gave opinions I could take or leave.

We built the house in the Hills as if it was a joint venture. A day didn't go by without us talking, no matter how much distance was between us. And when there was no distance between us, we twisted around in bed as if we were trying to shred the sheets.

Which we did, that one time. And that other time when he came home from twenty-four straight hours in the studio.

He'd always be Justin with the slouched posture and a "nah" for everything, and I'd always be Kayla of the quick temper and fierce fuck-yous.

"You're wearing that?" I asked from the bathroom when he came upstairs in yellow sweats with the crotch six inches too low and a bleached-white T-shirt with a wide neck. I took my mascara wand from the tube.

"Yeah," he answered from behind me, putting his arms around my waist and kissing my shoulder. "Problem?"

"It's your party."

We'd been living in his new house for a week, and it was time to celebrate. Downstairs, the housewarming guests hadn't arrived yet. The sound crew was testing the speakers. The sun had started to set over the miles-long view, the food was out and the staff buzzed around, and the benches on the little overlook where we'd first kissed were surrounded in plants and flowers.

"It's our party," he said, jerking his thumb to the window overlooking the courtyard.

"Sure." I brushed the mascara on, trying to lean forward with him holding me from behind.

"What?"

With only one eye done, I put the mascara down and twisted to face him.

"You spent a lot of time and money on this house, and you should be proud." I poked his chest. "You. Justin Beckett."

"You were there for the entire thing."

"Lots of people helped." I pushed him away. "I don't want to get makeup on your white shirt."

"Maybe I'm not wearing this, then." He pulled me closer.

"It's perfect on you."

"Oh yeah?"

"Yeah. It says, 'This is my new house, and I'll wear whatever the fuck I want.'"

"Okay." He let me go. "I was going to wait on this, but nah."

He left without a word, and I followed him to the bedroom. His closet door was open, and he'd disappeared into the depths of it, flicking lights on.

"Wait on what?" I called.

"I figured, after a year and a half or whatever, you'd get the hint." His voice was muffled by the L shape of the walk-in closet. "But you're stubborn. You know that? You've got some garbage in your head you've got to let go of."

"What garbage?"

"Stupid garbage," he said, reappearing and closing the closet door behind him.

I was about to chide him for his way with words, but he held something in the palm of his hand that stole my breath. A small box covered in light-blue velvet.

"Justin . . . ?"

"It's easier if you sit."

I sat on the edge of the bed without complaint. He knew how to ask me to do something in a way that didn't trigger my resistance to being bossed around.

"Like I said." He tossed the box between his hands. "I was gonna wait until your birthday, but you're making me crazy."

"You are crazy, player."

"Yeah," he said, dropping to one knee, stretching the low crotch of his sweatpants and throwing him off balance. I caught him by the arm, and he hitched a pant leg up so he could kneel properly.

"You don't have to kneel," I said. "Because the answer is—"

"You're ruining this."

"Okay, okay. I'll shut up."

"A'ight," he started, opening the box to reveal a diamond ring the same size as the top button on my jeans. "This is the deal. Straight up. We're not a normal couple, but that's cool. You're my woman. You're always going to be my woman. No matter what you say, this heart, right here?" He tapped his chest. "When it's quiet at night and I can hear it beating, it's saying your name, and it's gonna keep saying it until it stops. So, I figure we might as well make it official. We don't have to. It's up to you."

"Oh, Justin."

"Figure it's easier for the kids that way. I mean, if you want a couple or three."

"You know I do."

"Cool. Yeah. Cool. We don't have to be married for that, though, but I just want to." He scoffed at himself. "Yeah, I know. I'm really selling it."

Outside, the sound system went on, testing with our only song request: "The Long and Winding Road."

"You're doing great," I said.

From the courtyard below, Louise's voice interrupted.

"Louder! Crank that baby!"

"Jesus, Weezy," he said, as the volume went up a notch. "The neighbors."

"Did you tell her about the sound ordinances?" I asked.

"I will, but . . . you wanna marry me or nah?"

With my hands on his cheeks, I kept his head still and his eyes on mine so he'd know the answer was true.

The music cut out, and the crew's voices drifted up to us.

"I want to marry you, Justin. I've never wanted anything as much as I want to call you my husband."

"Yeah?" His eyes went a little wider, and under my hands, he smiled. "Yes."

He took the ring out of the box, and I held my finger out. When he slid the ring on, I smiled, too, and when he put his lips to mine, we could barely kiss around our grins. He pushed me onto my back, and I wrapped my legs around him. We had two hours before the guests arrived. More than enough time to shred the sheets.

"Justin!" Louise knocked, calling from the other side of the bedroom door. "Are you in there?"

"Weeze! I'll be right out."

"These people you hired don't seem to know this is a party."

He bowed his head against my chest, and I laughed.

"We have our whole lives," I whispered. "Take care of her."

He picked his head up, kissed me on the lips, and turned to the door.

"I'll be down in a minute," he said and got on his knees.

"Fine!" She stomped off.

Justin ran his fingers down my chest to the edge of my pants.

"Where were we?"

"You told her you'd be right out."

"I did." He bent down to kiss me and slid his hand under my waistband. I reached under his shirt to the sides of his rib cage, grasping hard muscle and velvet skin, digging in and wiggling my fingers until he twisted away, laughing.

"Stop!" he cried, trying to tickle me back. I ran away, downstairs, taunting him all the way out to the courtyard, where early guests had started arriving.

"Kayla!" Dad said. "What's that on your finger?"

"We're getting marri—"

Justin picked me up, knocking the wind right out of me, and jumped into the pool.

I had a split second in his arms before we hit the water together, and that was all the time I needed to realize that I was happy. I had arrived at my destination.

No matter what the future held in store for me, I was home.

ACKNOWLEDGMENTS

This is where I usually acknowledge not only the people who made this book possible but the long list of things I don't know, facts I fudged, and places I fell short.

In the case of Kayla's profession, I stuck to an area of expertise. I was a garment designer and technician in New York, London, and Los Angeles for twenty-five years. I was not a costume designer for film, however, so if I missed a bit of lingo or a part of the process, let me know.

There's not a book I've written since 2015 that hasn't gone through my legal fact-checker, Jean Siska. No matter the story, there's always legal content, and Jean always sets me straight. If there are legal or contractual maneuverings that aren't appropriate for the State of California in the 2020s, it's probably my fault for changing something I shouldn't have.

I'd like to thank my editor Lauren Plude for being able to support this story in its nascent five-sentence form, and then continuing her support when it came back totally different.

Krista Stroever, my developmental editor, was gentle, kind, and patient, prodding me to do better when I got too loose with the stets and laughing when I freaked out about the identity of "the reader."

Amy Tannenbaum deals with me in a way I always hoped an agent would.

I don't usually use beta readers, but when I told Jana Aston that the hero was a cross between Justin Bieber and Shawn Mendes, she demanded to see it immediately. This was how I got one of the best set of early notes I could have asked for. Jana's a goddess. Read her books.

My family is awesome, and they know it, especially my husband, who keeps me honest and organized so I have the space to work.

Everything is cool here. I hope everything is cool with you too.

If you're troubled or sad, if things in your life are confusing or bleak, I hope this book gave you a few hours of peace.

ABOUT THE AUTHOR

Photo © 2017 Liz Lippman

CD Reiss is the *New York Times* bestselling author of *Only Ever You,*
Iron Crowne, Bombshell, Bodyguard, The Edge series, and The Games
Duet. Born in New York City, she moved to Hollywood, California,
to get a very expensive master's degree in screenwriting from USC. In
case you want to know, that went nowhere. She started writing novels
in 2013, and though that went better, her student loans still aren't paid
back. If you ever meet her in person, bring dark chocolate and call her
Christine. For more information, visit www.cdreiss.com.